Praise for SIX DEGREES ©

Winner of the Governor General's Literary
Award for Fiction (French)

"Rich and skilfully constructed, *Six degrés de liberté* is a tender and finely written novel. Nicolas Dickner, well versed in the advances of technology, describes with intelligence and humour the ravages of globalization and unbridled capitalism while creating characters who push back all the boundaries."

—Jury statement, Governor General's
Literary Award (French-Language), 2015

"Brilliant, beautiful and poetic with moments of pure reading pleasure! You read it with a smile on your lips—it's a book that makes you happy. Which is just as well when the subject is ship containers."   —Anne Michaud, *Bernier et Cie*, Radio-Canada

"*Six Degrees of Freedom* is even richer [than Dickner's previous novels] whichever way you look at it. Even more masterful and with a remarkable structure and rhythm."

—Danielle Laurin, *Le Devoir*

"The formidable analytical mind of Nicolas Dickner is what marks him as one of the most interesting writers of his generation. This incisive intelligence, coupled with an irresistible humour, runs through the whole novel, taking us to places we never thought possible. All you have to do is let yourself go."

—Martine Desjardins, *L'Actualité*

"A novel with action, about friendship, about obsession. Nearly every sentence makes you smile."

—Anne-Josée Cameron, *Cet Après-midi*, Radio-Canada

"More than ever before, Nicolas Dickner's *Six Degrees of Freedom* has achieved the fine balance between narrative and emotion, inspiring in the reader equal amounts of admiration and pleasure."

—Isabelle Léger, *Bible Urbaine*

"Dickner's third novel is a fabulous treasure hunt. . . . There's much to love: the shipping container as dream machine, poetic and subversive thanks to the author's talents; the incisive and lively humour; the tenderness with which he treats the two adventurers; the feverish pace of the narrative."   —Monique Roy, *Chatelaine*

BY THE SAME AUTHOR

Nikolski
Apocalypse for Beginners

NICOLAS DICKNER

SIX
DEGREES
OF
FREEDOM

Translated by

LAZER LEDERHENDLER

VINTAGE CANADA

PUBLISHED BY VINTAGE CANADA

Copyright © Éditions Alto and Nicolas Dickner, 2015
English Translation Copyright © 2017 Lazer Lederhendler

Published by arrangement with Éditions Alto Inc.,
Quebec City, Quebec, Canada

www.penguinrandomhouse.ca

Vintage Canada and colophon are registered trademarks.

Library and Archives Canada Cataloguing in Publication

Dickner, Nicolas
[Six degrés de liberté. English]
Six degrees of freedom / Nicolas Dickner ; translated by
Lazer Lederhendler.

Translation of: Six degrés de liberté.

Issued in print and electronic formats.

ISBN 978-0-345-81118-9
eBook ISBN 978-0-345-81120-2

I. Lederhendler, Lazer, translator II. Title.
III. Title: Six degrés de liberté. English

PS8557.I32S85913 2017   C843'.6   C2017-900584-7

Book design by CS Richardson

Cover art © Tom Gauld

Printed and bound in the United States of America

10 9 8 7 6 5 4 3 2 1

Penguin
Random
House
VINTAGE CANADA

ONE

— 1 —

LISA IS THINKING ABOUT MONEY.

Dust mask strapped to her face, pitchfork in her hands, she flings cakes of guano and gangrene, rhinoceros skeletons and moth-infested mink coats out the attic window—and she is thinking about money.

She thrusts her pitchfork into a pile of old *Lundi* celebrity magazines glued together with damp and excrement. She plunges into sedimented crusts of culture like a palaeontologist of bad taste. Boy George. Pop singers Michèle Richard and Michel Louvain when they were young. Drew Barrymore's suicide attempt. Loto-Lundi, ten thousand dollars in prizes, weekly draws. Michael Jackson's plastic surgery. Another Loto-Lundi ticket. Lisa must have shovelled five hundred thousand dollars' worth of Loto-Lundi. And to think that all that money was won and spent ages ago—and on what? Gadgets, clothes, trips, Christmas presents—all of it now buried in the landfill, burned as calories, dispersed in the atmosphere.

Lisa toils away at the pile. The magazines sail out the window, plummet, and thud into the Dumpster two floors below. Between thuds there are the sounds of the neighbour's lawn mower, cars rolling down the road, bobolinks in the fields, and the New Holland car dealer's dog barking at a muskrat. The white noise of summer, like the faint static of an FM radio.

Lisa feels as if she is stuck between two stations. From September to June she navigates the narrow scholastic channel on automatic pilot. No ambiguities, no decisions to make. Summer, however, constantly reminds her that she does not control her destiny. She devises Towers of Babel and voyages around Cape Horn, treks across the Sahara and particle accelerators, but there's never any money—not even a modest sum—to carry out even the slightest project. The money needed to get a bicycle. Money to see a movie at the drive-in. Money to build a drone, buy a compass, a microscope. Money to take lessons in sailing and kung fu. Money to go out and conquer the world.

At age fifteen, Lisa is in an in-between place: old enough to conceive projects, too young to find anything resembling a real job—and it's not as if the area is teeming with interesting positions. This summer she had her choice between picking strawberries with seasonal workers from Mexico or helping out her father for a nominal wage; now, as she cleans out the attic of the Baskine house, she wonders if she'd have been better off choosing the strawberry fields. At least she might have picked up some rudimentary Spanish.

For two days now, she has been defenestrating prehistoric pump shoes, coat hangers, rattan chairs with splintered seats, dress forms, peacock feathers, globes, folding stools, bundles of velvet curtains. On her pitchfork she skewers mouse nests, wicker baskets, stacks of the parish bulletin. A cradle adorned with pink and greenish rabbits. Dismantled furniture. A Grundig shortwave radio with its back panel missing, revealing a row of burned-out vacuum tubes. Hotel stationery, props for a stage play. Cap guns. Water guns. Bones.

Dozens of cardboard boxes marked *Standard Oil* and *Чарльз Баскин* overflowing with travel souvenirs. Hand-painted maracas. A velvet painting depicting a full moon over a copse of coconut palms, with the caption *Punta Cana* at the bottom and *Hecho en China* on the back. Bottles of spiced rum (empty) and bottles of coconut oil (full). Diving masks, antique Indigenous craftwork blackened with shoe polish. Necklaces made from nuts, seashells, spices, small bones, feathers, Pepsi bottle caps.

The major trade routes of the twentieth century led to this attic, and as she wields her pitchfork, Lisa muses on the geopolitical madness that caused these objects to be desired, bought, accumulated, used, cherished and then piled up in this squalid space, layer by layer in a heap at times indistinguishable from the guano and bat carcasses.

Okay, one last push—another hour and she's done here.

Nicknamed, first, the Haunted Mansion, then the Chemist's Estate and finally the Fire Trap, the Baskine house is a colossal ruin located halfway between Huntingdon and the US border. Six consecutive owners had renovated it tastelessly and ineptly before it was abandoned to the elements. Its freestone walls, as thick as those of a fortified castle, are crowned with a pretentious cornice and a copper roof that has seen many an economic crisis come and go. It was erected when the Dominion of Canada was spreading gradually westward, and even its current decrepit state exudes the brutal optimism of empires.

Robert Routier had had his eye on the Baskine house for years. For a professional renovator, it represented a sort of ideal, a sublime, artistic version of his renovation business—a kind of antidote to the string of nondescript bungalows he had been fixing up for years, the result being the financial straits in which he currently found himself. He had just turned sixty-four and felt that time was slipping away. He regarded the Baskine house as his last chance to accomplish something, to go out in grand style.

Alas, the thing he coveted belonged to a Chinese multinational. The Chinese were snapping up everything in the vicinity, from woodland to farmland and this heritage homestead along the way. They could be seen combing the region in rented Fords, armed with hard-shell cases and satellite telephones. This discreet annexation of the area did not generate any visible commercial activity or profit. It was a purely fiscal offensive, one that eluded common sense, but even in the realm of irrationality and tax strategy, the Baskine house could not be justified, and after languishing in a real estate portfolio for a few years it was finally put back on the market during the financial crisis.

Robert Routier pounced on the opportunity with the zeal of a drug addict.

The Fire Trap was sold without legal warranty, and a cursory visit was enough to understand why. While its appearance on the outside was unprepossessing, the inside was worse still. The place looked like a deserted squat, an impression amplified by the huge hazy mirrors that hung facing each other, thereby creating an infinite corridor flecked with nebulae and black holes and inducing nausea when contemplated for too long. Aside from this gloomy Hall of Mirrors, what characterized the building was the general absence of anything approaching a right angle. The whole place sagged and tilted. The air stank, the wallpaper was peeling, the floors were rotten. But the building's condition in no way impinged on Robert Routier's determination: love is blind, deaf and even a bit stupid around the edges. The transaction was notarized in forty-eight hours, as if there was an urgent need to founder once and for all.

Robert and daughter got down to business on *la Saint-Jean*, the June 24 civic holiday, and since then every day has brought its share of hidden defects. Now the work threatens to drag on until Christmas, and Robert has started to wonder under his breath if he hasn't, by the by, just made the latest in a spectacular run of wrong moves.

The afternoon is drawing to a close when Robert pokes his head through the attic trap door, eyebrows white with plaster, eyes ringed with the outlines of his glasses. His daughter has done good work; the floor has been cleared, scraped and brushed to a relative degree of cleanliness. Lisa, whose grey silhouette can be made out in the dust-laden air, is busy inspecting the contents of one last cardboard box. Robert wrinkles his nose. It smells of soot and pulverized mummies.

"Five o'clock!"

Through the round, glassy eyes of her goggles, Lisa looks up at her father. Spread out around her on the floor, garage sale–style, are a dozen antique cameras. She pulls off her dust mask and examines the Leica in the murky light falling through the dormer window.

"Can I keep them? Please?"

He picks up the folding Polaroid and leans his nose closer. The camera stinks of carrion.

"What are you going to do with them?"

She shrugs. "Dunno. I'd just like to keep them."

Robert rubs his moustache—he does this whenever he's bemused—raising a small cloud of plaster. After a while he gestures magnanimously with his hand: having cleaned out the Augean stables, his Lady Lisa has certainly earned the right to keep a handful of knick-knacks if she so wishes. To each her spoils.

They go back down into the open air. Lisa has hitched her mask up onto her forehead like a warrior's helmet and balances her box of foul-smelling cameras on her hip. She wears an enigmatic smile. Contrary to what she has just claimed, she knows very well what she intends to do with the cameras.

After pulling the garden hose onto the front lawn, they wash up with a broom and blasts of water. Lisa looks at the pile of carcasses brimming in the Dumpster, unable to believe she pitched all of it out through the window.

They drive back home in Robert's old Dodge Ram with the windows rolled down. There's a nice breeze, but Lisa feels congested. She coughs and blows her nose and curses. Stupid attic.

They ride through the woods and fields as if they're going nowhere fast. Just past the road sign announcing *Frontière É.-U. U.S.A. Border 500m*, they reach their destination. The road on the right leads to a gravel parking lot edged with a row of mailboxes. A sign near the Dumpster proclaims *Bienvenue au Domaine Bordeur*. The sign was targeted a few years ago by an inspired vandal, and one can still see *Bienvenue au Domaine Boredom—capitale mondiale de l'ennui* spray-painted in Day-Glo orange.

The reason this insignificant trailer park bears the name Domaine Bordeur is unknown. It's commonly thought to be a deformation of the word *border*. More disconcerting, however, is the term *domaine*, which suggests the inhabitants dominate something. No one harbours any illusions on that score.

The streets beyond the parking lot are laid out more or less haphazardly. The oldest houses were towed there as hunting cabins when the forest still stretched in every direction. Back then, the place was inhabited only during the summer. Gradually, the cabins gave way to summer cottages and the cottages to permanent homes. The most recent houses of the Domaine were mass-produced on assembly lines, wrapped in plastic like new iPods, delivered by truck and unpacked on site.

But old or recent, now the supposedly mobile homes all rest on concrete pilings and boast the hookups of modern civilization: electricity, telephone and septic tank. Yet, despite this, the Domaine has retained its transient character, its demoralizing fragility.

As soon as she gets home, Lisa hops down from the van with her box of cameras and makes straight for her father's workshop, an old Maersk container sitting behind the house.

The fluorescent tubes flicker on and illuminate the walls lined with an astonishing set of tools: handsaws dating back to the interwar years but finely honed; screwdrivers the likes of which are no longer produced; chisels and gouges forged by anonymous master smiths. Lisa often wondered where the tools came from. When pressed, Robert would mention yard sales or obscure inheritances, but his stories always smacked of things left unsaid, kept secret. All Lisa knows is that on Saturday nights when his spirits are low, her father visits his tools as one might visit the altar of a malevolent divinity, or a box of dog-eared *Playboy*s.

She spreads her cameras out on the workbench. She doesn't know the first thing about cameras, but this looks like a good haul: a Kodak Retina IIa, a Leica III in its leather case, a Mercury Satellite 127, little black plastic Instamatic 110s, not to mention the patriarch of the box, the folding Polaroid. Lisa switches on the work light, takes out a can of methanol, some brushes and rags, and sets about restoring lustre to these ancestors.

As she brushes away, she can't stop sniffling and coughing. What exactly did she pick up in that filthy attic? Asbestosis or neurotoxic spores, or remnants of the Spanish flu? Or maybe that disease the bats have brought up from the States, white-nose syndrome.

By the time her father calls her in for supper, the cameras are gleaming under the lamp, but they still reek of the attic. They'll need to be aired out. She delicately stows them in the box and washes her hands three times with lots of soap.

On the table are two steaming platefuls of spaghetti à la Bob—tomato paste and imitation bacon bits—which they wolf down in devout silence. Lisa feels a gentle warmth radiating down her arms. She may not be learning Spanish, but she is knocking her biceps into shape.

Once she has gulped down her last mouthful, Lisa gives the dishes a hurried wash and announces she's going out for the evening. On the way out, she grabs her grey hoodie and the smelly box of cameras and shoots out of the house like an artillery shell. No need to say where she's going.

Outside, the night is perfect in the way only an August night can be. Somewhere on the edge of the park a dog barks. Some neighbours are engaged in a shouting match. Venus has sunk low on the horizon. In front of the house next door, Mr. Miron labours away at his Datsun's motor, a portable lamp suspended over his head. Focused like

Kasparov up against Deep Blue, he seems to be asking himself if in the end he will take the lazy route and replace the whole engine block.

Lisa walks up Bonheur Street, dodges the young Evel Knievels killing time by jumping the speed bumps on their BMXs, cuts across the yard of the house that has been on the market for two years, and goes up Allégresse Street to the Gaieté cul-de-sac.

The Le Blanc residence sits at the end of the blind alley, where the strawberry fields of the Covey Hill farm begin. Dozens of Mexicans are flown in each summer. Mexicans, Guatemalans and soon Salvadorans, Hondurans—Olmecs of every description. They land in May. Harvest the lettuce, strawberries, cabbage. Leave when corn season is done. But this late in the summer, the strawberry fields are deserted and the Le Blanc house stands there like an outpost of civilization.

Lisa goes in without knocking. The screen door snaps at her heels.

Sitting on the couch, Mrs. Le Blanc paints her toenails while reading *Danish for Dummies*, held open in front of her with a hair clip. She is an attractive woman and, contrary to Lisa's father, still has a substantial portion of her life ahead of her. Half turning toward Lisa, she greets her with a big smile.

"Hi there, sweetheart! Éric is in his sanctuary."

Éric's room actually measures up to its nickname. No dirty clothes lying around on the floor, no old socks, no pongy running shoes, though, truth to tell, Lisa can't remember the last time she saw Éric wearing socks or shoes. The desk is free of clutter, and the books on the shelves are arranged according to a complicated system. In the corner of the bedroom the birdcage is open, and three utterly identical budgies are perched atop the bookcase, each on its preferred volume.

Sitting on his bed, laptop on his knees, earbuds in, two litres of no-name grape juice within easy reach, Éric is debugging code. On the screen, ten stacked windows are downloading, compiling, calculating or silently standing by. Beside him on the bed there's a digital camera, a run-of-the-mill, low-end Canon PowerShot.

The three budgies take wing, circle the room and come back to roost on the bookcase, where one of them punctuates the spine of a Robert Heinlein novel with a tiny semicolon of droppings.

Lisa removes her shoes at the door and silently sets the box of ancestors down on the bed beside the PowerShot. A century of photographic technology in one square metre.

Éric pulls out his earbuds and mutely contemplates the box for several seconds. He finally picks up the Satellite Mercury. Moulded into the plastic, a Sputnik, lightly embossed, describes an elegant elliptical orbit.

"What's this?"

Lisa, beaming, drops onto the bed. "The answer to our money problems."

$$— 2 —$$

AFTER SEVEN YEARS OF HIBERNATION, Jay arrives
at Trudeau airport with her still-warm passport, her letter
of authorization covered with stamps and signatures, and a
simple shoulder bag. No checked baggage. The authorities
have given her seventy-two hours, and she is equipped for
seventy-two hours. She carries no computer, memory stick,
compact disc, SD card, camera or telephone, nothing that
could be suspected of containing sensitive data.

At security, they search through her things with a
fine-tooth comb. They empty her zip-lock bag, sniff her
toothpaste and hand cream. Every last seam in her bag is
turned inside out, squeezed, inspected under a flashlight.
She is directed to an office, where a female security guard
photocopies her address book and empties her wallet. The
guard examines the third volume of Jules Verne's *Œuvres
complètes*, a shockproof edition with a quilted cover. She
fingers the hot-air balloon embossed on the fake leather.
Evidently the guard has decided that the three cush-
ioned millimetres of the unknown represent a national
security risk, and Jay's opinion on the matter is of no
interest to anyone.

All this is the fault of Horacio Guzman.

After smoking enough Davidoffs to bump up the GDP,
after coughing for fifteen years, spitting up blood and

phlegm, after metastasizing to the very core of even the lowliest vital organs, including his brain, Horacio Guzman lay down on his bed on the second floor, near the window, and stated that he had no wish to get up again.

A little later, between two coughing fits, he asked that someone inform la Pequeña.

The request caught everyone off guard. No one knew anymore where or how to contact la Pequeña. She had disappeared years ago. Some had even forgotten she existed. Following two weeks of intensive searching, a friend of a friend of the family managed to locate Jay at an old spam-ridden Yahoo address.

The message consisted of five words (six counting the signature): "*El viejo se está muriendo.*"

Having bought an international calling card (paid in cash) and tracked down a telephone booth, she got in touch with the Guzman clan's headquarters. A nephew confirmed the news: Horacio was dying, Horacio was going to die. Jay promised to catch the first available flight, and hung up.

She instantly regretted it.

For one thing, she was not authorized to go back there. For another, she was no longer sure there was still a genuine connection between her and the Guzman tribe. The phone call had been their first contact in seven years.

But there was little time for metaphysical questions. Horacio was coughing up whatever was left of his lungs. Jay had to act fast.

To begin with, she had to get the travel ban lifted.

Jay got started on her uphill battle. She invited herself to a series of offices, pleaded her case, climbed the cliffs of the hierarchy. Everywhere, she was given a cool reception. The problem was not so much her leaving as her returning to visit Horacio Guzman. Wouldn't she rather take a ten-day all-inclusive holiday to Mexico?

Eventually, she reached the Parole Board. After a long teleconference with a probations officer, the RCMP's deputy divisional assistant commissioner and a mysterious Mrs. Bourassa, Jay was granted a "temporary suspension of paragraph 5(b) of Annex IV on humanitarian grounds, in consideration of her exemplary behaviour over the past six years, eight months, and twelve days."

The suspension would be in effect for seventy-two hours, take it or leave it.

Jay took it.

In the end, the Jules Verne cover was slit open with an X-acto knife and probed with a flashlight; this seemed to placate the border guard. Jay is now free to collect her belongings and move on to the international zone.

On her way to the departure gate, she expects all the same to be stopped by an airport security officer who will tell her they have changed their minds and she can no longer leave. The arrest will undoubtedly take place at any minute.

But no one intercepts her.

Incredulous, she clenches her jaw and holds her breath, not relaxing until ten minutes after takeoff, once the plane has turned south and left Montreal's airspace. The engine speed changes and the seatbelt warning lights are switched off. Jay still can't believe she was allowed to leave. She feels drained. It would not take much to make her cry.

She spends the greater part of the flight—including the stopover in Toronto—in the depths of a bituminous slumber and doesn't entirely wake up until the wheels hit the runway at Las Américas Airport.

Her eardrums hurt. The plane vibrates as it slows down and then taxis smoothly along the tarmac. Jay adjusts the pressure in her ears. Some sporadic applause breaks out. Her seatmate quickly crosses herself and kisses her fingertips. A few rows down, a lady goes about pulling a bulky suitcase from the overhead compartment despite the instructions given over the loudspeakers. She drops it on a man's head, a water bottle rolls across the floor, there's an angry exchange in English and Spanish.

The flight attendant makes a sudden announcement: all passengers are to remain seated and will be allowed to deplane only after airport officers have inspected the cabin.

The aircraft parks near the gate and all the on-board systems shut down. No engines, ventilation or lighting. Clinking noises made by the expansion joints can be heard here and there. People begin to grumble in various languages. There are already signs of disobedience in first class, where passengers are mistreating the overhead compartments and the flight attendants. The hatch finally opens and two police climb aboard.

Jay recognizes the first one. What's his name? It's on the tip of her tongue. He moves down the aisle looking at the seat numbers, not the passengers, as though mistrusting his visual memory. Eventually he reaches number 17B and stares Jay in the face. A few seconds of uncertainty go by; they recognize each other.

"*Usted no cambió.*"

Jay makes no reply, but she notes that, back in the day, this guy addressed her using the familiar *tú* rather than *usted*.

The two officers escort her to the front of the airplane. She looks straight ahead, her bearing royal, ignoring the surrounding commotion. Only once outside do they signal to her to hold out her wrists. The handcuffs are oddly warm to the touch, as if they have just been removed from someone else.

The trio walk up the boarding bridge. Through the thin walls Jay can smell the heat, the humidity, the scent of kerosene. At the boarding gate, two officers in battledress are waiting with M-16s cradled in the crooks of their arms. Somewhere in the terminal a bachata version of a Lady Gaga song is playing.

Jay looks down the corridor leading to the immigration counters. There will be no entry stamp for la Pequeña today.

In the airport security office, the two policemen have gone into a huddle. The older one, whose name Jay is still trying to recall, holds his cellphone to his ear while the other peruses her passport and letter of authorization. They appear to be working out the proper procedure.

The young officer ferrets around in Jay's bag, pulls out

volume three of Jules Verne's complete works. He examines the newly slit-open cover and leafs through a few pages.

"*¿Qué tal es?*"

"*Pésimo.*"

He nods.

"*A mi me gusta Émile Zola. Estoy leyendo* El paraíso de las damas *por tercera vez.*"

At the other end of the office, the policeman finally gets off his telephone and comes over holding the letter and frowning. The phrase "on humanitarian grounds" bewilders him.

"*Usted vino a visitar a Horacio Guzman.*"

It wasn't actually a question, but Jay nevertheless responds with a nod: yes, she expressly made the trip to see Horacio Guzman and, what's more, with the approval of the Canadian authorities.

The officer folds the letter.

"*Llegó tarde. Ya murió anoche.*"

The news seems unreal. Horacio died last night? Jay can't even muster the energy to call the officer a liar; the fact is, she takes him at his word. She knows he has no reason to mislead her. He wields total authority, absolute control over events. *Todopoderoso*, as they say: all-powerful, in sole command. He has Jay in the palm of his hand.

The only thing that niggles him is the letter; it attests to Jay's dual status—dangerous yet protected.

He walks away without saying anything more, and the situation is left in limbo. People come and go, no one pays attention to Jay. A drunken passenger is brought in, a lost little girl, a woman who has forgotten her medications. A teenager is shoved into the office handcuffed with tie wraps and wearing three layers of sweatshirts; he'd been discovered in the landing gear of a plane bound for Miami. Jay would like to reassure him: geography has always made her sweat too. The kid does not stay put very long—they take him away somewhere. Jay cools her heels. Everyone is waiting for something, a superior's decision no doubt.

The afternoon goes by and the sun sets on the tarmac. Jay's handcuffs are removed as she drowses in her plastic chair. The call comes in around midnight: immediate deportation.

The episode draws to a close. At dawn, Jay is put on the same plane for the return flight to Canada, and she counts herself lucky not to have had another taste of the *sistema penitenciario nacional.*

An officer escorts her to her seat and stays near the cockpit until it's time to close the hatch. Jay is impassive. She holds in her lap her still-virgin passport and the slightly creased letter of authorization. When the plane takes off—at long last—she leans against the window and looks down at the forbidden country far below. The aircraft turns seaward and flies over the Caucedo maritime terminal. In the terminal yard, thousands of containers are waiting, stacked like the multicoloured pieces of some unknown board game.

— 3 —

LISA WAS ÉRIC'S FIRST HACK.

As a small boy, he would sever words and sentences. His mother had to dissect every word for him like a crayfish. On his first day in kindergarten, when he was introduced to his neighbour, the little girl with blond braids who had just moved next door to the Mirons, he had been warned to articulate *É-Lii-Sa-BeTH. TH*, not *T*.

Éric took an instant liking to Élisabeth, and he was careful to pronounce every syllable of her given name. The elocutionary effort lasted a few days, until the *É* fell off. Lisabeth, Éric would say, and he said it often because they spent their days together, welded to one another. After that initial amputation, there was a brief period of wavering between Lisabeth and Zabeth before Éric finally settled on Lisa.

From then on, Lisa has been called Lisa, and the abbreviation has contaminated their community. Her father, mother, friends, teachers, school secretary, one and all now say Lisa.

Éric had a gift for programming.

To everyone's surprise, the two kids soon grew inseparable. They were thought to be different—but no, they were complementary. Éric had a geometric mind. He was fond of puzzles, detailed landscapes, symmetries. He always introduced himself the same way: "My name is Éric Le

Blanc. *Le Blanc* in two words, like Erik the Red." Lisa, on the other hand, was all synthesis and narrative; the overall picture and the subtexts were what interested her. When asked her name, she answered: "Lisa Routier-Savoie. About 95 percent Routier and 5 percent Savoie."

He was taciturn; she filled in the silences. He lived inside his head; she was constantly observing the world around her. She came up with questions and he found the answers, yet Lisa's questions were as clever and unique as Éric's answers.

They felt happy only in each other's company, like a brother and sister separated for too long. They were often found reading in a corner, seated back to back on the floor like two bodies extending from either side of a single spinal column.

This symbiosis lasted until high school, when Éric began to suffer from an extreme form of agoraphobia. Within six months, he was practically unable to leave the house, putting an end to his ambition of becoming an astronaut. The boy who had hoped to work in the International Space Station had to settle for his bedroom.

He enrolled in distance education and received his high school diploma eighteen months later, three years ahead of schedule. Too young to enter college—and incapable, in any case, of leaving his house—he suddenly found himself having to fill up days of solitude. How to keep busy during all those hours when his mother was at work in Valleyfield? He could have downloaded cars in flames, zombies, topless girls or the entire musical output of the 1990s. Instead, he took an interest in programming and soon began to pore over Python, C and Ruby manuals with confounding ease.

In tandem with this passion came a revelation: everything, absolutely everything, functioned through software and operating systems. From traffic lights to vending machines, microwave ovens, telephones and ABMs, all the way to medical devices. In fact, the only thing left that was entirely analog was Mr. Miron's Datsun Sunny.

All at once, Éric felt as though he were wearing X-ray glasses. His environment became eminently hackable, for better or worse. He undertook all sorts of more or less successful experiments. His attempt to hack into the firmware of the family's DVD player ended in complete and legendary failure, and Mrs. Le Blanc decreed that certain lines must not be crossed and that if ever Éric was caught hacking the neighbour's defibrillator, she would sentence him to Internet access via the old 14.4-baud fax modem that she kept tucked away in her closet. Beneath her kind-hearted exterior, Mrs. Le Blanc was well versed in the ancient art of the threat.

Each night, Lisa ran to the Gaieté cul-de-sac, where she took pains to disrupt Éric's quiet routine. He spent too much time in front of the screen, the bum, and Lisa concocted a raft of nonsensical plans for him. She proposed that they cook up explosives with lawn fertilizer, build their own Van de Graaff electrostatic generator, lob a ballistic missile across the US border. One day she had the idea of reproducing Benjamin Franklin's celebrated experiment:

they would tame lightning with a kite. How could Éric refuse? The project was fun and inexpensive, and—great Scott!—it wasn't every day you got the chance to handle fifty thousand amperes of electrical charge. Lisa prepared all the paraphernalia, but at the last minute Éric changed his mind: he already balked at the thought of leaving his house, and the muffled rumbling of thunder sealed his refusal.

Standing under the lowering sky, the kite held under her arm, Lisa watched the twenty-thousand-metre-high crest of the cumulonimbi with the distinct impression of having missed an important rendezvous. Oh well, she still had plenty of stratagems in store to shake up Éric's sorry carcass. The main thing was to keep their parents out of the loop.

Looking skeptical, Éric bends over the cardboard box. So these smelly old cameras are supposed to be the solution to their money problems? Lisa nods emphatically.

"We'll sell them on eBay."

Éric instantly sees the cameras in a new light. He examines them one at a time, presses the shutter releases, gingerly opens the bodies. One of the Instamatics still contains a film cartridge, which he does not disturb. Added value.

Over the past few months, Éric and Lisa have tried so many money-making schemes they've lost count. Lisa collected and returned empties and mowed lawns. She won't receive her wages for the work on the Baskine house until the end of the summer vacation. As for Éric, he debugged a few computers in the neighbourhood and did some free-lance website design. He keeps searching the Web for little-known machinations, but the legal system constitutes a perpetual obstacle on the road to wealth.

So, selling old cameras on eBay? No worse than lots of other silly ideas.

"How much are we short?"

"About two hundred and fifty dollars."

"We won't sell them overnight. It may take weeks. Or months."

"Maybe I should have gone strawberry picking."

"Waste of time."

He brings up eBay on his screen and keys a few model numbers into the search engine. The antique camera market appears to be flourishing. He adds up the prices. The plan looks workable.

While Lisa puts away the cameras, Éric points with his toe at the Cyrillic writing scribbled on the back of the box.

"Is that Russian?"

"Looks like Russian."

"We should do some research on who lived in the house."

"Someone rich, anyway. I spent the afternoon shovelling minks and martini glasses. We could have made a fortune on eBay if everything hadn't been coated in two inches of bat shit."

Abruptly erasing the box from his mind, Éric holds one of his earbuds out to Lisa and dives back into his work. Lisa takes the earbud and finds herself inside a cloud of Polish industrial punk. She glances at the lines of source code on the screen.

"You're making good progress?"

"Sort of. I'm trying to fix a bug with CHDK. I've got a 'lens error.' I think I've corrupted the ROM. My mother is going to kill me."

Lisa makes a face. "Hey, it's all for science."

As she says this, it occurs to her that this excuse really does allow you, really and truly, to do anything.

One of the budgies has just alighted on the top edge of the monitor and is eyeing the code, as if to scrutinize the naming conventions. It coos in disdain. There's nothing more annoying than a psittacine who knows code.

Lisa leaves Éric to his labours. When he is possessed like this, nothing can draw him out of it. She leaves the cameras behind so that he can post them on eBay tomorrow.

In the living room, Mrs. Le Blanc has stretched out on the couch and is drowsing in front of a gangster movie shot in a Germanic language that the protagonists must chew on at length. There are gunshots, and English subtitles.

Lisa slips out, taking care not to let the screen door slam, and goes back home.

JAY COMES INTO TOWN FROM the airport and goes directly to work without even making a detour to her apartment. Three-fifteen on the clock, not much of the day left to salvage, but Jay couldn't care less. The radio in the taxi is playing for no one in particular. A news report announces the start of another cannabis season in Montreal's outlying northern suburbs. Some guy in Mascouche was shot to death at dawn in a cornfield.

Jay shuts her eyes.

When she opens them again, the taxi has pulled up in front of the headquarters of the RCMP's C Division.

She takes the elevator wearing her solemn expression and dirty clothes. In the seventh-floor vestibule, she waves her access card and pushes open the bulletproof glass door. She immediately finds herself enveloped in the muted rustle of ventilation, crumpled paper, photocopiers and conversation.

Jay veers off toward the washrooms.

Swaying in front of the sink, she splashes water on her face. As she brushes her teeth, she thinks of Horacio, buried in the Guzmans' lot in the municipal cemetery, inside one of those little concrete pods reminiscent of Japanese capsule hotels.

Jay's office is in the Enclave, a workspace that, despite being in the middle of the seventh floor, is completely isolated from the surrounding cubicles by a wall of filing cabinets and movable partitions, a forest of artificial ferns and the cluster of photocopiers. This is a satellite of the Port Investigation Unit, whose main office is situated at the Cast Terminal, at the other end of the city. Jay ended up in the Enclave due to a bit of organizational happenstance: there was no room in Fraud but there was here.

So it was, through the workings of chance and circumstance, with the coffee maker supplying the lubricant, that Jay was integrated into the local population.

The first desk on the right, unoccupied 99 percent of the time, belongs to Sergeant M.F. Gamache, the dean of the Enclave. He devoted the better part of his career to the main national imports sector, narcotics, and now spends most of his time at the Cast Terminal. He is what is known as a field person, meaning he prefers to be "on site," even when it serves no purpose.

He drops by C Division once a week, with a dozen sesame bagels and first-hand information about ongoing investigations.

The occupant of the first desk on the left is Laura Wissenberg, criminal intelligence agent. Officially, she's assigned to the Sub-divisional Section of Border Analyses, which straddles the Divisional Section of Criminal Analyses, the National Security Intelligence Section as well as the Sub-sub-divisional Section of Unclassifiable Cases, but Laura usually works for the Port Investigation Unit.

She wears glasses, and has a librarian's brusque sense of humour and a keen awareness of political issues. Each day at lunch hour, she memorizes long-dead cases from the eighties while eating her pre-wrapped sandwiches. Even though she essentially deals with port-related matters, she never goes on site; contrary to Sergeant Gamache, she believes that geography is an abstract construction that can just as well be managed remotely.

Laura, what's more, is a major source of anxiety for Jay, who, after working alongside her for seven years, still has not been able to figure out what her omniscient colleague knows about her.

Mahesh Chandratreya Gariépy's desk is at the far end on the right and is the only one equipped with its own coffee maker. A computer analyst, he arrived seven years ago, a few months before Jay. He was barely eighteen years old and he had to beaver away for several years before he was taken seriously. He functions on code, caffeine and minimalist Scandinavian music.

At the far end on the left is the desk of Jay-full-stop, the asocial-Internet-fraud-girl who, glued to her keyboard all day long, an expensive pair of German noise-reducing headphones clamped over her ears, performs a task that could be listed in the DSM-IV.

Despite their undeniable cordiality, her colleagues know nothing about Jay. They don't know where she grew up and went to school. They don't know if she has travelled, if she has brothers or sisters. If she is self-taught or holds a degree. If she has a boyfriend, a lover, a child, a hamster, a collection of succulents. They don't know if she knits, trains for triathlons or saw the last season of *Breaking Bad*. They don't even know where she worked before the RCMP— this last point being especially irksome for Laura. She has often tried to question Jay, but the answers she got were vague and variable. *Independent consultant. Electronic media. Self-employed. A start-up. Transactional Web freelancer.*

Telecoms. There wasn't the slightest trace of her anywhere on LinkedIn, Facebook or Google.

In fact, her colleagues are unaware that Jay is not Jay's real name.

Jay enters the Enclave dragging a bag of dirty laundry behind her. All's quiet in the shadow of the ferns. Sergeant Gamache is on site, Mahesh is represented by the coffee machine, and Laura is so deeply absorbed in her monitor that she doesn't notice Jay's arrival.

Jay sits down in front of her computer. She has two (2) years, three (3) months and seventeen (17) days left to serve in this chair. One thing, at least, can be said about the conditions of her confinement: they are ergonomic. She boots up the computer—unofficially known as the slowest machine on the seventh floor—and cracks her knuckles. She sometimes wonders if her job isn't just a sophisticated way of convincing her this is all she is worth. The new flavour of rehabilitation: belittlement.

Whatever. They want her to triangulate, she'll triangulate.

Suddenly, Laura turns toward her, glasses poised on the tip of her nose.

"Absent yesterday. Late today."

Jay flashes back to her round-trip flight, the night spent in the airport security office. She feels paragraph 3(a) of Annex 1 pulsating around her like a force field.

"A funeral in Sainte-Foy."

"My condolences. Any inheritance on the horizon?"

"I doubt it. Mahesh call in sick?"

"Nah. He's at Cast."

Laura has already gone back to work, and Jay is fighting an urge to give the computer a whack to hurry the boot along.

"What's Mahesh doing over at Cast?"

"Gone to look for a phantom container."

"A phantom container?"

"A forty-foot refrigerated container. Called Papa Zulu."

"The reefer already has a name?"

"You know Mahesh . . ."

The connection window finally comes up. Jay keys in her password (5+e'@>»0~#8vcP) and hits the Enter key with calculated brutality.

"And what exactly does little Papa Zulu contain?"

"Fifteen tons of Empire apples."

Jay lifts her eyes from the screen, all at once intrigued. "Since when does Quebec import apples in October?"

"I didn't say it was import."

"Export?"

"Mmm, yes."

"That cuts down the possibilities. Stolen cars?"

"We have no idea what's in the box. It could be anything at all, including fifteen tons of Empire apples."

Laura chews on her Bic pen with a blank stare, looking as if she finds the idea genuinely amusing. What if, for once, reality actually coincided with appearances? That would be a refreshing change.

Jay folds her arms, perplexed. Nothing is more commonplace than a phantom container; there's one on every ship. No one knows who owns them, where they are from, where they are going. They travel in the cracks of the system, and so long as they stay on board, no one pays attention to them. Even once they're unloaded, they remain in administrative limbo until cleared through customs. If no one comes to claim them, they can sit idle for months among the abandoned containers—and since the 2007 financial crisis there are many, many abandoned containers.

Laura, who can tell from Jay's face what she is thinking, gestures vaguely.

"Actually, we're mainly interested in the way it disappeared. It was delivered to Cast five weeks ago. It was scheduled to stay on the wharf for two days and then leave for Hamburg. But in the meantime, it evaporated. Poof."

"Poof."

"That's the long and the short of it. It wasn't loaded onto the ship, it's not in the terminal yard anymore, and it was even deleted from the database. As if it had never been there—a real phantom. It was found accidentally, because of the invoices for dockage and electricity. We started from there and followed the trail."

"What about the exporter?"

"Can't be found. Not registered anywhere. An outfit with an odd name."

Her Bic clamped between her incisors, Laura swivels back to her computer and opens a PDF, which she zooms

200 percent. Jay can see it is a bill of lading for container number PZIU 127 002 7. Laura points her pen at the exporter's name.

"Rokov Export."

"It's Russian?"

"It *looks* Russian."

"False address, apparently."

"Apparently. The e-mails bounce, the street doesn't exist. The fax number rings at Pizzeria Stratos in Saint-Hyacinthe."

"Pizzeria Stratos."

"Probably just a random number."

Laura's telephone emits a double ring: outside call. She decides to ignore it.

"What was I about to say? Ah, yes. Papa Zulu wasn't on anyone's radar until we discovered the dockage bill. The exporter couldn't be located, the container was erased from the database . . . It attracted attention. They dug up the bill of lading, the delivery voucher, and Mahesh went down to analyze the databases."

"So you know where the container was shipped."

A red light starts to blink on the telephone. *You have one new message.* Laura gives the device a peeved look. "Not yet. I assume Mahesh will come back from Cast with an answer."

Pause. Jay scratches the nape of her neck. "So there's no complaint, no complainant, no victim and no evidence."

"There's a presumption of illegal activity. I'm trying to link this to the West End Gang, but there's not much to go on."

Laura's cellphone is vibrating on the desk. A picture of her girlfriend appears on the screen: blond, braids, and mean as a miniature Valkyrie.

"Sorry, I have to take this."

Jay beats a retreat to her desk, where her computer has finally finished booting up. She yawns and suddenly realizes she hasn't really slept in forty-eight hours. She decides to go have a coffee.

When she walks past Laura's desk, Laura is still on the telephone. The discussion has to do with the finer points of work-life balance.

As she watches the coffee machine dispensing the light brown liquid, Jay recalls the coffee she drank back then: endlessly boiled at high heat, flavoured with cinnamon, served with too much sugar. Horacio would down a dozen thimblefuls every morning, with cigarettes bridging the gaps and the radio blaring, before he deigned to utter his first word of the day.

When Jay returns to the Enclave, Laura has disappeared; all that's left of her is a zealously chewed Bic pen. The red light is still blinking on her telephone and the office chair is spinning, as if an intelligence officer was ejected from it an instant ago. Instinctively, Jay turns her eyes toward the ceiling, and then watches the chair rotating more and more slowly. Laura Wissenberg has gone to meet new challenges.

— 5 —

LISA IS STRIPPING THE VERANDA, and she's thinking about money again.

More specifically, she is thinking about the wealth of the house's erstwhile inhabitants. Yesterday morning, Robert discovered a bottle of Châteauneuf-du-Pape 1939 in the cellar, lying on the earthen floor behind a pile of boards. The wine was undrinkable and unsellable, full of suspended particles.

Lisa's imagination went into overdrive. How did the bottle get there? Come to think of it, how did a bottle of Châteauneuf-du-Pape get into Quebec before the Second World War? No doubt through a private importer. A bottle like this suggests a wine cellar, a luxurious wine cabinet, roasted game, a well-laden candle-lit table, and a 78 of a Mozart concerto playing on the phonograph.

Lisa is of the opinion that money buys happiness—and the people living in this house were obviously very happy.

For three days Lisa has been stripping the endless veranda girdling the house. At first it seemed preferable to emptying the attic full of bat shit, but now she isn't so sure anymore. Scraping guano or scraping paint—what's the difference? As she rasps away the eight layers of oil-based enamel covering the boards—mint green and jujube yellow and salmon pink—it occurs to her that each species stratifies a different variety of excrement.

Headphones covering her ears, she scrapes to the 4/4 beat of an obscure Byelorussian group that Éric introduced her to. She abruptly raises her head. She puts down her scraper and shuts off the music.

Robert is calling her.

She follows his voice to the vestibule, down the corridor, past the living room with its hall of mirrors, through the dining room and kitchen. She finds Robert kneeling at the far end of the pantry, half hidden behind a heap of wallpaper that has been torn to shreds, busy examining a triangular aperture.

"Look at what was under the wallpaper."

In front of him, the flowered paper has brought down a section of lath and plaster, exposing the entrance to a space between the partition and the exterior wall. Lisa instantly notices that the hole's dimensions are ideal for a somewhat skinny fifteen-year-old girl to slip through.

Robert moves aside to let Lisa poke her head through the opening. The inexplicable void extends several metres to the left, where she can discern in the half-light, leaning against the side of the chimney, a crude ladder leading to the floor above. Lisa licks her index finger with the assurance of a veteran speleologist. No hint of a draft.

"There's a ladder."

Robert nods.

"Going where?"

"No idea. Want to go see?"

Her father hands her the work light, which is plugged

into a twenty-metre extension. Coiling the cord in her hand, like a deep-sea diver with her air line, Lisa squeezes through the hole and makes her way to the ladder. She imagines the treasure tucked away at the other end of the shadowy passage—for what would be the point of building one other than to stash Aztec mummies and halberds? The ladder goes up to a trap door cut into the floor of the second storey.

She puts her foot on the first rung. The wood creaks but holds fast. Robert seems all at once to regret sending his daughter into this recess.

"Is it sturdy?"

Lisa nods. The little planks were nailed to the uprights decades ago, but they still appear to be sound. She starts to climb. Running along the walls are some ancient electric wires secured with porcelain insulators. Century-old forged nails protrude through the plaster lathing. Lisa brushes her finger against the tip of a nail. She thinks about the rich man who built the house, the mysterious Mr. Baskine. Was he thin or fat? She has trouble picturing him inching his way through this darkness bristling with metal.

When she reaches the top of the ladder, she sticks her head through the trap door. The passage continues for another five or six metres before disappearing behind the western corner. It probably runs all the way around the house. Does it possibly worm its way into the partitions between the rooms? Lisa remembers her father's observation a few days earlier that the second-storey walls were abnormally thick.

A drop of sweat slides down Lisa's temple. She starts to feel a throb in her stomach. She knows that the claustrophobia gene runs in her family and could manifest at any time. The Routiers expect elevators to break down the way other people expect asthma attacks or psoriasis.

She hoists herself onto the landing and pulls up a length of extension cord. One floor down, in the half-circle of light, she glimpses her father's backlit head. She gives him a thumbs-up—although the truth is she still feels that alarming throb in her stomach. She advances along the secret passageway clutching the extension cord. To cheer herself on, she imagines forgotten Monets and busts of Anubis.

Once she gets past the corner, Lisa ends up in a room—not much more than an enlargement of the passage, really—fitted out as a sort of hideaway. On the floor lie an almost brimming ashtray, a bottle of Barbancourt, a stack of *Life* magazines, a military flashlight and a purple cushion with golden pompoms devoured by generations of stubborn moths. The ground is littered with fossilized mouse droppings that crunch underfoot. Lisa grabs the flashlight, wipes it on her sleeve and flips the switch. The jinni in the batteries is long gone. The ashtray is heaped with Craven "A" butts and there are two fingers of syrupy rum left in the bottle. On the rim of a drinking glass Lisa can still make out a brownish trace of lipstick. A woman hid here, once, to escape from something, or someone. Or perhaps simply from boredom. Maybe the people in this house were not so happy after all.

Lisa shines the light on the walls, looking for clues to the identity of the woman who used this closet. Nothing, no graffiti, not even a tiny *Gertrude was here*.

She crouches to take a closer look at the February 1962 issue of *Life* lying open on the floor, face down, as though it has just been put there. John Glenn poses on the cover with his calm eyes, his freckles and his astronaut's helmet. Lisa picks up the magazine. Whoever came here left off reading right in the middle of an article titled "Six Degrees of Freedom."

After a last look around, Lisa turns and makes her way back to the ladder, coiling the work light's cord as she goes. Stationed at the aperture, waiting for his daughter, Robert fidgets as though he were expecting Jacques Cousteau. He relieves her of the lamp and helps her stand up.

"Does it go very far?"

"Dead end. It stops at the corner of the house."

"See anything?"

Lisa brushes off her jeans. "Nope. Pipes, spiderwebs, old electric wires."

Without saying any more, making a show of youthful, imperial indifference, she goes back to stripping the veranda. After a moment of doubt, Robert shrugs and sets about patching the hole with a piece of drywall. In forty-eight hours, with four layers of plaster and two coats of latex, every trace of the secret passageway will have vanished, and Lisa can't imagine a more fitting outcome: a secret room is of no value unless it is kept a secret.

— 6 —

IT IS ALTOGETHER POSSIBLE FOR someone, given enough time, to acquire a reasonable grasp of modern Greek from listening to the neighbours quarrel.

As Jay mounts the staircase to her apartment, she reflects on this strange osmosis. Through the imitation wood partition as thin as corrugated cardboard, Mrs. Xenakis can be heard shouting her head off. As a rule the range of topics is limited. At the moment they include tea, TV and feet. The cramped lexicon of a closed-circuit life.

Mr. and Mrs. Xenakis have owned this duplex for forty-five years. They have no children, no pets. Mrs. Xenakis's legs trouble her and she has not left her apartment—and possibly her bedroom—in the last two decades. This puts something of a strain on their relationship, and they lay into each other from ten in the morning until a quarter past midnight.

At the head of the stairs, Jay automatically reaches for the switch. The Sputnik lamp on the ceiling flickers, dithers and dies. For two years Jay has asked again and again for an electrician to come and fix it, but the lamp, along with the rest of the apartment, is part of a long-term experiment on the laws of universal deterioration. One day an electric arc will form and the fire will spread through the ceiling.

Jay has lived in this apartment since she was released on parole seven years ago. At the time, she no longer knew anyone in Montreal—no one, at least, that she was permitted to contact. She had been airdropped into hostile territory. No connections, no opinions, no moving allowance. In the tightly controlled ecology of the public service, her case defied classification. It did not come under labour standards or the collective agreement—it was, instead, an *arrangement*. Her status was that of a perpetual intern. Her probation officer claimed she was getting off easy, but Jay took the liberty of doubting it.

Be that as it may, she rented this little one-bedroom at the northern edge of the Villeray district, a hundred metres from the Metropolitan expressway. Neither glorious nor well lit, but affordable. There were children in the alley and a Portuguese bakery at the corner of the street that sold decent *pastéis de nata*. The headquarters of C Division was at the other end of the city, on the far side of Mount Royal, eight kilometres as the crow flies, which suited Jay perfectly. Better to keep one's distance.

For several months the apartment stayed almost completely empty. At first, Jay owned neither furniture nor dishes, just a clock radio dating from the Reagan era, whose face shone like a lighthouse in the dark. She drank water and beer as she followed the London bombings. She ate very little, slept on the floor with the windows open, listening to the roar of the air conditioners nearby and the quarrels on the ground floor. The paycheques piled up in her bank account.

In the early autumn, Jay resigned herself to furnishing her domestic space by searching through that infinitely renewable resource, the garbage. Everything in her place, from the flimsy futon to the rococo fondue forks, came from the sidewalks. Jay was secretly convinced she would end up a bag lady. All she had to do was wait a little—it would come. In the meantime, she was getting her hand in.

Seven years have gone by, and Jay still sleeps on the futon as thin as hope, where she is harried by strange dreams that she rarely remembers.

Jay's arrest had not really been covered by the Quebec media; she had been lucky enough to be apprehended the day the NHL announced the cancellation of the hockey season.

The trial was expeditious, and Jay was preparing to spend her three-year sentence in a squalid penitentiary with a view of eucalyptus trees. An embassy representative explained to her that there was no extradition treaty with Canada and that, anyway, extradition was never simply a matter of waving a magic wand; instead, the image one should have in mind was of a kind of bureaucratic tar. A high-viscosity process. Did she know a good lawyer?

She nevertheless was transferred after two months so she could be brought to trial for infractions committed in Montreal ten years earlier. Her eyelids flickered when she heard the news. They could bring her to whatever they liked, so long as she was transferred to a Canadian detention facility. But six months elapsed and there was still no trial. There was talk, and then more talk, but the preliminary inquiry was slow in coming. According to her lawyer, they were going to propose a deal.

And indeed, one Monday morning she was informed that a probation officer was there to see her. The officer, a woman, had come to make her a generous offer: Jay could get out of jail and serve her sentence working for the Royal Canadian Mounted Police. If she refused, the process would take its course and her three years were likely to turn into a nice round decade, with a remission of sentence once she had completed two-thirds of the term.

The probation officer had brought the contract with her. It contained a great many clauses, but the main ones were meant to ensure a clean break with the "Beneficiary's," to wit Jay's, past life:

2(a) The Beneficiary pledges to adopt a new identity.
3(a) The Beneficiary pledges to sign a non-disclosure agreement (Annex I).
5(a) The Beneficiary shall refrain from leaving Montreal without prior permission; an itinerary may be required (Annex III).
5(b) The Beneficiary pledges not to communicate either directly, indirectly, or passively with any of her former accomplices, specifically (but not exclusively) the members of the family of Horacio Mejía Guzmán (Annex IV).

7(c) This accord will remain in effect until the end of the
Beneficiary's sentence, eight (8) years, six (6) months,
and three (3) days from the signing date, unless otherwise recommended by the Parole Board (Annex VII).

The exhaustive document, which ran to seventeen pages
and of which Jay received no copy, pronounced her gone,
erased from the face of the planet. She was to be stripped
of her identity, her right to speak, her freedom to travel or
make choices, and the frail social fabric she had created
for herself in Montreal and abroad.

One tiny concession: they let her choose her new name—
the ultimate irony for a girl indicted for identity theft.

She throws her travel bag onto the comforter, unzips it and
pulls out seventy-two hours' worth of dirty laundry, stum-
bling on volume three of Jules Verne's complete works
sandwiched between two T-shirts. She found the book on
the sidewalk at the end of the summer—the garbage works
just as well as the Gutenberg Project—and every night for
the past three weeks she has tried to like Jules Verne, and
every night the book has fallen from her hands. She waded
through *Five Weeks in a Balloon* and *Journey to the Centre of
the Earth*, and now she is bogged down in *From the Earth
to the Moon* with the nagging feeling she won't make it alive
to *Twenty Thousand Leagues under the Sea*.

Her passport is wedged inside the book. There is no entrance or exit stamp—she might as well have dreamed of the trip. The only evidence is seventy-two hours' worth of dirty laundry spread out on the floor. She slips the passport into her shirt pocket and pitches the book into the pile of clothing, where it disappears without a sound. All of a sudden her mood has gone sour.

She walks around the apartment but can find neither hide nor hair of the cat. She ends up in the kitchen and comes to a standstill, as if there were nowhere else to go. Leaning against the counter, she yawns. She looks at the bowls on the floor: the kibble has been partially depleted and the water dish is nearly empty. Three turds have been deposited equidistantly in the litter box. Erwin is alive and holed up somewhere, as is his habit.

How the creature manages to disappear in a cramped one-bedroom apartment—there lies an enigma. He must know passageways to parallel dimensions. Sometimes in the silence of her apartment Jay calculates how long ago the cat last showed up. Eight days? Two weeks? Despite the missing pellets of kibble and the turds left behind, Jay wonders if Erwin is still alive, and in the absence of hard data she must assume he is at once living and dead.

For the time being, the situation appears to be stable. Jay tops up the dry food, changes the water and cleans out the litter box.

She unenthusiastically opens the refrigerator door. For years now her appetite has been poor. In any case, there's nothing interesting left there. A tiny bottle of habanero sauce. A tortilla that has turned leathery. A package of ham whose best-before date probably needs checking.

She chucks all of it in the trash and chooses a pizzeria menu stuck on the refrigerator door. She stares at the telephone number, momentarily imagining just for fun that it belongs to an exporter of phantom refrigerated containers. Her thoughts are interrupted by the rumbling of her stomach. She dials the number, orders a twelve-inch veggie with extra green olives, no drinks, thanks, and hangs up.

Back in the bedroom, she kicks aside the travel bag and stretches out on the futon. There's a Macedonian soap playing downstairs on the first floor; this is still as close as it ever gets to silence. She tries to recall Horacio's face, but the image appears veiled with noise and parasite pixels. She has no photo of him—she was never one to document her past in neatly arranged albums.

She falls asleep fully dressed and does not wake up when the pizza deliverer insistently rings the bell and bangs on the door.

— 7 —

THE SUN IS GOING DOWN over the lowlands of the St. Lawrence. Lisa watches the immense ball of hydrogen fusion rolling across a perfectly flat horizon and she tries again to picture the ocean that once covered this land.

As on every last Friday of the month, Robert and Lisa

are driving to Huntingdon. They've just finished a gruelling day's work at the Baskine house, and Lisa's hair is flecked with white paint. She can't wait to take a steaming hot shower. In the travel bag lying at her feet are clean clothes and everything she needs for the weekend.

Lisa's life follows a bimonthly cycle that was determined in court long ago: twelve days at Robert's place, two days at Josée's. Initially, the reason for the imbalance was her mother's health. Her condition has since improved, but the routine is so entrenched that no one has considered asking for a review, especially not Lisa or her mother. Two consecutive days add up to a fair dose. Best to leave well enough alone.

Lisa recollects—ever so vaguely—a time when her mother would blow up over any number of trifles. The colour of the sky at suppertime, the scent of Earl Grey or the texture of a cushion was enough for her to descend in flames like the Hindenburg. Her divorce from Robert took place during that time, and her extreme flammability was probably the main cause, but Lisa can't say for sure. Her memory has blotted out most of the significant family scenes, with no distinction made between joys and traumas. She never questioned her parents about it. Their separation is a reality all the more firmly established because Lisa has completely forgotten what their life together was like, and is in no hurry at all to remember.

Things are better now. Her mother is on regular medication at proven dosages, the result being an exceedingly uniform mood and an addiction to vanilla-scented candles, but then, everything has a price.

Her foot resting on the dashboard of the old Dodge, Lisa sings gibberish over the radio to stave off Robert's glumness. She knows that the moment he gets back from Huntingdon he'll return to the Baskine house and work until late into the night. He'll do overtime toiling away all weekend, and when he fetches Lisa on Sunday night, the poor man will be drained and undernourished.

Just before reaching the town, they come across a long line of cars parked on the side of the road. Cups of coffee in hand, a crowd of motorists have taken ringside seats to enjoy the sight of a hot-air balloon being inflated.

Robert stops the van and Lisa immediately leaps out onto the shoulder of the road. The preparations have barely begun, and it looks as if a gigantic jellyfish has plopped down in the middle of the pasture. People are bustling around the tricoloured envelope. The basket is lying on its side while an industrial fan pushes air into the mouth of the balloon. Lisa takes in every detail of this clockwork choreography, where every crew member knows exactly when and how to pull on this guy line or that section of fabric. Gradually, the shape of the polyester emerges. On the white stripe in the middle of the balloon, the registration number and part of a logo come into view. The pilot ignites the propane burner and the roar of the flame catches everyone by surprise. Jokes are made about a giant barbecue.

A few minutes later, the balloon towers over the motorists, as tall as a six-storey building.

Lisa is as excited as a little girl, and Robert finds it amusing to see her hopping about at the sight of what amounts to no more than a large polyester bag filled with hot air. Still, he has to admit there is something ineffably delightful about the balloon's roundness and colours that makes it impossible not to smile.

Very slowly, the balloon pivots and reveals the huge RE/MAX logo printed on the nylon. The magic of the moment goes as flat as a whoopee cushion.

Robert sniffs and climbs back behind the steering wheel, looking sullen. He spots an old Tim Hortons cup that's rolled out from under the seat. He starts to unroll the rim to see if he's won a new truck. The stiff paper resists, so Robert goes at it with his teeth. The verdict finally appears under the shredded brim: *Please Play Again / Réessayez s.v.p.*

As always, Robert drops Lisa off in front of Josée's house. He waits for her to mount the stairs, knock on the door and go in. As soon as he and his ex-wife have exchanged a wave, he drives away.

Josée Savoie rented this house on Lorne Street because it was next door to Cleyn & Tinker's No. 2 mill, where she worked until quite recently. The location is its only asset; otherwise, it is unattractive, soulless and minuscule. The house is not so much a one-family as a sub-family model. The rooms are small and there is only one bedroom. What's more, the geographic advantage no longer holds now that Cleyn & Tinker have closed their six mills. In addition to leaving three-quarters of Huntingdon's labour force—including Lisa's mother—unemployed, the series of closures focused the entire media's attention on the term "single industry." Ever since the barriers went up on Route 138, Huntingdon has turned into a national symbol. Today, everyone holds an opinion about globalization, the demise of the textile industry and the economic crisis. Each time the Canadian dollar goes up, the same scenario is played out: jobs move to Ciudad Juárez, Shenzhen, Dhaka. There is a silent war going on, and its front line runs through the heart of Huntingdon, QC.

For her part, Josée Savoie has no hard and fast opinion on globalization, though she does think it's not about to slow down. Better get used to it. She is still young and sometimes thinks about leaving. When there is talk of a call centre being set up in the old No. 2 mill, she slaps her thighs.

"The day that happens, Lisa, the telephone operators will be flown in from Bangladesh."

In the meantime, she cashes her unemployment insurance cheque and religiously takes her lithium pills.

When Lisa spends the weekend with her mother, she stays in a large closet her mother calls the guest room. Shopping bags and boxes as well as a humidifier and some boots have to be shunted aside so that the sofa bed can be unfolded. This cubbyhole also contains a baffling number of winter coats (one of which, a two-tone fake fur, Lisa has never seen her mother wear), floor lamps (three in all), a disassembled artificial Christmas tree whose sections are always stored pell-mell in a box with no lid, a profusion of hangers, the skeleton of a Poäng armchair, and an obsolete stationary bike, its chrome pocked with rust. The door doesn't close and the microscopic window looks out on a city lamppost, but it is a window all the same, a detail that justifies counting this closet as a room.

Despite these inconveniences, sleeping at her mother's place does have one advantage: Lisa can use the old turquoise iBook and the Internet connection to her heart's content.

Her back propped against a pillow, the computer resting on her lap, she trawls the Web. Typing away, she tilts her head somewhat to the right, a tic unconsciously picked up from Éric, and in point of fact she does rather resemble him, what with the computer and that look of concentration. Éric would no doubt appreciate the cubbyhole's scant dimensions. All that's missing are the budgies.

There are aquatic sounds coming through the wall from the adjoining bathroom. Every Friday night, in the wavering glow of vanilla-scented tea lights, her mother marinates for ninety minutes amid the ripple of dried petals.

Lisa is searching for a particular piece of information, and this explicit goal prevents her from asking herself if she isn't also pursuing an implicit goal, a hidden goal, one that involves mitigating the banes of her existence: her mother's quirks, the closure of mill No. 2, widespread unemployment, shared custody and—peripherally—Éric's agoraphobia and that other agoraphobia, her father's, indefinable and unstated, which is expressed in aberrations such as the Baskine house.

On the other side of the wall, her mother starts to hum, too quietly to make the song recognizable but loud enough for some of the notes to travel through plaster, tiles, studs. The effect of specific frequencies getting filtered by the walls, like sea water by sponges.

On the computer screen, Lisa wanders from site to site, strolls among florists, toy stores and welding shops. Or appears to wander—actually, she knows exactly what she wants. She brushes off the ads that are pitched at her. Used Ford dealer, single women in Huntingdon PQ, non-prescription anti-inflammatory drugs. She rewords her query, tries different postal codes.

She eventually ends up at the website of Animations Herbert. In a jumble of animated GIFs, a generic clown flourishes a bouquet of balloons. Specialty children's partys (*sic*), corpret events (*sic*), batchlor partys (*sic*). Disco, lighting, decoration, balloon bouquets. Valleyfield area and a little farther. Appelez Herbert the Clown Call Herbert the Clown.

This is perfect.

Lisa opens a chat window with Éric and announces she has found the Grail.

Éric: Where?
Lisa: Vallefyield.

She copy-pastes the site's address. This one is truly a classic. On the home page, a brutally Photoshopped Herbert holds a bouquet of Herbert-balloons: three miserable, pixelated clown heads floating at the end of their strings. A hasty glance makes it look as if Herbert has three heads. Cerberus the three-headed clown, guardian of Hades.

> **Éric:** wow. He does dachshund balloons too.
> **Lisa:** I know.
> **Éric:** How are things going at your mom's place?
> **Lisa:** Same as ever. Anything new on eBay?
> **Éric:** Nothing yet.

They chat a while longer, but Lisa starts dozing off, so they cut it short. Better get some sleep. Tomorrow morning, mother and daughter are going on their traditional IKEA spree. No matter the state of the world, there will always be goods to buy. This is the dominant religion, and Josée Savoie does not joke about spiritual matters.

Lisa makes note of Herbert the Clown's contact information, turns off the lamp. From next door comes the sucking noise of water returning to the sea.

— 8 —

IT'S ALREADY LATE WHEN JAY arrives at C Division armed with a large coffee. Laura's office is frozen in the same futurist still life as yesterday afternoon: deserted chair, chewed-up pen, blinking voice mail. Jay is lost in conjecture about her colleague. She imagines her on a stretcher in the emergency ward of the Jewish General Hospital. Stuck in traffic. Summoned to the Cast Terminal for a top-level meeting about a container full of spectral apples.

Mahesh hasn't come in either. Jay pulls out the filter from the coffee maker and stabs her finger into the grounds. Dry, crusty. The day-before-yesterday's percolation. No sign of life on Sergeant Gamache's desk. Alone as ever, Jay sips her jumbo family-sized coffee. Despite having slept for thirteen hours, she drags her feet. She has the unpleasant sensation of looking her age.

She can remember the pace she used to maintain, when she would follow a long day's work with a night of overtime and get by on four hours of sleep at dawn. This went on six days out of seven. She kept it up for almost ten years, and not once did she falter. Her personal heyday.

Now Jay looks at her hand trembling over the keyboard as if it doesn't belong to her. Big gulp of coffee. There are two (2) years, three (3) months and sixteen (16) days left to serve.

Someone on the floor can be heard pounding away on a stapler, a punching duel with a sheaf of paper.

Whenever she is asked to describe her work, Jay never uses the official nomenclature of her job description. She simply says "triangulating."

She learned this verb from her seafaring grandfather. He

was given to nostalgia and was forever going on about the good old days before the invention of loran and the GPS, when you put out to sea with maps made of real paper that ripped, with sextants and dividers. Drawing directly on the worn wood of the kitchen table, he had taught Jay how to locate one's position in space by measuring the angle between two known objects. Triangulation amounted to far more than playing with optics and mathematics: it was crucial for reaching port alive. But Jay suspected her grandfather's lesson had metaphorical implications.

Years later, the verb came to mind while she was spinning her wheels in the offices of the RCMP. Triangulation was a means of confronting figures and boredom, and getting home alive each night.

Officially, Jay is a financial fraud data analyst. She spends her days searching through Babylonian databases populated with hundreds of thousands of transactions made with cloned credit cards, an immense magma of legitimate purchases sprinkled here and there with cash advances in Bucharest, Lagos or Minsk. Her task involves detecting patterns, recurrences, coincidences. Over time, through cross-checking—triangulation—it is possible to determine which pizzerias, martini bars or Dollaramas show up a little too often on transaction statements in the months preceding a fraud. The work does require a degree of intellectual acuity but not exactly a degree in aeronautical engineering. It's more a matter of statistical abrasion—rubbing a problem for as long as it takes to pulverize it—and Jay often wonders why she was assigned to this position, which could be filled by any newly graduated technician.

Perhaps they yielded to a sort of fad that consists in hiring repentant cybercriminals? Divisions B and D each had their own hackers, and C Division could not afford to fall behind. But once the hacker had been delivered, what then? After all, she had to be given a job.

At first, Jay was treated like a kind of consultant. She took part in meetings, analyzed cases, and her advice was sought for investigations. She possessed the empirical knowledge of someone with first-hand experience of the terrain. She easily unpacked behavioural and strategic issues. She thought like a criminal.

Undoubtedly, she could have made her way up the hierarchy, despite her somewhat unusual situation, but it soon became obvious that she worked best in Asperger mode, with her headset over her ears. She could not be fired—she would have had to be an employee first—so instead she was gradually sidelined. For the past not quite four years she has not been invited to any meeting whatsoever. Sometimes months go by without her leaving the Enclave. She has become just one more resistance in the vast printed circuits of the civil service.

Every morning, she downloads fresh data and tracks fraudsters. She watches the parade of humanity's great passions and petty vices translated into perfectly neat rows and columns. She tries to picture, behind this cold numerical facade, the fates that are made and unmade, life advancing like a gummy flow of cross-country skis and scooters, souvlaki trios, MP3 files, airport novels, vibrators, regular gasoline, winter tires, California massages and roofing nails, IKEA cabinets, mint-flavoured chocolate pretzels, window cleaner and garbage bags.

She triangulates.

The morning goes by and the Enclave remains unusually deserted. Jay busies herself inside a closed circuit, head-phones over her ears, until the hunger and fatigue become unbearable. A quick glance at the clock. One p.m. on the nose. That's enough.

There are only a handful of stragglers left in the cafeteria. Most people have already gone back to work, but their presence lingers, scattered throughout the environment: bagel crumbs, ring-shaped coffee stains, molecules of Lise Watier and *pâté chinois*, heat signatures on the chairs. The sound system is playing an instrumental version of *Madame Butterfly* that blankets the acoustic space like a low-pile carpet and serves to mask conversations. Giacomo Puccini, white noise department.

Jay pulls out a random chair. She is still fried despite her three morning coffees. She takes out of her bag a snugly wrapped ham sandwich from the grocery store. Practical food in the shape of a torpedo. Load tube Number Two, prepare to launch. She bites into the bread without appetite, her eyes blank. Even eating a sandwich exhausts her, but she keeps at it and chews. The six inches between her and the end of this baguette stretch out like the road at the end of the world.

She finally swallows the last mouthful, short of breath, jaws aching. She rests her forearm on the table and her forehead on her arm.

When she awakes, Mahesh is sitting across from her. Since it's Thursday, he has just finished running seven imaginary kilometres on a treadmill, and he is about to plunge his chopsticks into some shrimp chow mein.

Mahesh snags a stray shrimp and holds it in front of his eyes. "What were you dreaming about?"

Jay rubs her eyes. "I was dreaming?"

"You spoke, anyway."

Mahesh pops the crustacean into his mouth and spits out the tail. Jay massages her temples and looks around for a source of caffeine. Her surroundings swim in a fog.

"I slept for thirteen hours last night. Dunno why I'm still tired."

"You're coming down with something."

He probes the noodles with the tips of his chopsticks, on the lookout for that mythic second shrimp. It's said all legends are grounded in truth, but this remains to be substantiated. Jay grabs the plastic wrapping of her sandwich and squeezes it into a compact sphere the size of an eyeball.

"So, have you found Papa Zulu?"

Mahesh slurps down a few decimetres of noodles with an air of amusement. "Laura told you about it."

"The bare bones. I didn't get the complete course on the art of making a container disappear."

"They doctored the database."

"Hack or penetration?"

"Penetration. *Several* penetrations, actually. They altered four or five databases with different authorizations. They manipulated the data to have the container loaded onto another ship, and then they erased everything. A one-two punch—it's as if the container had *never* transited the port. I retraced it in the database's backup copy."

"So we know where it is."

"Yes and no. We know it was shipped to Caucedo."

"Dominican Republic?"

"Correct. But according to official records, the carrier never had the container on board, and the Caucedo authority never received it. It may have been off-loaded on the sly at the Newark–Elizabeth port of call—that still needs to be verified."

Silence settles in at the table. Mahesh sucks up his noodles, Jay is thinking. Her brain switches on, one circuit at a time.

"And the carrier? Don't they have the exporter's contact information?"

Mahesh, looking jubilant, abruptly stops his sucking. "Laura didn't tell you?"

"Tell me what?"

"Oooh, you're going to love this. The killer detail. The container was delivered by a trucking company in Lachine, Transport Tor."

"Tor? Thor?"

"Tor. A family business, not registered at the port. Around twenty employees, a dozen tractors, a few trailers. Early June they get a phone call from a strange company . . . Korov Export."

"Rokov."

"Rokov? Okay. Whatever. They want to rent a trailer for a forty-foot container. Normally, Tor doesn't do rentals, but business is slow and they happen to have a trailer rusting away at the back of the lot. You know what they say: take the money and run."

Noodles, bok choy, noodles. Jay is getting antsy. Mahesh looks for something under the paper napkins (probably just a way to draw out the story). He locates the little packet of soy sauce and starts to tear it open.

"So one of the drivers delivers the trailer to a transfer point in Longueuil. The parking lot of a KFC that's gone out of business. The trailer didn't stay there, obviously, but since it wasn't equipped with a GPS tracker, there's no way of knowing where it was taken afterwards."

The soy sauce packet stretches but doesn't tear. Mahesh gives up.

"Long story short, early October the exporter calls Tor: they can come pick up the trailer, same place as in June, the KFC parking lot. A slight change: there's a reefer on the trailer, and it needs to be delivered to the Cast Terminal."

"They didn't find that suspicious?"

"Sure, but hey, it's a little late for scruples. The exporter faxes the information: reservation number, temperature setting. Everything seems to be by the book. So they make the delivery and wash their hands of it. The upshot: no one has any idea where the container spent the summer."

"Distributed trucking."

"Correct. They segmented the transportation. Another trucking outfit took over, but which one? Where did they move the container? Straight to Rovok?"

"Rokov."

"Rokov, Korov. Who cares?!"

"I sometimes wonder how you've managed to hide your dyslexia from everyone for the past seven years."

"Next time, I'll come better prepared. I'll have a Power-Point."

Jay smiles dreamily as she fidgets with her ball of Cellophane. "Anyway, they're clever."

Mahesh lifts a flaccid piece of bok choy with his chopsticks and subjects it to a stern examination. "Clever, yes, which is also our main reason for presuming criminal activity. Why would a bona fide exporter of Empire apples want to make their containers invisible and untraceable?"

The question hovers momentarily over the table. Jay takes the opportunity to pitch the Cellophane ball, which lands directly in the trash can. Mahesh abandons the bok choy on the heap of noodles and closes the container. He pretends to sweep the crumbs off the table but finds none.

"My grandfather used to say that a meal that leaves no crumbs is a suspicious meal."

"Your grandfather was a wise man."

"No doubt about that."

Packing the food container back into the plastic bag, Mahesh discovers a fortune cookie and hands it to Jay. On their way back to the Enclave, Jay toys with the cookie as if it were a subversive idea.

The two co-workers return to their ergonomic chairs. Mahesh starts up his coffee machine and brings up the file of container PZIU 127 002 7 on his monitor. Jay puts on her headset and cracks her knuckles. Just as she is about to turn on the music, her eyes fall on the fortune cookie. She unwraps it, breaks it in half and extracts the slip of paper.

You are one of the people who go places in life.

She wonders if the statement should be taken literally. She crunches a piece. Edible but not really meant to be eaten. A fortune cookie isn't a food—it's an information storage unit.

While she chews, she watches an endless column of credit card numbers shimmering on her computer screen. Sometimes this feels like a life sentence.

— ⑨ —

THE MIRONS ARE NOT PART of the landscape; they built the landscape.

Most people move to the Domaine Bordeur simply as a result of circumstance: a divorce, a death, a reversal of fortune. The Mirons, however, live in this bleak place of their own free will. They laid claim to this plot of land long before the streets were paved, long before they had names, when all you could see were some trailers scattered among the spruce trees. The bears would attack the garbage and the bird feeders on a daily basis. It was the Far South.

Back then, Sheila Miron taught an intro to technology course at the Huntingdon high school and Gus was a foreman on various construction sites in the area. They had known each other since childhood. They both hailed from a hamlet somewhere in Ontario called Milles Roches, which no one had ever heard of. This is not a subject Gus Miron likes to talk about. When questioned about his little hometown, he just mumbles, "Don't waste your time. It's not down on any map."

When Lisa is not with either Éric or Robert Routier, chances are she can be found at the Mirons'. Not so long ago, the legs of Mr. Miron and those of his young assistant could often be seen sticking out side by side under the Datsun. She would hold the flashlight, hand him tools, ask questions. At 4 p.m., Mrs. Miron brought them tea and scones. Lisa would come home stained with motor oil and plum jam.

The Mirons never had children, and Lisa is the closest thing they have to a granddaughter. The Mirons are there for her whenever she needs a hand. Even in touchy situations. They help her deal with algebra homework, bake a birthday cake for Robert, repair a window broken by a catapult prototype, improve the catapult prototype. So, naturally, it was to them that Lisa turned to fashion a parachute.

The Mirons didn't know why their young neighbour needed a parachute, but they didn't ask any questions.

She spent several days drawing plans and cobbling together small-scale models with grocery bags and glue sticks. Her parachute was not going to look like a sack of potatoes. It would be worthy of Leonardo da Vinci, with an elegant canopy and a vent to reduce oscillation. A first-rate piece of work. Three times she calculated the surface area in relation to weight, air density, altitude, drag coefficient and terminal velocity. Éric reviewed the calculations—two heads are better than one—but found nothing wrong.

Lisa pushes open the Mirons' screen door and goes in without knocking. Inside, the house smells of boeuf bourguignon and vanilla. Sitting at the kitchen counter, Sheila Miron looks up from her crossword puzzle and fixes her piercing gaze on Lisa.

"I was waiting for you."

"Am I too late?"

"No. I even have a surprise for you."

She gets up, and Lisa follows her to the sewing room. Madame Miron turns on the light and rubs her hands together. The workshop is the only untidy room in the house. Whereas the rest of the place is impeccably neat, this room is overflowing with rolls of cloth, tailor's dummies, patterns, bobbins, vintage and modern machines. Not everyone is allowed in here. You must earn the right to enter, show the proper attitude. For Sheila Miron, sewing is a serious matter, to be ranked alongside marble sculpture or aluminum welding. Beyond this door, she is Chief Textile Engineer.

Near the overlock machine, on a large work table, lies a carefully folded parachute: prototype number three.

The past week has been a veritable obstacle course for Lisa. She has simultaneously learned the basics of sewing and how to operate an overlock, plus the art of drawing a pattern and choosing a fabric. The first two parachutes were sewn, analyzed and unstitched several times before being rejected. The Chief Engineer was adamant: these were merely test models that did not deserve to cross the threshold of her workshop. Lisa continued to unstitch, measure, draw and sew together again. The nylon resisted, slipped, puckered. Peering over Lisa's shoulder, the Engineer supervised the stitching without saying a word, while an old cassette tape deck played operatic arias.

Despite Lisa's efforts, prototype number three did not receive the stamp of approval. Lisa inspects every seam— she doesn't understand. It all seems quite acceptable. But Mrs. Miron insisted: this parachute does not leave the workshop. Try, try, try again, etc. Lisa sighs. There's not enough nylon left for the fourth parachute and she has no time to return to Valleyfield to buy more. While Lisa is stewing over it, Mrs. Miron hunts through her closet and pulls out an old Eaton's garment bag.

"You can get the overlock ready. We're starting over from scratch."

Lisa is stunned. "From scratch? But . . ."

Mrs. Miron solemnly unzips the bag and reveals five or six coal-black shirts. She cautiously takes out one of the shirts and proffers it to Lisa.

"Pure Guangxi silk. Ebony buttons. My brother had them made in 1957 for his part in *Madame Butterfly* at the Metropolitan Opera in New York. There are five left. The sixth he wore in his coffin."

Lisa fingers the silk in wonderment. Sewn onto the inside of the shirt is a thin golden label like a signature: *Jacob Weisberg & Sons*. Mrs. Miron smiles dreamily.

"At the time, they were the best tailors in Montreal."

Lisa shakes her head in protest. "It's much too beautiful to . . ."

"Not another word. Fit the overlock with a new pair of needles and let's get to work."

Parachute number four receives Sheila Miron's approval just before midnight. The object is strangely elegant, dark and delicate as a Japanese bat. On the reverse side, Lisa has sewn the Weisberg & Sons golden label. Designer parachutes are not exactly a dime a dozen.

When Lisa steps through the door of the workshop, victorious and worn out, her creation rolled up under her arm like a Picasso that has just been purloined from the Prado, she not only is proud but feels as if she has just discovered the antidote to the primal sense of vertigo. As she crosses the few metres of lawn to her house, she looks up at the starry dome overhead. Conditions are perfect—if only they could finally sell the damned cameras.

She goes to bed with a silent prayer addressed to the obscure deities of eBay.

— 10 —

AT JARRY METRO STATION, THE escalator is under repair. Two technicians are toiling away in the pit like a pair of surgeons in Hell, surrounded by mysterious steel organs and tool boxes, amid wads of chewing gum and Doritos bags and used metro tickets. Without access to their mechanical staircase, the passengers are forced to use the conventional one.

Jay grumbles as she takes on the seventy-two thousand steps separating her from the surface. Her thighs are burning and she is out of breath. She feels ridiculous and geriatric. Sooner or later she will have to emulate Mahesh and go sweat on a treadmill Tuesdays and Thursdays at noon. March across the austere geography of repetition. Take protein supplements and vitamin D.

She exits the metro shelter still short of breath and, at the corner of the street, leans her back against the traffic-light post.

The whistle of compressed air makes her start. The light has turned red, and a China Shipping Lines container looms up a few metres in front of her, filling her field of vision almost entirely. It's as though a chunk of industrial park has broken off and gone adrift. Somewhere on the outskirts of the city a glacier is calving containers.

The box is painted the strident green used in filmmaking for image substitution, and Jay notices that the container has the same effect: reality bounces off its sides. No one pays any attention to it. Just behind, sitting in her BMW, a woman refreshes her lipstick in her rear-view mirror. On the sidewalk, the people waiting for the bus seem to be looking right through the giant box. They filter its presence as if it were an optical anomaly, a fifth dimension their brains would be unable to interpret. Only a young child, strapped into its stroller, scans the container with big round eyes.

Jay is engrossed in the white Chinese ideograms printed on the container. She recognizes at least the two characters signifying China, the 中 and the 國, but the rest—航, 運, 公 and 司—could be anything. A furtive box with mysterious contents, adorned with incomprehensible symbols: a colossal fortune cookie.

The light turns green, the truck starts up, the container moves off. An idea begins to germinate in Jay's head. She walks the rest of the way home, immersed in her thoughts.

When she arrives in front of her door, she stops short. During the day, someone has affixed a RE/MAX sign to the fence. She recognizes, set against the tricoloured background, Alex Onassis, his smile showing six dozen immaculate, perfectly symmetrical teeth. She has already seen this face posted on houses here and there around the neighbourhood. While she is examining the sign, Mr. Xenakis appears on the doorstep. Behind him, his wife can be heard whining at the far end of the house. He motions to Jay with his hand.

"There's someone upstairs."

"Someone?"

"The electrician."

"Ah."

"You saw the sign."

"Yes. It would have been nice to let me know in advance."

Xenakis gives his nose a noncommittal scratch. Over the past forty years he's become inured to female disgruntlement.

"There will be visits."

Jay frowns. The last thing she needs right now is to see strangers parading through her private space, probing electrical outlets and drainpipes. Xenakis rocks from one foot to the other, as though struggling to compose a difficult statement. From inside comes a volley of rapid-fire sentences.

"*Nai! Nai!*" Xenakis answers, turning halfway around. He sighs. "You have to keep the apartment clean. For the visits."

Jay shrugs. It'll take a lot more than a clean apartment to sell this dump.

When she gets to her living room, she finds the promised electrician standing at the top of a ladder. He has deposited the carcass of the Sputnik on the floor, next to a half-open box from which its replacement peeks out, a garish chrome fixture manufactured in Malaysia. Life expectancy: eighteen months.

"I'll be another fifteen minutes," the electrician says without taking his eyes off his work.

He has pulled a bunch of wires out of the ceiling, like a tapeworm parasitically ensconced inside the apartment's walls. Mineral wool and flakes of plaster are raining down, and Jay beats a hasty retreat.

In the bedroom, the floor is littered with dirty laundry. She yanks a large duffle bag out of the closet and starts to cram it with clothes. Grabbing a bra, she sends Jules Verne's complete works, incised cover and all, spinning through the air. She collects her laptop, a minuscule Eee, and stuffs it between two T-shirts. She hoists the bag onto her shoulder, scoops a handful of quarters out of the loose-change bowl and leaves without even glancing at the electrician.

The laundromat is deserted, which amplifies the shockwave of the purple walls. A narrow vestibule has been fitted out with a condom vending machine, a display case of postcards and the last remaining pay phone in the city.

Planted in the doorway, Jay lets out a sigh. At the age of thirty-nine, aren't you supposed to have a washing machine and a dryer? She suddenly misses the days when she lived oblivious to the objects that a human being should own as a matter of course. She overloads two machines, inserts the change and installs herself on a bench, legs stretched out. The walls are really very purple. Jay shuts her eyes, leaning her back against a dryer. The soapy backwash of the machines eventually calms her down.

Eyes still closed, she turns the distributed-trucking affair over and over in her mind. Somewhere in Montreal, a Russian illusionist is having fun making refrigerated containers vanish.

That said, she can't see what's so complicated about this investigation. The chain has been broken up into segments, fine, but all that's needed is to draw up a complete list of carriers in the Montreal area and call them one by one to find out which of them was entrusted with container PZIU 127 002 7. This wouldn't even require a warrant; you can get quite far with an RCMP badge and a good attitude. You just have to slog your way from one call to the next. A tedious but simple procedure.

The clothes in the washing machine tumble over themselves like a heap of entangled identities.

Jay opens her eyes. The purple of the walls hits her full on. She lifts her computer out of the bag and locates an unsecured wi-fi connection. With the screen's brightness at the lowest setting, she logs on to Canada411 and chooses the category "Containers—Carrier Services, Montreal QC." The list comes up on the screen: Transport Globalex, Tremblay Express, CargoPro, Transport Nguyen, RTF Express, Logistique Robert, and so on for another twenty-five pages. It's impossible to display all the results on a single page. What's more, she would have to click on each carrier to access the contact information. This means copy-pasting everything manually. Pure drudgery.

Closing her eyes again, Jay works out a more efficient method. She could code a script in Python to identify the relevant links on each of the twenty-five pages of results and then extract the contents of every linked page. Afterwards, she could filter and organize the addresses, which would enable her to automatically transpose them onto OpenStreetMap and determine a route by means of combinatorial optimization.

Jay feels a weight building up on her chest.

She opens her eyes again—that purple!—and casts them at the vestibule of the laundromat. Suspended under the old pay phone is a copy of the Yellow Pages, swollen from age and humidity.

Jay has not opened a paper telephone directory for at least twenty years. Propped against the condom vending machine, she flips through the thin, crinkled pages until she gets to *Containers—Carrier Services.* A single page. She delicately tears it out, folds it in four and slips it into her pocket. Anyway, what sort of dinosaur still uses the Yellow Pages?

CONTRARY TO EXPECTATIONS, HERBERT THE Clown does not have three heads. He's neither funny nor sketchy, and he doesn't reek of cigarettes or stale beer. He's only a fifty-something, ill-shaven guy who lives in a former convenience store on the corner of a busy street. Resting against the door jamb, he looks as if he's just awoken from a nap.

In front of him, tiny Lisa nervously shifts her weight from one foot to the other.

"I called to reserve a gas cylinder."

"Lisa?"

"That's me."

Herbert yawns and, after sizing up his customer, points to a hundred-and-twenty-five-cubic-foot cylinder standing at attention near the door. Lisa is surprised to see how massive it is. She was expecting something easier to handle, more clownish, pink and shiny, not this big welder's cylinder. She apprehensively strokes the cold metal. Thor's hammer comes to mind: it could be used to slay giants.

Standing on the sidewalk, Robert Routier watches in stupefaction as the deposit and rental fee are duly paid. Herbert scribbles the amount on a receipt, which Lisa stuffs into her pocket. What Robert does not know is that the rental of this gas cylinder results directly from the long-awaited sale of the old cameras his daughter found in the attic of the Baskine house.

The outcome hinged on an eleventh-hour eBay surge. The Instamatic 110s weren't worth anything, except for the one containing a film cartridge, which, thanks to the curiosity factor, got up to fifteen whole dollars. Collectors spurned the Retina IIa and the Mercury for reasons to which only collectors are privy, and the magnificent Polaroid might have had potential if not for the subtle aroma of bat guano permeating the bellows—a detail that could hardly be kept secret. Just when Éric and Lisa were about to lose all hope, the Leica III, the dark horse that was off everyone's radar, pulled up on the outside track and, with an astonishing burst, finally, on August 17 at 2 a.m., attained the sum of $245.

Seventy-two hours later, nearly all the money is gone and now in the possession of a fifty-something clown from Valleyfield.

As soon as they've loaded the cylinder into the van ("It has to stay upright!" Herbert yells from the doorway) and firmly secured it, father and daughter head back to Domaine Bordeur. Not a word passes between them during the ride back. The radio is playing a retrospective of Willie Lamothe's country music career. Two or three times, Robert seems to be on the verge of asking about the object strapped behind his seat. In the end, he thinks better of it. When they get home, he simply asks—affecting an air of detachment—if he can drop Lisa and her helium off somewhere. She shakes her head. No, that's okay.

As they unload the cylinder, Lisa is struck by how she receives the spontaneous consent of the adults around her. She's starting to wonder if she has acquired some sort of reputation.

She walks over to the Mirons', where, after ten years of heroic treatment, and by a fabulous coincidence, the Datsun has just now started up—oh, ever so briefly, scarcely long enough to produce a blackish fart—but start up it did, nevertheless. His hands smeared with grease, Gus Miron gives Lisa a disconcerting high-five. The car's awakening has taken thirty years off him in thirty seconds.

Then Mr. Miron looks hard at his young neighbour. He knows that expression: there is something she needs.

"I've got something heavy to move. Could I borrow your hand truck?"

Watching her hurriedly fasten the cylinder to the hand truck, Mr. Miron shows signs of apprehension. He notices the green diamond: *Non-flammable contents*. All right, no danger of an explosion.

Lisa carts the cylinder to her father's workshop, then she goes back to the house and fixes herself a pickle sandwich.

At 4 a.m., the clock radio begins to chatter, smothered under Lisa's pillow, where she has hidden it.

She pulls on her jeans and a thick sweater. On her way through the kitchen, she grabs an apple, which she will munch on while standing in the wet grass. There is a faint hint of dawn above the woods. She noiselessly removes the lock from the door of the workshop. Under the fluorescent lights, the cylinder appears even more massive than yesterday evening. Lisa takes a deep breath, takes hold of the hand truck and, with a spring in her step, sets out on the long trek to the Gaieté cul-de-sac.

When she arrives at the end of the blind alley, she is relieved to see a lamp shining in the sanctuary window. She scratches on the screen and Éric's head pops into the rectangle of light. He eyes Lisa and then the cylinder.

"What's up?"

"I don't want to wake your mother."

"She's not here."

Lisa is taken aback. She parks the cylinder at the bottom of the stairs and goes in. She finds Éric still in pyjamas, bare-chested, doing his prison routine. Every morning—whether it's 4 a.m. or 9 a.m.—the gentleman starts his day with a series of push-ups and sit-ups, uses as dumbbells whatever objects are to hand, jogs in place, and concludes with ten minutes in the low squat position. He'd read somewhere that prisoners stayed in shape with this sort of minimalist workout, and what's good for a prisoner is good for him.

Lisa, meanwhile, feels she has already done her share pushing the cylinder this far. She mops her forehead with her sleeve.

"Your mother's spending the night out?"

"She's seeing someone—a colleague."

The silence is charged with innuendo. Éric moves on to his dumbbells du jour (four Stephen King novels).

"Do you really have to finish your exercises?"

"Uh-huh."

Lisa settles onto the bed, an appealing warmth still emanating from the sheets, and leafs through a shoddily printed booklet titled *Manual Operation for GPG Beacon Garmik 55*. (Warning: May contain Chinglish.)

"Is that something new?"

"What?"

"Your mother sleeping away from home."

"It's been going on for a few months."

"I never noticed."

"My mother is a ninja."

"And do you know this colleague?"

"Haven't met him yet. My mother never talks about him. But I googled him, just in case."

"Jealous?"

"Well, before you know it, *poof*—there's a psychopath."

"And?"

He lays the Stephen Kings down on the floor, checks the time and directly assumes the squat position. With his striped pyjamas, half-closed eyes and slow breathing, he looks like a suburban Zen monk.

"And nothing special. His name is Anker Høj. He's from Copenhagen. Civil engineer specializing in pre-stressed concrete. Published a number of articles on winter additives. Anyway, the Danish police aren't after him for some brutal quadruple murder."

He finishes his workout and gets dressed. As he slips into his sneakers, he hesitates momentarily, and Lisa wonders if he has completely got out of the habit of wearing shoes or if he has simply outgrown his sneakers. They finally go outside carrying a large cardboard box and a backpack.

When he sets foot on the street, Éric looks up at the star-studded sky. The horizon has begun to glow toward the east, but the Milky Way can still be easily recognized tilting down over the U.S. border.

"I'd forgotten how big the galaxy is."

"You should get out more often."

The strawberry fields on the other side of the fence are empty. It's been several weeks since the Mexicans left. The two conspirators stride across the rows of strawberry plants. They've hidden the hand truck in the ditch on the edge of the field; Lisa carries the cardboard box and the backpack, and Éric lugs the cylinder (he insisted).

Having reached the far side of the field, they clamber one at a time over a rickety fence, passing their load over the wire. They handle the box like a newborn baby and the cylinder like an old, cantankerous torpedo. The pasture has been grazed down to the ground, and far off, where the farm lies, the cows can be heard lowing as they line up at the milking machine. Lisa turns around to gauge the distance they've covered.

"Don't you think this is far enough?"

Éric shakes his head and points to the neighbouring field. Lisa shrugs. The sky is growing brighter and the surroundings are more sharply defined. The space around them expands as the night retreats; suddenly Éric stops dead. He puts down the cylinder and drops to his knees.

Ohshitohshitohshit, Lisa is thinking. She has never witnessed one of Éric's attacks of agoraphobia and has no idea how to cope with it. She'll just have to wing it.

"Okay, don't panic. You need to keep breathing, all right? Do you hear me?"

No response. He has turned white, his eyes glued to the

ground. His forehead is beaded with sweat. Lisa is at a loss for what to do. Should she go get help? On the far side of the strawberry field, the roofs of the mobile homes seem to be on another continent. Mrs. Le Blanc is the only person capable of helping her, and right now she is in Valleyfield with her Danish winter-resistant-concrete expert.

Lisa crouches down beside Éric and, as gently as possible, presses her lips against his ear.

"Listen to me. There's no one here. Just you and me. It'll be okay. You have to calm down."

She keeps on murmuring like this until, after several endless minutes, Éric gives her a feeble nod. He finally resurfaces and draws a few deep breaths. Lisa silently wraps her arms around him. The attack is over. Éric stands back up like a boxer who has been down on the mat for the last minute: pale, beat-up, but operational. He rubs his face, shoulders the cylinder and without a word heads off toward the line of corn. Lisa frowns as she watches him move away.

They finally reach the electric fence that separates the corn from the cattle. Vibrating between the two orange filaments is an enormous spiderweb speckled with dewdrops. After slipping the equipment between the two wires without receiving a shock, Éric and Lisa plunge at right angles into the cornfield. They go through row after row, which stretch like so many walls forming narrow corridors. The fragrant leafage brushes against their faces.

Once they have covered what Éric considers an adequate distance, they set about flattening the corn plants until they've cleared a nice round circle rimmed by cornstalks standing at attention. It looks for all the world as though a flying saucer landed here during the night.

Éric is rather pleased with the results, but Lisa is jumpy. She knits her brow and pricks up her ears. The only sounds are the calls of bobolinks and red-winged blackbirds. Éric is about to ask her what's the matter when it hits him. In two or three weeks, the cannabis harvest will get under way. This isolated cornfield is the perfect spot for stepping on a bear trap or being blasted by a .22 rifle. He sees these surroundings in a whole new light, as though a Bengal tiger were lurking among the stalks.

Lisa gestures: there's no time to lose.

They spread a tarp on the ground and lay out the contents of the cardboard box. First Lisa takes out a disposable white cooler, organ-donation size, bristling with snap-hooks. A porthole has been carved into the side of the cooler to accommodate the black eye of Mrs. Le Blanc's Canon PowerShot, sequestered in the name of science. Éric has managed to reprogram it so it will take a picture every fifteen seconds until the batteries run down or the memory card is full, whichever comes first. Lisa has jammed hot packs around the camera to prevent the batteries from freezing.

In addition to the camera, the box contains the Garmik 55, a GPS beacon designed to trace motor vehicles. All that's needed is to turn the gizmo on underneath the body of an automobile and the beacon's geographic coordinates stream into a mobile phone—in this case the one belonging to Mrs. Le Blanc—in a highly instructive but (admittedly) rather spartan form:

```
GARMIK (3:03PM) > 06-08-25-190231-UTC-0,
44.9962973, -74.0864321
GARMIK (3:18PM) > 06-08-25-191808-UTC.0,
44.9975719, -74.0866145
GARMIK (3:33PM) > 06-08-25-193354-UTC-0,
45.0008417, -74.0867325
```

When she received this little series of test messages on her phone yesterday afternoon, Isabelle Le Blanc cast her son a dubious look.

"Who is this Garmik?"

"Nobody."

"And what does all this mean?"

"It means Garmik is working."

She shrugged. What in the world could these two kids be up to?

Having turned on the camera and the GPS beacon, Lisa seals the cooler with three strips of duct tape. She fastens the parachute to the snap-hooks set into the sides of the box and starts to carefully coil the suspension lines. If the parachute fails to deploy properly, the cooler will plummet thirty thousand metres, Mrs. Le Blanc's PowerShot will shatter into thousands of tiny fragments of plastic and printed circuits, and the two young scientists will have to put up with a parental lecture on the topic, "Do our children have too much free time?"

They finally connect the weather balloon to the cylinder and Lisa opens the valve. After a short while the balloon has expanded to the size of a small car, a diaphanous white Fiat 500 floating in the cold air, visible from far above the sea of corn.

Lisa knots the opening, removes the hose and lets the rope run through her fingers. The balloon rises with the cooler and then stops four metres in the air, still tied to the helium cylinder. To the east, the sky is turning blue. Unlimited ceiling, zero turbulence. Lisa looks for a signal from Éric. Without a word, he hands her his Swiss Army knife. Lisa pulls out the saw, the file, the scissors and the awl before finally locating a blade. She presses it against the rope and, holding her breath, cuts it with a single stroke.

The balloon lifts off at an astonishing rate. It ascends almost vertically in the still air, and then begins to drift slightly eastward. When it comes level with the angle the sun has already risen to, the membrane is set ablaze like a Chinese lantern. Their mouths agape, Lisa and Éric watch the glowing sphere shrink against the dark blue of the sky, climb faster and faster, as if it has just been caught in a high-altitude wind, and disappear barely five minutes later behind the tops of the cornstalks.

What happens next will unfold far beyond their range of vision. The balloon will ascend through the troposphere, higher than Mount Everest, pass the cruising altitude of commercial flights, and—with a bit of luck—reach the stratosphere and brush against the ozone layer. In that rarefied atmosphere, it will expand to the size of a mobile home and burst. The Weisberg parachute will deploy—Lisa's fingers are crossed—and the cooler will fall back down while a steady flow of coordinates are sent to Mrs. Le Blanc's telephone. And then all they have to do is retrieve the cooler later that afternoon.

According to Éric's simulations, the flight should last two to three hours.

For the moment, there's nothing left to see; in the wake of the liftoff, the place feels empty and somewhat grim. They collect their paraphernalia and retrace their steps: wall of greenery, electric fence, pasture strewn with cow pats. Lisa thinks about the balloon, somewhere up there, spooling out a slender string of numbers and pictures as it ascends. She glances toward the east and sees nothing but empty sky.

Beside her, Éric advances with long strides, obviously in a hurry to return to his sanctuary.

"What are you doing today?"

Lisa stops looking at the sky. "Baskine house, as usual. We're painting the ceilings. I've already asked my father if we could go fetch *something* later this afternoon."

"Did he say we could?"

"Yes. But I didn't mention we might have to drive three hundred kilometres. Hey! See that?"

She points to a cluster of multicoloured balloons limply floating through their field of vision, skimming the roofs of the Domaine Bordeur.

Éric stops, dumbstruck, and sets the cylinder down on the ground before realizing it's simply a bouquet of balloons that have broken loose from a children's party and, after drifting through the night, are slowly starting to deflate.

"Weird coincidence, don't you think?"

Éric nods.

"For a second, I had the feeling another you and another me had also just launched a high-altitude balloon."

Lisa smiles at the thought of another Éric and another Lisa in another nearby cornfield. Now there's an unlikely idea. Éric watches the multicoloured cluster float away, as if expecting the sky to soon fill up with balloons from one horizon to the other. The human race storming the stratosphere. The balloons are on the verge of disappearing just above the woods. In an hour they'll be found snagged on a tree branch.

Éric lifts the cylinder onto his shoulder, and they set off again.

— 12 —

HIS NAME IS ZHŌU PAVEL.

He picked up the Russian given name while working in Nakhodka, carried it all the way to Singapore, then

Montreal, and now it's been so long since he used his real first name that he's begun to forget it. He'll be turning eighty-four next week. He's entitled to let a few details escape him. What's in a name, anyway? Pavel knows he'll never be going back to Shenzhen. He will die in this North American city wearing this Russian name, and it doesn't bother him one way or the other. Right now he has papers to classify, a skyscraper of papers with a Rubbermaid container of cold noodles and a Thermos of tea perched at the very top.

He looks up. It's drizzling on the parking lot, the tractors and the rust-brown containers. The camouflage colour of a furtive economy, and the fact is even Pavel doesn't see them anymore. His gaze goes right through them.

He takes a sip of tea. Adds up some figures.

A white Dodge Charger appears between two tractors and parks in front of the office. Pavel frowns. He knows what kind of car this is. It's not so much a vehicle as a sort of non-verbal language. There was a time when the police drove Crown Victorias. These days they're equipped with Dodge Chargers or SUVs with tinted windows. Always an American make, never Asian or European. There is something subtly political about the way police services put together their fleets of vehicles.

A woman gets out of the car. Pantsuit, leather jacket, high-heeled shoes. Her face is hard and tired, as if this were the Friday of a hundred-day week.

Pavel drains his cup of tea.

She walks through the door, scans the place and steps toward Pavel. In her heels, the woman towers over him. She pulls out an RCMP badge and holds it up long enough for him to get a good look at the buffalo head and the crown and to take in the motto *Maintiens le droit* inscribed in the top banner.

Pavel nods his head. He says nothing, has no intention of doing so unless obliged to. His grasp of French was never very strong. The woman opens her briefcase—he catches a glimpse of lists of addresses struck through with a red pen—lifts out a sheet of paper and places it on the table.

He pretends to adjust his glasses, basically to stall for time. Written on the paper are *Rokov Export* and *PZIU 127 002 7*. The woman explains something, but Pavel doesn't really listen. He knows exactly what she's after. He knew it as soon as she stepped into the office, as soon as he saw the white Dodge Charger pull into the parking lot. It's about that damned container. He was sure someone would come to ask about it sooner or later.

With a thoughtful expression, he places his finger on the sheet of paper and then withdraws it.

Acting as if he is in no hurry, he pours two cups of tea and offers one to the woman. She looks at the cup but doesn't touch it. Pavel turns toward the venerable Pentium, wakes it by jiggling the mouse and then keys in a search request. The hard drive squeals and squawks. A few seconds later, at the other end of the room, the printer spits out an invoice in the name of Rokov Export. The history of PZIU 127 002 7 is summarized on this page in the terse dialect of management: addresses, travel dates, terms and conditions. At the very bottom, in the Means of Payment section, there is a check mark beside *Cash*.

The woman seems to be on the verge of smiling. She asks if Rokov Export often does business with them. Pavel shakes his head and raises a finger. *Just once.*

After a brief moment of silence, he brings the cup to his lips. The woman does the same—the insignificant sip gives her away. A real police detective would never have taken the tea. Pavel follows her gesture attentively, their eyes meet and he instantly realizes that she knows he knows. But it doesn't matter anymore. She finally allows herself to smile.

She drains her cup, slips the invoice into her briefcase and goes out without another word.

— 13 —

SEPTEMBER GOES BY, RAINY AND FOUL, without Mrs. Le Blanc's telephone ever receiving the GPS signal.

Lisa spins endless hypotheses. Maybe the balloon rose so fast it ended up beyond the reach of the cellphone relay towers? The device could then have fallen into the river or a bank of electric transformers or another similarly fatal location. Éric calculated the trajectory based on speed, wind direction and the balloon's capacity to dilate, but Lisa is well aware that the effort was futile. There are too many unknowns left in the equation. The capsule could have landed anywhere between thirty and three hundred kilometres from the launch point inside a fifteen-degree wedge, an area equivalent to tens of thousands of cornfields.

As he waits for a sign from the heavens, Éric compiles notes toward a kind of manual for beginner stratonauts, a detailed user's guide that will make things easier for another Éric, another Lisa, who, at some indefinite time and place, may want to launch their own high-altitude balloon. Rather than blindly fishing around for information, they can simply consult the manual. Éric takes some pleasure imagining this future alter ego hunkered down amid the corn at dawn, the manual in his hand. You can be reclusive and altruistic at the same time.

While Éric writes his notes, Mrs. Le Blanc searches high and low for her camera. Her son has managed to avoid the subject so far, but how long will he be able to hide the truth from her?

This bad state of affairs is briefly—and only partly—mitigated by the resurrection of Mr. Miron's Datsun.

The car hasn't touched asphalt for fifteen years. Gus Miron salvaged it from behind a barn, where it was hibernating on railroad ties, and he's being trying to resuscitate it ever since.

For Lisa, the unstartable Datsun, perched on cinder blocks, deserved to figure prominently in the Hall of Fame of vehicles, alongside chariots of fire, enchanted pumpkins, the Saturn V, farcasters, witches' brooms, balsa wood rafts, and flying BMXs. Actually, Lisa is starting to wonder if the car's function isn't purely symbolic. On several occasions she has surprised Mr. Miron sitting behind the wheel late at night with his elbow protruding through the open window, a cigarette stuck between his lips, daydreaming. Maybe he didn't really want to resuscitate it.

In any case, the engine kept on turning over more and more often and for longer and longer periods of time, until it eventually appeared reliable, so much so that on the second Sunday in September, shortly before supper, Mr. Miron comes knocking on the Routiers' door to ask if Lisa would like to, quote, *go for a spin*, unquote.

The automobile gleams in the sunset light. Indulging in an unusual bit of vanity, Mr. Miron spent two hours waxing the bodywork and polishing the chrome. Having got wind of the impending takeoff, a few inquisitive souls came over to make sure they would not miss the unlikely event. This part of the street has taken on a Barnum & Bailey atmosphere.

The pilot and co-pilot climb into the cockpit and shake hands ceremoniously. The Datsun starts up instantly. Mr. Miron rolls down the window and listens. To anyone who might have followed the trials and errors of the previous months, the engine's performance is a harmonious concerto. As if it was finely tuned, 440 Hz on the nose. No suspicious ping, no whistle. Clutch engaged: the transmission groans a little, but the gravel can be heard crunching under the tires like coarse sugar. There's excitement among the curious spectators, timid applause. All that's missing are confetti and streamers.

Gus Miron pulls out, turns right and begins to drive up Bonheur Street. He must deal with a slight gradient, but the Datsun shifts into second gear without a hitch. There is a quick jolt as the gear changes, but the engine holds steady. This is the best show of the year, with the sunlight flooding the car's interior. Two kids provide an escort on their BMXs. Lisa can imagine Éric's face when he sees her pull up in front of his house, her arm draped nonchalantly over the car door. It will take a couple of honks of the horn to get that recluse to pay attention to anything that's happening in the street.

Just as they shift into third gear, the engine coughs and stalls. Gus Miron immediately puts it in neutral and tries to restart it. It's no use. The car comes to a stop right in the middle of the road. They get out to estimate the distance they've covered: a hundred and fifty metres all told. Mr. Miron gives the car an affectionate pat.

"Well, anyway, we outdid the Wright brothers!"

The way back is a lesson in humility. To the amusement of the onlookers, the two of them push the Datsun back to its usual spot. People chatter as they drift away. From the bushes comes the sound of the first crickets of the night.

Having fetched his work light, Mr. Miron inspects the engine for the ten thousandth time, and a feeling of admiration wells up inside Lisa. *That's the spirit!* she thinks. Never give in to adversity; keep fighting, always.

She suddenly feels foolish for waiting all these weeks for the GPS signal, as if the point of the operation was actually to take pictures from the upper atmosphere. The pictures were just a bonus. The real goal of the balloon was its fabrication, the evenings spent coding, sewing, debugging, finding answers to questions, and answers to the questions raised by the answers to the questions. Lisa must stop thinking about the balloon; she still has a long list of projects she'd like to suggest to Éric.

Leaving Mr. Miron to attend to his engine, Lisa does an about-face and is on the point of dashing over to the Gaieté cul-de-sac when she spots Mrs. Le Blanc approaching—on foot, no less!—looking determined, with that expression she wears on bad days.

— 14 —

WHAT USED TO BE THE garage of Autocars Mondiaux, at 230 Gibson Street, apparently has been closed for a few years. Clumps of wildflowers are slowly colonizing the cracks in the parking lot. A large poster for MVGR Global Rental pasted inside the window is the only indication that the place has not been totally abandoned to the elements. The garage does not look like the headquarters of a dangerous group of Russian terrorists—but how to know for sure?

Zoom out: what comes into view is the Saint-Laurent industrial park, its lifeless warehouses, its deserted streets below the approach corridor of the airport. Zoom out farther and the frame of Google Street View appears, followed by the Orweb navigation window and, finally, the screen of the Eee sitting on the living room floor.

Strewn around the computer are a black leather briefcase, an invoice made out to Rokov Export and greasy wrapping paper flecked with grains of salt, the sole remnants of what for a short time was a double cheeseburger.

Zooming out still farther, one comes across a trail of clothes leading away from the Eee: a pair of high-heeled shoes, a leather jacket, a grey woollen pantsuit and a pearl-coloured blouse with the price tag still attached (SALE $39.95). Another couple of metres and one discovers an RCMP badge in its textured leather case purchased on eBay for $24.99, forty-eight-hour delivery. A collector's item, not exactly identical to the badge used by officers in Montreal but indistinguishable to the uninitiated.

Pull back and pan across: the trail of apparel continues—nylon stockings, panties, bra—and ends in the bathroom, where Jay has been marinating for nearly an hour, eyes shut, submerged up to her nose in scalding water. One more centimetre and she would need a snorkel. The adrenalin level in her blood has dropped back to normal for the first time in three days. She has a feeling of post-orgasmic plenitude; she never would have believed that the invoice of a transport company could bring her such joy.

The water level rises and falls imperceptibly with her breathing. All is calm. Jay is barely aware of the sound of a soap opera playing on the ground floor.

In a recess of her consciousness, she wonders if it is wise to interfere with an RCMP investigation. She has only two (2) years, three (3) months and eight (8) days left to go—not very much longer. When she gets caught—and she will get caught—they'll drag her back to Joliette to serve out the rest of her sentence. Come to think of it, how much time would be left? The Parole Commission must use an equivalency algorithm, like the one that converts bonus points on an Air Miles card. If it comes to that, she has six years of jail time left with no possibility of sentence reduction or another parole—and that doesn't take into account a new trial with a fresh batch of charges. Using forged documents. Identity fraud. Breach of conditions. Breaking and entering. Obstruction of justice. Obstructing police work.

Jay takes a deep breath. She feels good.

Then suddenly she feels hungry. The double cheeseburger wasn't double enough.

Stepping out of the bath, she wishes she owned a bathrobe. At what age does one start wearing a bathrobe? She pulls on a pair of pyjama pants and an old grey hoodie. As she dries her hair, she grabs a handful of menus from off the fridge and spreads them out on the counter, like a musical score. Symphony number three for fried foods and pickle.

As she compares the respective merits of bacon poutine and the egg roll combo, the telephone rings. The display shows a number in the 450 area. Jay is surprised to hear

Laura's voice, since she doesn't recall giving her her phone number. After three days of sick leave, her co-worker began to worry.

"They say you've got a cold?"

"Some sort of virus, aching muscles. I'm starting to feel better. I'll be back at work Monday morning. Have I missed anything important?"

"I can see you haven't lost your sense of humour."

At the far end of the apartment, the bathwater can be heard gurgling down the drain.

"Actually, now that you mention it, we did get some news about Papa Zulu."

"You found it?"

"Yes and no."

This is one of Laura's favourite answers—along with *hmmm . . . yesss* and *it's complicated*—which usually precede long, nuanced explanations.

"You remember what they did at the Montreal terminal?"

"Like hacking into the database?"

"Yes. The famous 'one-two punch,' as Mahesh puts it. First they redirected the container, then they erased it from the database. They did precisely—*very* precisely—the same thing at the port in Caucedo."

With a look of mild disgust, Jay hesitates between the tempura sushi combo number seventeen and the Hawaiian pizza with extra pineapple.

"It took them a week to confirm that?"

"It's a case of an old backup on tape. And maybe some

bad faith too. In a nutshell, Papa Zulu arrived with a trans-shipment code for Brazil. It stayed in the Caucedo terminal for forty-eight hours, then it was redirected to Long Beach, California."

"You think they're trying to get it into the States?"

"Not likely. They would have already tried at Newark–Elizabeth. Anyway, we'll know soon enough. It was supposed to be unloaded about ten days ago . . ."

"If it was in fact unloaded at Long Beach."

". . . *if* it was unloaded at Long Beach, naturally. Everyone's on the case. The FBI, Homeland Security, Border Services. Montreal is a bit peripheral, but there's more and more pressure to find Rokov."

Jay pushes away the menus; geopolitics is incompatible with the goings-on in her stomach.

"There's a problem."

A brief silence ensues. Laura was about to wrap up the call and wasn't expecting this new development.

"What problem?"

"According to Mahesh, it's impossible to hack the shipping industry. Not because it has a high level of security but because the systems are too diversified. They've got numerous software layers and all sorts of redundancies. Information is spread over many databases that are under the jurisdiction of multiple administrative bodies: customs, the port, the longshoremen, border security, shippers, exporters. Everyone operates with different kinds of software and protocols. There are a large number of standards that are not necessarily compatible. Not to mention back-ups and photocopies."

"Yes, Mahesh already talked to me about this. He says that ports practise security through opacity."

"Right. So when he saw that the Cast Terminal's database had been tampered with, he immediately assumed it was an inside job: one or more infiltrators with passwords and the security certificate, capable of modifying the database on site. But . . ."

". . . but it's a little far-fetched to imagine that Rokov could have infiltrated several security zones in the port of Montreal and in Caucedo simultaneously."

"Exactly."

"Far-fetched, but not impossible."

Laura's voice modulates in a way that betrays her uncertainty. She will investigate further.

When Jay hangs up, a faint smile flickers across her face, as if she were playing a complex game whose rules she is just now beginning to understand.

— 15 —

AS SOON AS SHE SETS HER duly unshod foot in the sanctuary, Lisa senses a definite change in the atmosphere, although at first glance everything looks the same, except perhaps for a slight hint of untidiness. Perched on the bookcase, the budgies are hatching a plot.

Éric sits cross-legged on his bed; he's thrown the comforter over his head to make a tent/bunker. The power cord of his computer snakes under the comforter, like an umbilical cord brimming with electricity, and there's the muffled sound of fingers on the keyboard. Without asking permission, Lisa slips inside.

The glow of the screen and the purring of the fan create a cozy ambience. It feels like the inside of a high-tech igloo. Lisa squeezes in next to Éric, who stops typing. Stacked on the screen are lines of very compact code flanked by lengthy, incomprehensible comments.

"I was just talking with your mother."

"What did she tell you?"

"Not much. The basic details. Engagement to Anker. Two-year contract. Copenhagen."

"Copenhagen."

"When are you leaving?"

He shrugs. "This winter."

"Does your mother speak Danish?"

"She can get by. She's been learning it for months. I didn't clue in."

"You mean she was preparing without talking to you about it?"

"She swears she wasn't. She said it was just to surprise Anker."

"You believe her?"

"I dunno. Yeah, I guess."

Outside the tent, the budgies can be heard cooing, flying around the room and returning to their usual perch. With the tip of his forefinger, Éric toys with the cursor. Makes figure eights over the whole screen. Then abruptly tires of it.

"Did she say anything about me?"

"No."

There's nothing more to add, and they stay there, sitting side by side, without saying a word. The computer screen goes to sleep and suddenly they are plunged into darkness. There's no sound except for the purr of the fan and the budgies squabbling. Lisa wonders how long their oxygen supply will last.

"Can you suffocate from carbon dioxide poisoning under a quilt?"

"I can google that if you like."

He brings Google up on the screen and keys in *submarine + single-seater + endurance + "carbon dioxide."* Out of the corner of her eye, Lisa sees him smile. Well, that's something, anyway.

— 16 —

THE SAINT-LAURENT INDUSTRIAL PARK is as calm as a Japanese print. All that's missing is some bamboo and the silhouette of Mount Fuji on the horizon. No sign of life anywhere along the short length of Gibson Street, aside from the white van approaching number 230, which rolls by very slowly before disappearing at the corner of Griffin Street.

Then, silence once more. It is 7 a.m. on the last Saturday of November. Nothing stirs, not even a sparrow. This place is Montreal's blind spot.

After a minute, the van comes back in the opposite direction and stops in the parking lot of the former Aeroflot office, a hundred metres kitty-corner from number 230. The engine stops running, and the street once again sinks into a prehistoric calm.

It's an ideal vantage point; from here, Jay can see all of the Autocars Mondiaux garage while maintaining a healthy distance just in case. She slides her seat back and turns the radio on very low.

As she half listens to the news, she reaches for her binoculars and carefully scans the decrepit surroundings. The landscape is filled with a blend of warehouses, workshops and garages. Stretching down the north side is a windowless distribution centre perforated, however, by a series of loading docks with a trailer attached to each one. The south side is occupied by the Total Sexe bar, teleported to this hole by a species of incompetent aliens. Directly opposite lies an empty lot guarded by a lonely hydrant, which seems to be dreaming of faraway fires.

The Autocars Mondiaux garage looks especially dilapidated in the low-angled dawn light. Jay examines the building carefully, sees no camera, no trace of human activity.

She does not want to take any risks; the reflections in the windows prevent her from seeing inside.

Deep in thought, she lowers the binoculars. She's studied this location so much on Google Street View that it now seems strangely familiar to her, like a false memory.

Jay tilts her seat back slightly. This rental van is as clean as an operating room. It smells of solvents and new carpet. Not a scratch, inside or out.

On the radio, they're recycling the annual Black Friday story. Customers pressed against the windows as they wait for the stores to open. Trampled kids, sprained ankles, cracked ribs. In order to reach a pyramid of marked-down Xboxes, a woman in Los Angeles cleared a path using pepper spray. Next year, tasers will be in vogue. And then Molotov cocktails, machine guns, bazookas. You can't stop progress.

The news ends with the weather. Sun in the forecast. It's zero degrees at Trudeau airport. The van will start to freeze like an old can of food with holes in it; in fact, the windshield has already begun to frost up. The highs and lows of stakeouts. Jay opens her window a crack, zips up her parka and takes out the Thermos of coffee. Holding the steaming cup, she is beginning to enjoy her situation. She settles comfortably into her seat. She has no lover, no children, no future. She can take as long as she wants to spy on haunted garages.

The hours drag by, empty and static. No sign of life at Autocars Mondiaux. The entire neighbourhood would look deserted if not for the patrol cars. Garda, Montreal police, Sûreté du Québec, Contrôle routier—even the RCMP monitors the area, no doubt because the airport is so close. No one takes any notice of the van.

In the passenger seat, Horacio fiddles with a dead Cohiba.

"¿Esos coches, tendrán cámaras?"

Jay frowns. Good question: patrol cars are now equipped with cameras. She congratulates herself for parking the van so that the licence plate can't be seen from the street.

Aside from the unhurried patrols and the occasional UPS truck, the area is decidedly lifeless. Uninterrupted dead calm. Evidently because it's a weekend. The only sound is the noise of airplanes taking off from the nearby airport at regular intervals. When she hears an Airbus flying overhead, Jay realizes she rented the Dodge Charger near here a few days ago. She sits up in her seat and, looking west, spots the apple-green lampposts of the Park'N Fly. The rental office is located somewhere in that direction, just a five- or six-minute walk away. Horacio chews on his cigar with a teasing expression.

"No hay coincidencias, Pequeña."

Jay shrugs.

The day goes by, the sun describes its habitual parabola and sets behind the airport control tower. The neighbourhood is as quiet as ever, as if it were trying to crush Jay under the weight of boredom. No such luck. Seven years with the RCMP have made her monotony-proof. She bites into a Portuguese chicken sandwich without taking her eyes off the garage.

⬡

When the sun goes down, the neighbourhood shifts like an Escher engraving.

To the west, the Park'N Fly lampposts go on. The first trucks gradually show up. At the Total Sexe bar, the pink neon lights start winking and very soon the parking lot is full. Jay points her binoculars and examines the cars. Audi, Mercedes, Jaguar. Apparently, the Total Sexe is used as a hangout by airline pilots. Wednesday special for co-pilots: bonus Air Miles on cocktails.

Still no sign of life at Autocars Mondiaux. The garage is completely dark and a municipal lamppost floods the parking lot with an orangey glow that makes it appear especially bleak. The trucks and tractor-trailers multiply, arrive and drive off again, guided by distant and mysterious dispatchers.

The supply of sandwiches runs out toward midnight. A radio interview with a hockey analyst drones on. Jay gets out to stretch her legs under a mandarin-coloured sky. She notes the warehouse next door, with its loading docks arrayed like intergalactic portals. She takes stock of the situation: seventeen hours of surveillance and zero human activity at number 230. She can move on to the operational phase, but not without a night's sleep.

She climbs back into the van, locks the doors and unrolls a mummy sleeping bag rated -40°C. The floor is made of corrugated steel, but she has slept on surfaces even less hospitable. She eases herself into the sleeping bag and rolls up in a ball. A few minutes later, she is fast asleep inside the down.

A little before 7 a.m., she is awoken by the cold and discomfort. She sits up and rubs her eyes. What was she dreaming about a few seconds ago? The action took place in a cornfield. She can't remember anything else. She wants a steaming hot shower and a coffee. The Thermos has been empty since the night before. Her teeth chatter as she gets dressed. The temperature dropped below freezing during the night.

Outside, the neighbourhood is deserted again. Other trailers, other containers stand at the loading docks. Different, but indistinguishable. Not a single car remains in the Total Sexe parking lot.

The roar of the first Airbuses of the day can be heard as they arrive from Europe. On board, passengers yawn, brush the crumbs off their laps, roll up their headphone cords. Soon they'll pass through immigration and customs. Take the shuttle over to the Park'N Fly to retrieve their cars. Return to normal life.

Jay stretches, cracks her joints. She is shivering from the cold, hunger, caffeine withdrawal. She starts the van and heads off in search of a place where they serve coffee at dawn on a Sunday morning. She ends up at the drive-through window of a Tim Hortons. Whatever—it's civilization. Orders a large, double cream, and a bagel. The coffee smells burnt, the bagel is a crime against humanity. Whatever. She eats while driving back to Gibson Street. Still not a soul.

She backs up the van in front of the Autocars Mondiaux garage, cuts the engine and slips into the back. She pushes the sleeping bag into a corner, squats down by a knapsack and pulls out a mechanic's coveralls, a cap and a black plastic pouch.

She opens the pouch. Inside it are a hook, a half diamond and a few torsion wrenches—the classic set of a dozen instruments. She bought them at the last minute on Kijiji, and it's easy to see they don't compare with Horacio's tools. The old bandit fashioned all his hooks himself, like a luthier, using windshield wiper parts and umbrella ribs. Jay will have to make do with this beginner's set.

She slips on a pair of nitrile gloves and, after quickly scanning the environs, steps out of the van looking busy and professional. She has to decide which lock to pick: the glass entrance door or the huge garage door. There may be a way to get in through the back, but for Jay time is of the essence.

She approaches the main entrance and looks inside. No keyboard, no indicator light. The peeling *Alarmes GPR* sticker must date back to the seventies. She tries the doorknob. Locked, of course. She strokes the lock with her thumb. An old Weiser deadbolt. Nothing exotic, but Jay has the jitters all the same. She opens the tool kit, chooses a torsion wrench and a simple hook and pick. The torsion wrench instinctively drops into place between the fingers of her right hand.

Without even noticing, Jay begins to whistle an old Antonio Morel merengue tune.

She tests the cylinder. It turns counter-clockwise. She inserts the hook and gently probes the pins, making two or three passes. The fabric of the universe contracts around the lock: Jay's attention is wholly focused on tiny sensations, minuscule clicks. She works with half-closed eyes, clenched teeth, convinced that over her shoulder Horacio is watching her every move. She can smell the tobacco and rum on his breath. The lock is slightly clogged and the pins don't slide easily. Without releasing the tension, Jay sprays some lubricant into the keyhole. Then, still whistling, she takes hold of a half diamond.

After an interminable minute, the lock gives. The sound of the cylinder turning, the latch sliding free, is music to Jay's ears. She swings around to give Horacio a triumphant look, but there is no one in the parking lot.

Jay steps inside and locks the door behind her.

It's dark. The opaque windows allow only a fraction of the wan November light to get through. Jay feels as though she is submerged in an abandoned swimming pool. She listens. Not a sound. There's a thick odour of dust, oil and paint.

She turns on a tiny flashlight and sweeps the beam over the reception area. It could easily be mistaken for a museum of industrial ethnology. Business cards covered with a fine layer of dust litter the counter, and one corner is dominated by a half-empty peanut vending machine. A 2003 Shell calendar hangs on the wall, with the pages torn out until November. Nothing of interest behind the counter—the drawers and shelves have been emptied. In the toilet, the air freshener stick deodorant has shrivelled to the size of a jujube but still gives off a faint scent of cherry.

It's hard to believe the place has been used recently, but the floor leaves no doubt: the dust is criss-crossed with footprints. Jay shines the flashlight directly on the counter. The surface must be covered with fingerprints and genetic material. The human body crumbles and scatters data around, but Jay is not equipped to collect eyelashes or fingerprints, and she can't avail herself of the RCMP labs or databases. What she is doing here is akin to a pastime. Some people build boats inside bottles; Jay tracks feral containers.

Holding her breath, she moves on to the garage.

First observation: there is ample room here for a forty-foot container loaded onto a trailer. Finding an industrial space like this in Montreal must not be easy. Most containers are moored to outdoor docks, which should still allow access to the contents without a person being seen. So why stash Papa Zulu away in a garage? The staff of Rokov Export obviously wished to be especially discreet.

Along the wall is a large steel workbench strewn with

screws, bits of electric wire, an empty grease tube. Some construction debris is piled up in a corner of the garage. Now Jay notices the cardboard boxes stacked against the wall, marked *Pommes du Québec—Quebec Apples*. She flips over one of the boxes. Empire.

Jay reels a little. The excitement makes her head swim. She shuts her eyes. After three deep breaths, she regains her composure. Her brain shifts into high gear.

She starts by cataloguing the debris. She notes a dozen folded-up apple boxes showing signs of wear, probably salvaged from the trash of a wholesaler or at the Jean-Talon market. The scraps of wood are many and various. Ditto for the scrap metal: sheet metal, rods, copper piping and a number of parts from an indeterminate electrical appliance. However much she examines this trash, she's unable to figure out what it means. Alongside the heap are some rolled-up plastic tarps splattered with white and black paint. They must have done some cosmetic work on the container, changed its serial number.

Jay scrutinizes the rest of the shop. She immediately spots, hanging on the wall, a hook scale like those used by butchers to weigh carcasses. Under the workbench, someone has stowed a long watering hose. There's also a red plastic jerry can with some liquid still sloshing inside it. Jay unscrews the cap and brings her nose closer to the opening. Gasoline.

She can see signs of DIY activity here and there. Nails, screws, sawdust. She picks up a grease tube. Empty. As she puts it back on the workbench, Jay notices a red stain on the tube. She looks at her thumb. The nitrile glove has a three-centimetre-long incision and is smeared with blood. She must have cut herself on a piece of scrap metal. The wound is oddly painless.

Jay looks around, trying to recall where she might have put her hand down in the past few minutes. She rummages in her pockets hoping to find an old tissue. Nothing. And her thumb is bleeding more heavily. Large drops fall on the floor, leaving red ideograms imprinted in the dust. The wound is starting to burn.

"Shit, shit, shit."

She runs to the washroom, holding her arm up. Next to the toilet bowl, all that's left is a cardboard tube with a shred of paper clinging to it.

"Shiiiit."

Gripping the flashlight between her teeth, she removes the glove as gently as possible to avoid splashing and wraps it around the cut. And, wouldn't you know, it had to be her left hand. She wipes the drops of blood off the floor with her sleeve, carefully inspects the surrounding surfaces. Apart from the grease tube, everything looks clean.

She leans back against the wall. All at once her morale has collapsed, overcome by the cold and her exhaustion. She looks despondently at the clues scattered around the huge shop. Did she really believe she could single-handedly do the work that would ordinarily require a whole team of technicians? Through the grimy windowpanes she discerns movement, hears the muffled sound of an engine in the street. She abruptly comes back down to earth. It's time to clear out.

It's only as she is about to exit the shop that she notices the trash can.

It's an oversized, battered blue steel drum, so nondescript as to be practically invisible. Jay lifts the lid and discovers a bulging garbage bag. She folds back the plastic with her good hand. Papers, remnants of fabric, wrappers. Jay considers her bloody hand. No use hesitating— her mind is made up.

She knots the bag and sets about extracting it from the drum. The bastard won't budge—too stuffed, too heavy. She tips the drum over on its side with a solid kick and tugs the bag horizontally, but it's no use—the drum slides along too. She jams her foot against the rim and pulls the bag with all her might. The plastic stretches, tears in a few places, but the bag finally yields with a sucking sound.

Jay catches her breath. She is sweating. She dreams of a bathrobe and a café au lait.

She hauls her booty across the room like a carcass, leaving an incriminating trail in the dust. Before going out, she pauses long enough to glance around the neighbourhood. No one in sight. She loads the bag, heavy and full of promise, into the van. She half smiles at the thought that her prediction is coming true: here she is, a bag lady.

A minute later, the garage is deserted and the van already far away.

— 17 —

THE FIRST SNOWFALL OBLITERATES THE MONTÉRÉGIE region, blanketing Mr. Miron's Datsun and the fields spiked with stubble, erasing the US border, capping the For Sale sign Robert Routier has finally planted in front of the Baskine house.

Through the living room window, Lisa watches the snow-laden sky come down. She can just barely make out the silhouette of the maple tree twenty metres from the house.

It's been two weeks since Éric went away. Anker starts in his new position right after Christmas, and Isabelle Le Blanc wanted to cut short the melodrama. Lisa refused to accompany them to the airport, and the whole thing ended with the grace of a wrecking ball.

A short time later, Robert put the final touch on the Baskine house: the painstaking restoration of the built-in bookcases, which, with their fresh coat of varnish and cut-glass doors, lend a princely aspect to the living room. Robert outdid himself.

The very next day, after enjoying a rare lazy morning and a third cup of coffee, and planting the *À vendre par le propriétaire / For Sale by Owner* sign in the yard, he immersed himself in the real estate listings in search of his next site. When questioned, he swears it will be a less ambitious project, without financial hurdles or surprises, probably a good old bungalow.

As they wait for a buyer to materialize, father and daughter clean up and shiver (the furnace has been put on standby to save on heating oil). While Robert thrusts the vacuum cleaner into every nook and cranny on the upper floor, Lisa mops the floors downstairs. She finishes in the living room with a series of leisurely meanders and stands back to contemplate the end result. Gleaming wood and the smell of vinegar and latex paint. The bookcases are magnificent, and Lisa catches herself picturing them filled with books. There would be a huge armchair near the window, with a reading lamp. And a fire crackling on the hearth.

She goes to empty her pail in the large porcelain sink in the kitchen. As the floor juice spirals down toward its dark destination, Lisa looks at the pantry door. She thinks about the secret passage hidden in the house's entrails, sealed under plaster and paint, forever inaccessible. She recalls the trace of lipstick on the rim of the glass and the piles of *Life* magazines.

She wonders if it's snowing in Copenhagen.

She immediately dismisses the question. She has no idea what Danish winters look like and has no wish to find out. She's been in denial since October, refusing even to consult the page on Copenhagen in Wikipedia. Who the hell cares about that backwater of neurasthenic Vikings!

The last time she saw Éric, he was packing his personal effects. The bulk of their possessions had been boxed, stacked in a container and shipped out. One bonus: in all the commotion of the move, Mrs. Le Blanc ended up writing off her PowerShot as lost. Despite the massiveness of the move, Lisa took note of signs suggesting the situation might only be temporary: several pieces of furniture as well as all the dishes and cutlery had been stored in Varennes. Isabelle Le Blanc wasn't quite burning her bridges. Lisa and Éric tried to convince themselves that the exile would last no more than a year, at most two. That Mrs. Le Blanc would hate Copenhagen. That her balloon would burst and she would come back to earth, that the wind would shift . . . and other reassuring aeronautical metaphors.

Éric took comfort in at least one thing: the famous Anker turned out to be a truly nice person. The slightly shy fellow was smart and partial to good beer, pretzels and late night epistemology. No sudden stepfatherly squalls—chalk one up on the plus side.

Then, all at once, the discussion turned into a quarrel. Just like that, in less than a minute. Lisa can't even remember what the subject was—just a mundane burst of steam. A valve yielding under pressure. Slamming the door, she stormed out of the sanctuary, and they didn't get a chance to make up before he shoved off.

Since then, she has been getting sporadic updates. According to the latest report, the fool wasn't even homesick; he had just changed rooms, after crossing the five-thousand-kilometre corridor of the Atlantic, as though it were floating amid the cumulonimbi and puffs of sedatives. The budgies, at least, had had the decency to die. The trip had disturbed their migratory patterns. The poor little creatures remained disoriented for days before succumbing one after the other within the space of seventy-two hours.

She finishes emptying the pail into the sink, wrings out the mop and comes back to the living room. Stationed in the doorway, holding the vacuum cleaner, her father surveys the premises. She steals over to stand beside him. Sheltered under the massive door frame, they seem to be waiting for an earthquake.

Lisa sighs. "We could celebrate Christmas here."

"Here?"

"In the living room. We could decorate it, put up a tree."

"There isn't even any furniture."

"We'll eat on the floor. On a tablecloth."

"A Christmas picnic?"

"We'll make a big fire in the fireplace."

Robert opens his mouth to articulate one or two of the dozen counter-arguments that come to mind, but he holds back. He gives her a long look, his Lisa, who handled this absurd project like a real trooper. He wraps his arm around her shoulders and squeezes a little too hard.

— 18 —

JAY TAKES A SCALDING HOT SHOWER, changes the bandage on her thumb. Pyjamas, coffee—real coffee—English muffin with lots of butter. The garbage bag sits regally in the middle of the living room, but Jay makes an effort not to look at it. She is prolonging the pleasure.

She looks out the window as she eats her English muffin. The first snowflakes are falling in Montreal. She brushes the crumbs off the table and makes herself another coffee. The first one didn't count.

Then she goes to sit on the sofa with her legs crossed, the steaming cup perched carelessly on her knee, and contemplates the bag.

She thinks back to an old discussion with Horacio, a recurring discussion, actually. Her former stepfather was especially picky about the garbage that went out of their residence. It was not enough to empty the trash cans into a green bag and then dump said green bag on the street corner. Each piece of trash had a status, an impact, a meaning. According to Horacio, some pieces of refuse had to be burned, some finely shredded, whereas others needed to be thrown into the sea at night under a new moon. He arranged the contents of his bags as meticulously as a visual artist preparing a major exhibition at the Guggenheim.

Horacio Mejía Guzman Retrospective
Treinta Años de Basura—Thirty Years of Trash

Jay was skeptical, but her stepfather insisted on inspecting every single bag that left his house, a cigar jammed between his molars.

"Nunca te olvides de Abimael Guzmán, Pequeña. El cabrón no cuidó su basura."

This Abimael Guzmán—no relation—was his preferred

example. When he was captured, the leader of the Shining Path was holed up in a suburb of Lima above a dance studio suspected for some time of serving as HQ for the *senderistas*. The police kept an eye on the apartment but dared not take action. For a year, they inspected the garbage. In the morning, a fake garbage truck operated by fake garbage collectors would drive along the street and pick up everyone's bags. Once the truck turned the corner, the studio's trash was delivered to the offices of the national police. The investigators could easily see that the amount of trash was at odds with outward appearances. The director of the studio claimed she lived alone in the apartment upstairs; the bags, however, contained the refuse that a small commando might produce.

For months, gloved police officers analyzed the slightest Kleenex thrown away by the studio's occupants. There was no room for error. In the end, it was a tube of cortisone ointment that convinced them Guzmán was hiding out there. The fearsome terrorist was known to be afflicted with psoriasis.

"*¡Fíjate!*" Horacio said as he sorted the contents of the house's trash cans. "They had armed units stationed throughout the country, were responsible for thousands of deaths, threatened the police. They came within a hair's breadth of toppling the government—and it was a tube of cream that was their downfall."

Although Horacio was not particularly fond of Abimael Guzmán, he insisted: *esta historia lleva una lección, Pequeña.*

There's a lesson to be drawn from this story. Take good care of your garbage.

Years later, sitting in her living room, Jay catches herself coveting a jumbo-sized garbage bag with a greedy smile on her face.

She drains her coffee and gets down to work. She delicately unties the knot and fends off the temptation to split open the bag and spread the contents over the floor. The rubbish is packed inside the plastic in chronological order, with the most recent trash on top, the oldest at the bottom. Even the humblest garbage displays a coherence that commands perhaps not appreciation but at least respect.

Jay starts extracting the artifacts one at a time, sorting them as she goes. The contents, compressed under their own weight, immediately expand. In short order, Jay must divide them into little piles that soon surround her on all sides, like the shifting model of a boom town.

Right from the very first layers, she thinks she has hit the jackpot: a reservation voucher from Park'N Fly for three months' worth of parking, from October 11 to January 11. Someone has obviously gone abroad. The voucher bears no name, no credit card or licence plate number. Maybe the plane ticket will show up deeper in the bag.

While she is busy analyzing a handful of chocolate bar wrappers, the doorbell rings. She glances at the clock. Who in the world can be dropping by at nine o'clock on a Sunday morning?

Before she has a chance to press the buzzer, there's a key

rattling in the lock. Mr. Xenakis's face appears at the bottom of the staircase. He waves his hand as if to greet her, but no, he stands aside to let in Alex Onassis and his seventy-two teeth, followed by a young couple, potential buyers. Even at this distance, Onassis smells of toothpaste.

"Hello, we're here for the visit."

"Visit?"

No time to protest—the group is already on its way up the stairs. Jay retreats to the living room, in the middle of which sits what could hardly be taken—even with a great deal of imagination—for anything but a garbage bag in the process of being dissected. Behind her, Onassis has begun his pitch about the space and light and the building's exposure, while Xenakis examines the new light fixture with an approving air. Too late to conceal anything at all.

Onassis swerves to the left—". . . spacious bedroom . . ." —as Xenakis scans the room, distractedly jiggling his set of keys. His eyes land on the garbage bag surrounded by mounds of rubbish classified into concentric circles. Pointing at the mess with the key to the apartment, he attempts to utter a word, a sentence. *The horror, the horror.* Jay acts nonchalant.

"I threw a cheque in the garbage by mistake."

Looking dubious, Xenakis stretches his neck, thereby emphasizing his natural likeness to a giant Galapagos tortoise. At a loss for words—in Greek or any other language—he shakes his key in a way that suggests all this must be cleaned up before . . . Too late. Onassis and the young couple step out of the bedroom and plant themselves in front of the scene.

"And here we have, uh . . ."

Onassis skids sideways, as if having trouble negotiating an icy curve.

". . . the living room. The living room and its skylight."

He continues to skid (not altogether inelegantly) toward the back of the apartment, where the visitors pretend not to see the soiled dishes, the dirty dishcloth, the empty pizza boxes. They leave after three minutes and forty-five seconds. Xenakis brings up the rear. Just as he is about to go downstairs, he glares at Jay, who waves back cheerfully.

"Come again!"

It takes her almost an hour to empty the contents of the bag onto the floor. The various piles and sub-piles get organized into little neighbourhoods, move beyond the living room and colonize the corridor. As she takes in the scene, Jay strikes a conqueror's pose, arms akimbo. She is the Citizen Kane of garbage.

As far as receipts go, the pickings are slim. The oldest date back to June 15, the most recent to the first week of October. Everything was paid in cash. Not a single credit card number to sink her teeth into. The receipts point to a large-scale project: lumber, screws, rivets, soldering rods, compressor and spray paint gun. All told, Jay counts three dozen hardware invoices totalling several thousand dollars. She tries in vain to imagine an object whose construction would require such a diverse collection of material. It could be anything. She feels as though she is trying to put together a three-dimensional puzzle without knowing what purpose it serves, what it looks like, or even exactly how big it is.

Jay focuses on food-related clues. True hunters track their prey by way of its food and excrement. Size, texture, distribution: the least turd betrays its maker. Jay stacks Tim Hortons cups, examines pizzeria and supermarket bills, compiles the wrappers of chewy caramels.

After a long while, she reaches an unlikely conclusion.

She can hardly believe it, but the facts are unequivocal. The pizzas are never bigger than twelve inches and are invariably Hawaiian. The bills show just one size of coffee, medium, double cream, and always the same BLT sandwich. The menus and sizes recur without the slightest variation.

One person.

There was just one person at 230 Gibson Street.

One person shut up in that garage for the whole summer in order to build a secret device inside Papa Zulu.

All at once, the trash around Jay takes on a different colour. This isn't the collective testimony of a group but the story of one single life: intimate, detailed, yet abstract. Jay sets aside the least significant pieces of detritus. Tissues, greasy rags, an old toothbrush that was used to clean something filthy. No clues as to the gender, age, appearance or ethnic origin of this mysterious individual. At most, it can be inferred from the BLT sandwiches that this do-it-yourselfer was not a jihadi.

Jay feels as though she is listening to the monologue of someone whose self-expression comes not through Morse code or semaphore but by means of a garbage bag—a modern mode of communication if ever there was one. She would give anything to get a glimpse, if only for a fleeting instant, of that person's face.

The bag is empty now and flat as a punctured balloon. Jay is on the point of putting it in the recycling bin when she feels a strange object in the folds at the bottom of the bag. She turns it inside out like a sock and, amid a shower of crumbs, a camera crashes onto the floor like a brick. A sliver of plastic flies under the couch.

Flabbergasted, Jay scrutinizes the Canon PowerShot, which looks as though it has been through the war in Afghanistan. The lens cover is open like the eye of a dead animal. She instinctively squeezes the power button, but the camera is unmoved. Inside the battery compartment, an unknown hand has removed the memory card.

Jay points the camera at herself, examines the black pupil of the lens. It sends back her image, bulging and perplexed.

— 19 —

THE MONTHS SLIP AWAY LIKE a sigh, and Lisa is transformed. What for a long time was believed to be a contextual sadness soon turns out to be her true personality—along with a few grams of maternal anxiety, interspersed with the paternal propensity for self-destruction.

Otherwise, everything stays invariably the same; daily life has taken on a greyish cast since Éric's departure. The two confederates have patched things up, which is better than nothing, and now they Skype at least once a week. In the absence of the minutiae that lent a bland sort of charm to evenings at the Domaine Bordeur, their conversations take on more depth and substance.

While Lisa's life marks time, there's plenty of action on the far side of the Atlantic. The first thing Mrs. Le Blanc did was to cook up a half-sister for Éric; little Lærke Høj-Le Blanc is already six months old and equipped with a sharp pair of incisors. What's more, the expanding Le Blanc family have significantly raised their standard of living since arriving in Denmark, having traded the shabby trailer next to a strawberry field for a comfortable cottage near an arm of the sea. Éric now has a gabled room in a nineteenth-century attic, where he divides his time between intensive Danish lessons and a few programming contracts. That he was able to make a go of it so quickly boggles the mind. Still, Lisa suspects—even if the question remains off limits—that he's busy keeping his mind off something by working.

But then, doesn't everyone try to keep their mind off something?

Lisa is certainly of an age prone to mood swings, but, more to the point, she's of an age to borrow Dad's Dodge to go help out Mom, who has to "move an item that's too big for the Yaris"—a thinly veiled allusion to the Sunday trip to IKEA.

After mill No. 2 was shut down, Josée Savoie lost no time getting hired elsewhere. Nowadays she makes moulded plastic car parts. Her dignity and buying power have remained intact, together with her visits to the two-tone temple on Cavendish Boulevard.

Robert magnanimously agreed. He doesn't need the van. He is going through one of his lean times, between projects, during which he spends his afternoons in the garage honing blades while listening to jazz on an AM station from the US.

It took Lisa quite a while to grasp the extent to which her father hates IKEA—the knick-knacks and the furniture and the hex screws with heads that seem scientifically designed to tolerate a specific number of turns, not one more, and that get chewed up as soon as you venture to take apart or reassemble a piece of furniture one time too many.

Back when Robert and Josée still lived together, the winding aisles of the Cavendish IKEA witnessed many an altercation. Robert suffocated the moment he crossed the threshold, whereas Josée thrived inside the store like a lotus in bloom. When they got to the escalator, the couple went into passive-aggressive mode. The shopping inevitably ended—more often than not in the rugs and cushions department—with a full-blown shouting match. It would have been possible to summarize the enormous mistake this relationship amounted to by drawing their respective paths on a map of the store: Robert advanced in long, straight lines, like a tank, with minor swerves near the shortcuts he was itching to take; Josée proceeded in curves and loops, twisting back-and-forth movements punctuated by a thousand pauses. Meanwhile, seated at one end of the cart, Lisa manhandled the merchandise.

The scene was repeated every Sunday, fifty weeks a year. Toward the end, Robert, fuming, refused flat out to set foot inside the store. Two months later, the relationship fell apart. Since then, Josée has remained convinced that IKEA was the cause of their breakup. This narrative is one of the little fictions that help her to hold on—and who is Lisa to contradict her mother?

Which is why, on this rainy Sunday, with the parking lot overflowing in every direction, Lisa is hunting for a spot big enough for the Dodge. She must be at least three kilometres from the store. In fact, she's no longer sure—strictly in terms of the land registry—that she is still on IKEA property. The airport really does seem very close, and Airbuses are hedge-hopping above the cars.

The store appears to be crowded and Lisa regrets not having insisted on coming early in the morning, before it opened. Of course, her mother would have refused—the stampede atmosphere is an integral part of the experience. It's not enough to engage with her contemporaries; she needs to collide with them. Shopping at IKEA is an intensely civilizational activity—or perhaps, on the contrary, one deeply rooted in the vestigial insect within us. In any case, Josée Savoie likes her IKEA overcrowded.

At the escalator, Lisa is instantly struck by the indefinable scent of the place, a composite fragrance in which one's nose struggles to distinguish wood, resin and varnish, cleaning products, oil, vanilla, cinnamon and glue, solvents, flame retardants and a faint note of beeswax. A pleasant scent, comparable to the aroma of gasoline or a new car, and no doubt carcinogenic. Lisa wonders if the smell was synthesized by a chemist somewhere in a lab. IKEA No. 5.

Their mission, Lisa and her mother's, involves purchasing a new bookcase to replace the black Billy that stood in the corner of the living room, apparently still in good condition the last few times Lisa visited Huntingdon.

"What exactly is the problem with your old bookcase?"

"The problem?"

Lisa waits for the rest of the answer, but her mother doesn't deign to elaborate. That is her answer: just *"The problem?"* Though, come to think of it, Lisa isn't even sure she heard an interrogative inflection, so she's unable to determine if her mother wants her to specify the meaning of *problem*, or if this is the beginning of an answer or even a whole answer, or if the general ambiguity of the pseudo-answer isn't ultimately part of a general strategy of jamming the airwaves. The old Billy most likely does not have a problem.

The IKEA is even more labyrinthian than usual. The ongoing expansion has upset the customary geometry of the store. Here and there, plastic curtains block the way, masking aisles that have been put in or are in the process of being put in. Josée Savoie stopped finding her way in the IKEA after she broke up with Robert. She is no longer afraid of getting lost: she *wants* to get lost. Going astray constitutes a mystical act. To stop seeking one's way is to stop desiring.

In the bookcase section, she scribbles on her shopping list. She notes the product codes and their location in the warehouse, aisle and bin, she wavers between pale pink and ultra-gloss red, gets the code wrong, grumbles, erases and holds the product label out to Lisa.

"Could you read out the numbers for me?"

Lisa does as she's asked. The litany drags on. One label for the Billy, another for the glass door and still another for the little low unit. The lead breaks. Lisa spots a pencil dispenser nearby. All those pencils, like bullets in a machine-gun magazine. Somewhere in the depths of IKEA there are gigantic boxes containing millions of minuscule brown HB pencils with flawlessly sharpened leads. The lubricant of capitalism is made of graphite. Josée changes her mind about the colour five times, comparing light walnut and imitation birch. Each colour has a different code, which must be transcribed, struck through, underlined.

"What do you think? Walnut or birch?"

"Dunno."

"Come on, make an effort. Burgundy, maybe?"

"Do you know why IKEA furniture has names and not just numbers?"

"Hmmm. No idea."

"Ingvar Kamprad was dyslexic. He found it simpler to use a system with names."

"Who is Ingevar Kamprate?"

"The founder of IKEA."

"The founder of IKEA. Who knows this kind of stuff?"

"I had a school project."

After filling out, copying and tearing up three shopping lists, they finally have to think about getting out of the maze. The two women look around. It seems to Lisa that they are Hansel and Gretel in the middle of a medieval German forest. The arrows have disappeared from the floor and the information on the signs is contradictory. In every direction, all one can see are series of living rooms and offices, as if the rooms of hundreds of houses had merged into a single vast domestic magma. The store is a subduction zone: the real sinks beneath the showroom as though beneath a tectonic plate.

Lisa stops in front of a vase with a Cretan motif. "We already came this way."

"No."

"I've seen this vase before."

"There are several like this in the store. I saw two or three of them."

"I think we took a shortcut in the wrong direction."

"You think?"

Her mother plunks herself down on an ottoman bearing a Picasso-style bull, and reconsiders the vase. For a few seconds she tries to see it as a geodesic beacon and not a consumer item. So much for that idea. She writes the code down on her list.

In the end, they find the exit purely by chance. They collect the boxes at the warehouse and head toward the cash registers. The scene is straight out of Ellis Island. The immigrants, pushing their loads of lamps, rattan baskets, chairs, drawers, mirrors, line up in front of the counters, beyond which stretches the promised land. Bunches of items lie abandoned: candles, packs of clothes hangers, cushions, wineglasses.

Outside, the weather wages war. As Lisa runs to get the van, mammoth drops of rain explode like grenades.

Forty minutes later, Lisa gets down to assembling the new bookcase and its elegant patented glass doors. Her mother brings her a screwdriver, which Lisa waves aside.

"I already told you. IKEA uses Pozidriv, not Phillips."

"It's the same thing."

"It's not the same thing."

Lisa takes out of her bag the sockets she borrowed from Robert, and her mother retreats before getting another exhaustive lecture on the evolution of the screwdriver through the ages. Anyway, she has to check on the slow cooker. On her way to the kitchen, she switches the TV on to create a tapestry of sound.

Lisa lets out a loud sigh and focuses on the assembly guide. Ten steps, thirty pieces. She was hoping for something more complicated. In the background, the LCN news channel presents a story on Black Friday, which has just drawn to a close. When the Walmart in Long Island opened that morning, the surging mob almost demolished the glass doors, and a man was trampled to death. On the screen, customers can be seen storming towering stacks of Wiis and iPhones.

In the kitchen, Josée stirs the boeuf bourguignon. There's the clatter of the spoon and the lid of the slow cooker, the sound of the drawer sliding on ball bearings, followed by the distinctive pop of a wine bottle being uncorked. After a minute, Josée leans against the living room doorpost holding a glass of Pinot. Lisa thinks about the drug interactions but says nothing. After all, her mother is stable. Consistent, dull, sometimes annoying, but stable.

"How is your father?"

Lisa wrinkles her nose without taking her eyes off the diagram. She needs twelve 118331 screws, which she counts out and sets aside, and sixteen wooden 101351 dowels. Why the question about her father? Her mother rarely asks after him, and when she does, it never sounds genuine, more like the product of some internal calendar than spontaneous interest. On the television, the subject is the possible worldwide shortage of helium, which apparently is not a renewable resource. "Are birthday balloons an endangered species?" the commentator asks in a part tragical, part amused tone of voice.

"Papa is fine."

Sixteen 101532 metal pins and twelve 119081 tightening washers.

"He's fine. He seems a little tired. I get the feeling he doesn't enjoy remodelling houses as much as he used to. He'd like to stop, but . . ."

Lisa's gesture makes further explanation superfluous. Robert can't stop. He's in a financial and moral trap. Eighteen 101201 nails and a wall bracket. All parts accounted for; she can start to assemble.

Her mother takes a sip of wine, her gaze clouded over and a vague smile on her lips. Post-shopping empty-headedness: better than lithium.

— 20 —

THERE ARE ONLY TWO (2) years, three (3) months and four (4) days left to count down—five (5) days, considering the workday hasn't officially begun yet. It's 8:53 a.m., and Jay turns on the used Nokia she has just acquired at an Indian shop under an already forgotten alias. She is busy adding credit using a calling card when Laura arrives in the Enclave.

"Glad to see you survived your virus."

Jay raises a jovial thumb and Laura immediately notices the bandage.

"Hurt yourself?"

"Cut myself in the kitchen."

Laura puts on a pained expression and starts up her computer. "There's news about Papa Zulu."

"Already?"

"A lot happened over the weekend."

"They found it in Long Beach?"

"The container never arrived in Long Beach. It was transshipped onto a China Shipping Lines vessel. It crossed the Pacific, no port of call, and was *probably* off-loaded in Shenzhen between Thursday night and Friday morning."

"Same method as always?"

"Same method as always, confirming what you said on Friday. Rokov could not have infiltrated the ports of Montreal, Caucedo and Panama. That would be insane. So the only other possibility is a hack."

"Which would be just as insane."

Laura shrugs. Jay realizes she is still holding the Nokia in her hand. She crosses her arms to remove it from Laura's line of vision.

"It's strange, though. Papa Zulu is moving farther away from the US, yet the CIA is still interested."

Mahesh enters the Enclave and jumps right into the discussion. "Since when does distance make a difference for the CIA?"

"Good point."

"Laura is getting you up to speed on the Papa Zulu case?"

"Seems the gap is shrinking."

Mahesh fills his coffee machine; it's going to be a long day. "It won't last, if Shenzhen refuses to collaborate. In three or four days, Papa will be anywhere within a radius of two thousand kilometres."

"If the container actually leaves Shenzhen."

Jay has just hit a nerve. There is no indication the container was (or will be) transshipped toward another port, yet dozens of investigators are basing their work on that very assumption.

Laura shrugs again. "At any rate, Papa Zulu may not have been off-loaded there. We're still waiting for confirmation from the port authority. The Shenzhen government is probably trying to work this out internally. Either that, or they don't want to get involved at all."

Jay shakes her head. "I don't get it. The Shenzhen *government*? I thought Shenzhen was a sort of free zone?"

Mahesh makes a familiar gesture drawn from his repertoire: *please direct your question to Laura Wissenberg.* The subject in question rolls her eyes.

"I'm not an expert in Chinese geopolitics."

"You've got ten minutes to become one."

"Okay, okay, okay. As far as I know, Shenzhen is a city with provincial powers, within the province of Guangdong. Most of Shenzhen is basically a special economic zone. Half of the West's consumer products are made there."

"So we're talking about a large port."

"We're talking about a colossal port. Highest growth rate in Asia. Every quarter, they send hundreds of thousands of containers off to America—and in exchange, we send back raw materials and waste."

"Waste?"

"Yes indeed. For the past few years that's been our number one export sector. Scrap metal as well as paper and plastic. And electronic waste too. It's the modern version of triangular trade."

"You are a fount of knowledge."

"I can't take any credit. Three years ago, Division E investigated contraband waste. I can dig up the report, if you like."

"Contraband waste?"

"Highly lucrative."

All morning, Jay waits to finally be alone in the Enclave, but things don't quiet down. Mahesh doesn't stray from his coffee machine, Laura makes sixty phone calls, the office clerk comes to empty the recycling bins, and even Sergeant Gamache pops in (with bagels but no information).

Jay finally decides to choose another tack and goes to shut herself away in the washroom. She removes the Nokia from her bag. The signal is weak but adequate. She sits down on the toilet and dials a toll-free number. *Welcome to Canon Canada, bienvenue chez Canon Canada. To continue in English, please press 1. Pour continuer en français, faites le 2. Our customer support service is available Monday to Friday from 9 a.m. to 5 p.m., Eastern Standard Time. Thank you. We are transferring your call to one of our representatives. Please note that this call may be recorded for quality control purposes.*

"Hello, this is Mariann speaking, how may I provide you with excellent service today?"

Faint static on the line, a hint of a British accent. There's no way of knowing if Jay is speaking to an Indo-Canadian from Toronto or if her call was transferred to a suburb of Mumbai.

"Yes, hi, I . . . I don't know if you can help me. My mother-in-law's camera needs to be repaired."

"Yes?"

"She took an extended warranty, but . . . I know it sounds silly, but she can't remember the store where she bought the camera. She keeps saying she got it at Sears, but I know that's not right. I checked."

"Did your mother-in-law keep the receipt?"

Lowering her voice, Jay adopts a distressed tone. "No, you see, she's begun to . . . well . . . There's no diagnosis yet, but we think it's Alzheimer's. We try to keep her affairs in order, but it's not easy, you know."

"I understand."

"She loses a lot of things."

"Do you have the serial number?"

Jay turns the camera over and locates the number. Goose-bumps ripple across her forearm as she reads out the numbers. At the other end, Mariann taps away on her keyboard.

"The camera was purchased at Caméra Expert in Valleyfield."

"Aha, I knew it."

Underneath her confident air, Jay is actually baffled. Valleyfield? Which terrorist group worthy of the name would set up its headquarters in Valleyfield? She doesn't even know where it is, exactly. Her grasp of regional geography doesn't extend beyond the exit ramps of the bridges. West of Montreal, or maybe southwest? No, she's confusing it with Granby.

"Do you need the address?"

"No, no, thanks."

"Is there something else I can help you with today?"

Jay scribbles the name of the store on a piece of toilet paper. "No, that's fine, thank you."

Immediately on returning to the Enclave, she launches a search on Google Maps. A map appears with, in the middle, a salmon-pink arrow piercing a liver-shaped island: Salaberry-de-Valleyfield, QC, future terrorist criminal nexus.

— 21 —

LISA IS GOING TO MONTREAL. For good.

As she sees it, the Domaine Bordeur has become a degenerative disease. Saturday nights are deadly. The demographics keep going downhill. Mr. Miron has stopped trying to get his Datsun running again. Not to mention her father, who is foundering, one bungalow after another, without her being able to do anything about it.

Meanwhile, on the far side of the Greenwich meridian,

Éric is making great strides. He never mentions it, out of a sense of tact, so as not to annoy Lisa. He feels protected by distance and the language barrier, but Lisa knows how to google. She found out everything some time ago. Éric created a software company, and business is booming. Even once they've gone through the meat-grinder of online translation, the lengthy articles in the Danish newspapers about the young prodigy retain their gushing tone. The kid will go far. The kid has already gone far.

And Lisa must get away at all costs.

She enrolled in a Cégep in Montreal. In electronics, unsure of what she really wanted to study. She bought a rusted Honda with three hundred thousand klicks on the odometer. She rented a room in the Villeray district in an apartment shared by three strangers. She leaves tomorrow morning, the car crammed to overflowing, as though she were heading off to Oregon, with stuff and gear sticking out through the sunroof, without her father—she insists on doing this on her own—with the aim of conquering electric circuits, tin-based solder and analog signals.

Éric will go far, and Lisa advances a centimetre at a time—but at least she'll have achieved what matters most: leaving Domaine Bordeur.

At the age of sixty-seven, Robert Routier finds himself suddenly alone.

He acts like a man who's been through it all. He never needed anyone to cook his pasta or wash his socks. In fact, he hardly notices Lisa's absence; there's a new house to be renovated, a promising bungalow, where he's thinking of adding a sauna-Jacuzzi.

Late in January, he catches a virus. A garden-variety rhinitis, one of the bugs that are going around. But the cold persists, turns into bronchitis, transforms into a triple sinusitis, which degenerates into an exotic form of pneumonia. Robert is a rare case. Three labs vie for his lung biopsies. He is hospitalized for two weeks, intubated, aspirated, saturated and drained, then, on strict orders from his doctor, confined to a month of complete rest. He acquiesces under protest.

Up until now, Lisa has never been concerned about her father. There's a first time for everything.

Robert gets back to work toward the end of March, but he's not the man he used to be. At first glance, nothing has changed. Yet he starts to make uncharacteristic errors of judgment. Once sharp-eyed and sure-handed, now he gets things wrong at an alarming rate. The mistakes multiply to the point where they will soon jeopardize his meagre profit margin.

But it's the hammer episode that really raises the alarm.

During the day, Robert is permanently surrounded by tools, which act as extensions of his anatomy. Most of them hang on his tool belt, but some wait within reach, placed momentarily on a crossbeam or ribbon strip, between two joists, and it takes only a minute of inattention to close up a wall and leave behind a screwdriver, a hammer or a crowbar. Except, the minutes of inattention are becoming routine. Robert tries to laugh it off, but his laughter is less and less heartfelt.

When he walls in his third hammer in ten days, he stops laughing altogether.

He gazes for a long time at the plasterboard partition into which he has just driven a hundred screws, and all at once he hits it with his fist. Then he punches it again. And again, leaving the imprint of four bloody knuckles on the paper surface.

This doesn't calm him down.

He goes out of the house, walks to his van and back, and positions himself in front of the wall with his carpenter's axe: three and a half pounds of surgically honed steel mounted on a walnut handle. Robert pulverizes the sheets of drywall, dislodges the studs with the butt of the axe head and even rips out the electric wires. Two hours' labour wrecked in five minutes and twelve seconds.

Robert tosses the axe aside, reeling a little, and slumps to the ground. As he drops down, he feels something strike the floor. It's the handle of his hammer, hanging from his tool belt.

— 22 —

JAY IS STUCK IN FRIDAY night traffic. It's bumper to bumper for two kilometres, and the traffic update reports a series of disasters stretching from Dorval to Baie-D'Urfé.

Do people really put themselves through this dystopian experience every day?

She shuts off the radio and finds herself wreathed in the monotone noise of the engine. This sub-mini-compact Yaris is worlds apart from her recent rentals—the obscene Dodge Charger and the spotless surveillance van—but it's equipped with a GPS. Nevertheless, Jay has bought herself a road atlas; it's out of the question for her to enter even the most innocuous address into the device. The history of searches and routes is kept in the cache, and the contents of the cache can be consulted, searched, submitted in court. This is the shape of the modern world: bristling with cache.

Jay turned off the GPS when she took the driver's seat, and if the damned instrument hadn't been built into the dashboard, she would have wrapped it in three layers of aluminum foil. Such precautions are probably futile; another GPS beacon must be concealed elsewhere in the car so that it can be located 24/7. In any event, the chances that her colleagues will trace this particular GPS are slim. Jay is years ahead of the RCMP.

She finally reaches the tip of the island and takes the Galipeault Bridge. A quick glance at the atlas and then at the clock. All's well. She is in control of time and space. It's 5:16 p.m. and no one on Earth is thinking about her. As she drives under a huge sign that says *Salaberry-de-Valleyfield 28 km*, she recalls paragraph 5(a) of her contract: "The

Beneficiary shall refrain from leaving Montreal without prior permission; an itinerary may be required."

Fuck the itinerary.

On Victoria Street, the passersby lower their heads and hunch their shoulders. Twenty-six days before Christmas, there's incipient panic in the air.

Jay has parked the car in front of Caméra Expert. Sitting behind the wheel, she studies the shop, psychs herself up. She doesn't know what to expect behind that glass door. Small retailers have become so rare. Over time, shopping at Best Buy has distorted our view of the world. We've grown used to innumerable blasé employees, the constant turnover of personnel, the maze-like layouts. There's something intimidating now about the prospect of dealing in real time with an actual human being.

Jay slips the camera into her coat pocket and steps out to face the unknown. When she walks through the shop door, a bell rings, a real bell made of bronze, not an electronic chime. She is instantly struck by the atmosphere of the place, the almost artistic way the lighting delineates the different sections, like a museum where the artifacts are tripods, zoom lenses and lens cloths. In a corner, in a discreet display case, is an exhibit of antique cameras. Jay places her hand on the glass, fascinated by the massive, intricate devices with unfamiliar names: Ricohflex, Asahi Pentax, Univex Mercury, Leica III.

"Can I help you?"

The man behind the counter is pushing seventy. He looks like an old aficionado who may have opened the store during the Quiet Revolution. He has witnessed the passage of traditional film, Polaroids, cheap 110s, the first disposable cameras and the first digital models. He wears a moustache and reading glasses on a chain. No wedding band on his finger. Jay imagines him shut inside the darkroom every Sunday, developing old rolls of negatives dug up in garage sales. The opening of Expo 67. The construction of the St. Lawrence Seaway. The Saint-Jean-Baptiste parade of 1968. A train derailed in wintertime.

She draws the Canon out of her pocket and sets it on the counter as gently as possible.

"I had an extended warranty on this camera."

The man examines the camera with a perplexed look, assessing the damage. He notes the chipped plastic on the corner of the camera body.

"Did you use it to hammer nails?"

Jay smiles nervously.

"When did you buy it?"

"In 2005, I believe."

Jay is glad she googled the model number before coming, and that she memorized various facts, in particular the year it was introduced. She feels well informed. Being informed lends plausibility. Plausibility is power.

"What's the problem?"

"It doesn't come on. You press the button, nothing happens. Kaput."

"Otherwise just fine."

"It still took good pictures."

The man says nothing, but his gaze speaks volumes. His eyes spell out *euthanasia*. He straightens his glasses and enters into a long, tactful detour about the problem this wreck represents.

"You say you have an extended warranty?"

"I believe so, yes. I suppose there was a paper . . ."

"What's your phone number?"

Jay invents a number with the 450 area code. The man taps away on his computer, predictably to no avail. Jay slaps her forehead.

"Wait a minute . . . You probably have my old number. Now, what was it?"

"We can try something else."

"I'm really useless with numbers."

"Not to worry. Your name?"

"Nancy Ouimet."

More tapping.

"Nothing. Are you sure you bought your camera here? Hold on, I'll search with the serial number. Seven, four, five . . . Ah, here it is. Mrs. Le Blanc?"

"My mother-in-law."

"You did have an extended warranty, but it expired three years ago."

"Seriously? You're kidding."

He swivels the monitor around. "See for yourself."

Jay stares intently at the screen. She has ten seconds to memorize everything at once: first and last names, address, two telephone numbers and date of birth. She misses the photographic memory she had when she was twenty-five.

The man points at a field on the screen. "See? End of extended warranty, October 18, 2009."

"Ah, yes. Three years. Oh, well, too bad. The warranty has expired, so I guess that's that."

"I can still give the camera a closer look."

"No, thanks. It's not worth it. Sorry to bother you."

She collects the camera and leaves the store before her scenario unravels. Sound the retreat, all troops return to the trenches.

The interior of the car is already cold. Jay boots up her Eee, blows on her fingers and transcribes in one go what she saw on the shop's computer: Isabelle Le Blanc 5 Gaieté Street Domaine Bordeur Huntingdon date of birth May 14 1972 (same year as Jay, how about that). She's forgotten the phone numbers.

She starts the engine and opens the road atlas. She locates Huntingdon but not Domaine Bordeur. The car purrs while Jay ruminates.

First option: drive to Huntingdon and ask around. Second option: enter the coordinates in the GPS, let the satellites figure it out, and suffer from insomnia for the next twelve weeks. Third option: find a wi-fi signal and google the coordinates.

Jay launches the network finder utility. Nothing available within a radius of fifty metres. At least this is a task with a clear objective. She places the computer on the passenger seat with the screen facing her and sets off.

The streets in the neighbourhood are narrow; the houses were built in the interwar years. The car wends its way among the invisible profusion of secured networks, like a whale amid plankton. It certainly looks as if people have learned to secure their home networks after all, but Jay is patient. After five minutes she locates an ancient 802.11 router belonging to the Théberge family. The signal is good.

She parks, applies the handbrake and launches the password cracker. It takes only a few minutes to hack into the network. The password is something out of a game of charades for first-graders. First syllable: short for Edward. Second syllable: the fourth letter. Third syllable: not covered. The answer: "Teddy bear"—and the Théberges ought to buy a new router.

Once online, Jay searches "*Domaine Bordeur + Huntingdon.*" It loads—slowly—but it loads. Google presents her with the map of a microscopic hamlet, halfway between Huntingdon (pop: 2,587) and the border of the USA (pop: 317,095,000). She zooms in and memorizes the route. After hesitating momentarily, she captures a screenshot. As a precaution.

She has to cover an extra thirty kilometres, and even though no traffic jams are expected, she nevertheless must cope with the Larocque Bridge, which straddles the St. Lawrence Seaway and has been raised to let a ship go through. A dozen cars are backed up, sending plumes of vapour into the frozen night. Next to the red traffic light, a digital clock shows another seven minutes of waiting time.

Hands locked behind her neck, Jay muses. What exactly is she doing in the hinterland of suburban Montreal? Is she really tracking a reefer reportedly last sighted in Shenzhen, People's Republic of China—the term "sighted" being a misuse of language, said container being notoriously elusive—and which may currently be sailing off the Philippine coast?

An old CSL barge finally slips between the piers of the bridge and glides away, leaving behind the stink of poor combustion. A minute later, the bridge is lowered again. Jay closes her eyes, rocked by the mechanical grating. When she opens them again, the light has turned green and the other cars are already far ahead.

The bridge is unbelievably long, as if it were joining two worlds. Jay listens to the Yaris's antenna whistling in the wind, the cardiac beat of the tires on the expansion joints, and then solid ground again and the muffled swish of asphalt. In the distance, between two curves, the other cars are on the point of disappearing, their tail lights reduced to a few red pixels.

On the passenger seat, the computer gives off a bluish

glow. Every two minutes the screen goes into sleep mode and Jay has to prod it awake with her index finger, like a narcoleptic co-pilot. But the route is uncomplicated: continue driving straight ahead.

Once past Sainte-Barbe, she comes out onto an endless plain. Lifeless fields sown with stalks extend as far as the eye can see. The land of the zombie corn. The clouds have parted, revealing a dizzy, star-filled sky. On the horizon, the lights of a farm can be made out; the silhouette of a grain elevator.

Huntingdon is a more sprawling municipality than Jay expected, but, admittedly, she wasn't expecting much. Distracted by the excessive Christmas lights, she misses a bridge, backtracks, lurches along. She passes through the unmapped village of Hinchinbrooke, beyond which the signs become downright cryptic. Over here is Herdman, over there Athelstan, and down that way is Chateaugay, New York.

The Christmas decorations grow sparse and end abruptly with a dilapidated, nightmarish Rudolph, followed by a string of DuProprio realtor signs. All the houses are for sale. The real estate apocalypse has swept through the countryside, carrying off bungalows and barns.

After a few kilometres, Jay is convinced she is truly lost and needs to consult the map. She pulls up in the yard of a New Holland dealer, where combine harvesters hibernate under a yellowish street light. At the perimeter of the circle of light, a yellow dog barks and strains at its chain. The dog is not on the map. Jay ignores it. Where exactly did she go wrong? The scale of the map is inadequate at this point, but there is no way to download a new version without an Internet connection. She checks the list of available networks. Nothing. Adventures in the heart of No-Wi-fi-Land.

Jay looks up from her computer. On the other side of the road stands an oversized mansion completely unlit, deserted and bleak. The RE/MAX sign looks as though it was nailed to the door years ago.

Out of nowhere, a Honda Civic shoots past at a hundred and forty kilometres an hour—the licence plate framed in fleeting black LEDs—and vanishes into a parallel nowhere. The tireless dog keeps on barking, as steadily as a metronome.

Leaning over the road atlas with her fingers in her ears, Jay decides she is not lost. This country is a labyrinth not because of the complexity of the roads but the impossibility of distinguishing one road from the next. She starts up the car and abandons the dog to the night.

She plunges deeper and deeper into the plain. Corn-stalks, copses. Time stretches like a plastic bag. The stopover in Valleyfield feels as if it was hours ago, yet according to the dashboard clock only thirty-five minutes have elapsed. On the horizon, Montreal amounts to an orange streak of light pollution.

When she finally finds the entrance to Domaine Bordeur, Jay pauses briefly to examine the mailboxes. She counts about forty residents. No addresses or names on the boxes, just anonymous numbers. Attached with wire to a limbless spruce tree, a sign announces high-speed Internet. A bunch of advertising bags hang under a rudimentary shelter made of corrugated sheet metal. A floor lamp and a rusted propane tank have been discarded next to the Dumpster. Still life number twenty-seven.

Jay wonders what the time might be off the coast of the Philippines.

She enters the Domaine and makes her way among the mobile homes. After the drive through the desolate fields, this feels like a return to civilization. The trimmed shrubs are hung with Christmas lights. The roads are illuminated by a few street lights, yet one can still see the inhabitants going about their business inside the houses.

She drives up de l'Extase Street, turns at Bonheur, slows for the traffic bump, takes l'Allégresse and goes down the Gaieté cul-de-sac, with the vast black hole of a field looming in the background. The place is poorly lit, but it's impossible to go astray—a strategic advantage of blind alleys. She advances at a snail's pace, finds the scene almost touching. She feels she has reached a sort of epicentre, although she realizes she has no game plan. Does she really see herself knocking on the door with an innocent air and asking the first question that pops into her head? Excuse me, is the Rokov Export terrorist cell here? Do you recognize this camera? What were you doing on the nights between June 12 and October 12?

She drives past 1 and 3. Visual contact with the objective. Her foot slides off the accelerator and onto the brake.

The number 5 is still visible next to the door frame, even though there is nothing left around the door. The house is almost a total loss. The fire must have happened just a few days ago, and all that remains are minimalist ruins. The four walls and roof have collapsed, leaving only the naked frame of the trailer. Parked on the grounds, a backhoe waits for the impending cleanup. A sign announces the work will be done by Sinistres 3000, a Valleyfield company specializing in calamities.

Jay turns the car around and heads back to Montreal.

— 23 —

THE MONTHS GO BY AND Robert grows thinner. His last bungalow was sold at a loss, and the tireless worker has been put on forced rest for an indeterminate period, perhaps for good. He watches TV and sorts nails, while his health swiftly declines. His vocabulary escapes him, one word at a time, like sand in an hourglass. He soon struggles to name the handsaw, the coffee maker, the door. His environment drifts into a semantic fog.

Even so, he takes things with a gallows humour unfamiliar to Lisa: "I forgot a hammer in there," he grumbles, rubbing his skull.

From Lisa's point of view, her father's condition worsens even faster because she sees him only intermittently. She tries to call him every night and visit him each Sunday, but one missed visit is enough to put her half at sea. Robert has become a Venezuelan TV series where events move at an insane pace. Gus and Sheila Miron keep an eye on him, and a nurse from the local public health clinic sees him once a week, but already this help is no longer enough. Lisa often must stay with him until Monday morning and sometimes rush back at a moment's notice in the middle of the week.

It quickly becomes impossible for her to juggle the shuttling back and forth with her full-time studies. She has to severely prune back her schedule, keeping just two miserable courses per term. As a result, the Ministry of Education terminates the modest loans and bursaries she was receiving. Unable to study full-time, she now must study *and* work simultaneously—which, ultimately, doesn't help at all.

Some people have flight plans. Lisa has to make do with vicious circles.

One Sunday in November, she shows up at Domaine Bordeur with Portuguese chicken wrapped in greasy aluminum foil, fries and coleslaw. Robert doesn't eat much. He looks more demoralized than usual—or maybe just more lucid. The conversation drags on without content or cohesion. Robert's life is now devoid of narrative developments, and he finds it hard to show an interest in anything. He eats the fries with his fingers, seeming to be wholly absorbed in this task. He drifts off for long stretches, comes back down to earth, repeats the questions he asked ten minutes earlier, scarcely listens to the answers. Lisa is from another world, one he is no longer equipped to understand.

After the meal, he looks for the tea tin for several minutes, eventually spots it where it has always been for twenty years, forever, drops a teabag into the pot and pours the boiling water without saying a word. Then, while the tea is steeping, he conspiratorially motions to Lisa to follow him.

They take the back door and go over to the workshop. The Virginia creeper has invaded the surface of the old container, which seems to be covered with a thick layer of military camouflage.

Inside, the air is cold but dry. All of Robert's tools are there, many stored in their boxes or hanging on hooks, others fanned out on the workbench, under the blinking fluorescent light. Antique blades, several generations of clamps, squares that would delight the curator of an ethnological museum, but also the hammer drill bought the previous winter, the laser level and the orbital sander. There's a cross-section of a century and a half of woodworking in this place.

Robert advances, slowly rubbing his hands together. He respectfully grasps a maple wood plane polished by generations of palms. He strokes the wood, sets the plane down again, but his hand remains suspended over the workbench. He is searching for a tool, searching for his words. He draws S's in the air with the tip of his index finger.

"The oldest tools . . . the plane, the adze, the chisel . . . they belonged to Simon, your great-great-grandfather."

Lisa's eyes open wide. "My great-great-grandfather? But . . . you always told me that . . ."

Her sentence goes out like a match, sending up a whorl of vapour. Robert always claimed the tools came from garage sales. Flea markets. Want ads. Lisa never heard anything about this Simon. Robert does not stop there.

"Grandpa Simon worked in the dry docks, at the shipyard. The St. Lawrence Marine Works. Near the Old Port. Doesn't exist anymore. There's a highway there now instead. You know which . . . highway . . ."

"The 15?"

"No, the other one."

"Bonaventure."

"No, the other one."

Lisa shrugs her shoulders. Robert pushes on. He waves an enormous brace fitted with a bit long enough to sink a schooner.

"This was used to install bolts. And the adze here— Grandpa forged it himself. You see, this is his signature, here."

He points to the side of the blade, but Lisa does not see any signature, only wear and tear. He goes on enumerating: the caulking mallet, the male and female plow planes, the straight gouge, the spoon, the burin, the files. One tool after another, he resurrects the vanished docks of Montreal's Old Port. The vocabulary comes to him with no apparent effort.

Lisa marvels at discovering these bits of unimpaired memory, just as the rest of it is eroding, but she cannot help but wonder how much of this family history course is fabricated. It may be easier, when there's nothing left of a life but words, to summon up the distant past. In the end, it hardly matters if it's all invented or not, if the tools come from a mythical forebear or a Valleyfield flea market; at this very instant, in this icy container, Lisa can see the squared-off tree trunks at the edge of the dock, the massive hulls on their cradles, the steel rivets glowing red-hot in braziers, the smell of dross and the iridescence of oil on the water's surface, broken here and there by a dead rat floating belly up.

And Robert keeps on talking, indifferent to the landscape he is conjuring up in the cold air of the workshop, travelling back in time, talking about her great-grandfather Jean-Charles, about his whetstones and his scraper, his spokeshave, his marking gauge, his collection of squares and compasses.

Lisa's attention wanders as she listens. Not that the tools don't interest her anymore, but she suddenly realizes that three of her forebears worked at the shipyard, building and repairing steamships and schooners, until her grandfather Émile closed the works in 1950, so that Robert was the first one in four generations of Routiers to ply another trade.

At this point, Robert puts a large rasp back in its place and catches his breath. He hasn't spoken for this long in months. The steam rising from his mouth and his shirt collar envelop him in a silvery halo.

He points at the tools with a sweeping gesture. "It's all yours now."

To Lisa, this feels like an uppercut to the diaphragm. Yet there wasn't the slightest trace of melodrama in Robert's voice. These days, he is well beyond—or well below— dramatic effects.

"I don't have any room for it, Papa! I share a three-bedroom apartment with three other people."

"You'll make room."

"It's twenty years of your life. You can't give me all of it."

"I have the right to give you anything I want."

Robert strikes the workbench with the flat of his hand, then does it again, a little harder, as though wanting to add something. He stops, looking as though he has immediately forgotten the subject of the conversation.

Lisa feels her body temperature drop a few degrees. Mrs. Miron warned her that her father had been growing irritable after suppertime. The public health nurse called it sundown syndrome. It's best to avoid vexing him; tread carefully. Lisa decides to stall for time: if she claims instead that she intends to take the tools the following week, her father will have forgotten this business by then. But Robert shakes his head.

"You'll need to do several trips in any case. We'll load up your car. You'll take the rest of it next week."

Lisa sighs. "Okay. If you insist. But for now, your tea must be ready."

"What tea?"

— 24 —

AS SOON AS SHE GETS HOME, Jay first pulls out her computer and then unwraps her quarter grilled chicken with extra piri piri sauce, in that order. Sitting cross-legged, the aluminum foil unfolded on the floor, she digs in with her fingers while keeping an eye on the computer's charge level. The battery was completely drained on the way back, and she had to fall back on her memory. Huntingdon, the St. Lawrence Seaway, Valleyfield. The return run seemed shorter to her. The kilometre you know always takes less time than the one you don't.

Gnawing at a metacarpus, she takes stock of the evening. She has come back from Valleyfield with a name: Isabelle Le Blanc. She can't yet see the connection between this woman and Rokov Export, but it's only a matter of time. There are lots of little bones left to crunch, in this investigation.

She licks her fingers. The chicken is perfect—just spicy enough to wring a few tears from her.

What's the next step? Wait until Monday morning to do some research at the RCMP office? Negative. Civilians have no direct access to the databases; she would have to ask a co-worker to do the research for her. Very bad idea.

Rewrap carcass in aluminum foil, degrease fingers. Keyboards don't get along well with Portuguese grilled food. Jay cracks open a beer, wakes up the computer and loads the Facebook home page. She creates a fake account and immediately looks up Isabelle Le Blanc. *Le Blanc* with a space. Surely not very common.

In a nutshell: about fifteen Isabelle Le Blancs have a Facebook account, not to mention the Isabelle-Leblancs-in-one-word and the Isabelle-LeBlancs-with-no-space-but-with-two-capitals, as well as the Isa-or-Isabel-Le[ ] Blancs, who are still potentially in the running. Anyone can be subject to orthographic inconsistency, especially on Facebook.

Jay scrolls down the list. It stretches to infinity. She feels as though she has stepped into a parallel world populated exclusively by Isabelle Le Blancs—perhaps even a single Isabelle Le Blanc endowed with multiple extensions and outgrowths. A sort of distributed intelligence that is at once married, unmarried, underage, lesbian, menopausal. Who is young, old, ageless, wears a straw hat and a miniskirt. Who was a student at the Cégep de Saint-Hyacinthe, Université Laval, Paris-Sorbonne, MIT. Who is French-speaking, English-speaking, bilingual, who speaks Tagalog and Italian and even a little Vietnamese, who eats cucumber and citrus salad, who likes poutine and hot dogs, who does pottery and paragliding and cycling, and who just scored an eighty-three-point word in Scrabble. Isabelle has many friends, of all ages and all colours. People who are old, shy, loquacious, trolls, friends who like everything Isabelle posts, announces, reveals, shares. But above all, Isabelle lives everywhere. In Trois-Rivières and Montreal,

Paris, Kedgwick, Longueuil and Lévis, and again in Longueuil (Jay notes an impressive concentration of Isabelle Le Blancs per square kilometre on Montreal's South Shore), in Iqaluit, New York, Copenhagen, Tunis, Lyon.

In short, there are Isabelle Le Blancs everywhere, except—and this is beyond a shadow of a doubt—except along the Valleyfield–Domaine Bordeur corridor. It's as though a kind of perimeter had been established to create an Isabelle Le Blanc–free zone. A bothersome statistical gap.

How can each Isabelle be differentiated from her namesakes, and, especially, how can they be eliminated one after another until only one remains? Jay has nothing to go on but geography.

She takes a swig of beer, cracks her knuckles. She'll have to use triangulation.

She keys in the query *"Isabelle Le Blanc" + Huntingdon OR Valleyfield OR "Domaine Bordeur."* She needs to rephrase her query several times before Google deigns to spit out what she wants, but after a few minutes she feels a tug on the end of her line. Search result number thirty-five, after the genealogy pages and online dating sites, takes her to a LinkedIn account. An Isabelle Le Blanc was an administrative assistant for a Valleyfield consulting engineering firm from 2003 to 2006, before taking on new challenges with an engineering company in Copenhagen.

Jay rubs her hands together. There are some kilometres between Gibson Street and Copenhagen, not to say a great many kilometres, but it's her most tangible lead. In the picture, Isabelle looks intelligent and relaxed, early forties and radiant.

This is her target.

Back to Facebook, where Jay quickly identifies *the* Isabelle among the Isabelles. An explosion of sorts occurs, blasting away all the supernumeraries and leaving just a single survivor in the middle of a smoking crater. So Isabelle Le Blanc lives in Copenhagen. She has two children, Éric and Lærke, and is in a relationship with Anker Høj, a civil engineer with a friendly face. (A quick search indicates that he is a specialist in pre-stressed concrete and has published a number of papers on low-temperature additives.)

Isabelle is fond of winter sports, Discovery Channel and hot scones with *stikkelsbær* jam. She writes her status updates in English and Danish, and occasionally in French. She seems very comfortably integrated into her new country, considering she has been living in Denmark for only six years. Her last vacation was in Palma. She is quite active on the page of a Danish group devoted to agoraphobia. Scrolling down her page, Jay observes a slightly higher than average ratio of cat pictures. A notable percentage, not yet pathological or even abnormal, but one that attests to a marked interest.

A light bulb comes on in Jay's mind: it's not possible for this Isabelle Le Blanc to be mixed up either directly or indirectly in the hijacking of Papa Zulu. Jay can't say why, but she is certain of this. No doubt because of the cats. The number of cat pictures posted on a Facebook account is inversely proportional to the probability of the user being a terrorist. The people at Facebook surely must have developed algorithms to identify such social deviations. The relationship between pictures of reptiles and psychopathology. Frequency of posts and kleptomania. Eating habits and depression. The future is in data mining.

Jay peruses the photos one more time. Suddenly, there it is, plain as day. The album *Sommerferie 2012* shows Isabelle on the beaches of Palma in July, and then in the little village of Skagen in August. The album *Fødselsdag Éric*, dated September, shows her preparing a birthday cake. She could not have been in Montreal between June and October.

Isabelle Le Blanc, acquitted.

Jay stretches, snatches the camera out of her coat pocket and examines it from every angle. What was it doing at the bottom of the garbage in that garage on Gibson Street? Maybe Isabelle Le Blanc had simply lost it in a public place or sold it through the want ads. Maybe it was stolen from her. Maybe it was a combination of all those possibilities. Plenty of scenarios could explain how the camera might have gone from the (innocent until proven otherwise) hands of Isabelle Le Blanc into the (most likely criminal) ones of the Rokov gang.

Jay finishes her beer. Resists the urge to open another. She is losing the thread. Better turn off the computer and turn in. On the other hand, she could have another beer, try once again to read *Twenty Thousand Leagues under the Sea*. She starts to daydream. In two weeks, she turns forty. She wonders what the weather is like in Copenhagen. She mechanically scratches the label on the misty bottle.

Then she comes up with a fifth hypothesis. Isabelle may have lent the camera to someone in her circle, not knowing what would become of it.

Jay goes through Isabelle's friends again. A lot of Danes, not many Le Blancs. The account suggests a family that has drifted apart, and everyone has lost touch with each other. Perhaps Isabelle is an only child. Even better: the only child of parents who had no siblings either—no uncles, aunts or cousins in the picture. A modern family. In any event, Isabelle has surrounded herself with friends who don't exactly look like a group of radical Islamists. This Hilse could easily be a ballroom dancing instructor, and this one, Karl, you could lay odds that he enjoys salmon fishing, and Bjørn, here, no doubt collects hockey cards.

Click by click, Jay arrives at the profile of Isabelle's son, Éric. Éric Le Blanc, twenty years old, max. He looks like a younger version of his mother and bears the same surname, suggesting that Anker is his stepfather. The young Éric probably left Quebec at the same time as Isabelle, when he was still a minor, which means his biological father is completely out of the picture. Disappeared? Drug problem? Premature death? It's hard to draw conclusions merely from a Facebook account. What's more, Éric appears to keep quite a low profile. His statuses are in Danish and deal with a company called Weiss PSL.

Jay automatically goes to the company's site, and all at once the sky splits open and floods the room with light. Weiss PSL is in the business of intermodal logistics. On the home page, containers, gantry cranes, trucks and still more containers are on parade, a veritable orgy of containers, containers at night, at sunset and in the mist, photographed by keen-eyed professionals alive to the poetry of industry.

Jay trembles and watches the photos march past, too stunned even to smile. All these containers and container ships and lift trucks and gantry cranes. Never. Has she seen. Anything. More beautiful.

— 25 —

LISA NOW LIVES SURROUNDED BY tools in a rundown one-bedroom flat.

Every time she visited her father over the past months, she hoped he'd forgotten the whole business, but no. He forgets to take his medications, to eat, to change his underwear, he forgets the names of his neighbours, of the place he is in, he forgets which day of the week it is, which season, but never once, whenever Lisa came to visit, did he neglect to load up the Honda with a mitre-box saw, a set of sockets, clamps, a crate full of screws, a gas welder. From now on, nothing else matters to him but this final mission: to pass on the family hardware to his only daughter.

Twelve times, fifteen times, Lisa has returned from Valleyfield with the Honda crammed to bursting and riding low on shock absorbers weighed down by hundreds of tools, instruments and blades. Her father's tools gradually invaded all the free space in her little room, a corner of the living room and the shed on the balcony, until her housemates presented her with an ultimatum: this isn't working anymore, the tools have to go.

And so Lisa's new place is a stone's throw from the Notre-Dame-de-la-Défense church, on the top floor of a crumbling three-storey building. She doesn't really have more living space than before, but there's no one complaining about stubbing a big toe against a plane.

It's been barely twenty-four hours since she moved in; she hasn't had time yet even to hang up the roll of toilet paper. She climbs the stairs, teetering a little, with her last carton. She has just spent the day at the Domaine Bordeur because of a medical appointment, and her father seized the opportunity to unload a last volley of tools on her. The workshop is empty now, except for the workbench and a cast iron surface planer that weighs half a ton.

For once, her father appeared quite calm, almost serene. He had just closed an important chapter and could finally let go.

Lisa opens the door to her apartment and flicks the light on with her shoulder. There are tools everywhere—in the corridor, in the bedroom, piled up to the ceiling in the living room—and the air is permeated with the smell of resin and machine oil. Lisa keeps telling herself the situation is temporary, but the truth is, no solution has come to mind. She has a storage locker in the basement, but it's too damp to store anything there.

She walks along the corridor to the kitchen, strides over the tools, bumps her feet against the unscrewed heating grate. Her computer sits on the counter, between the microwave and a pyramid of canned food. She pours herself a large glass of milk and launches Skype. After a minute, Éric appears on the screen wearing a quasi-invisible headset straight out of a science fiction movie. He was waiting for Lisa's call while drinking his second cup of coffee.

"Does the doctor have a diagnosis?"

She shakes her head and drains her glass in one go. "Apparently it's the kind of disease that gets diagnosed in the autopsy."

"Delightful."

"They're trying a new drug, but I'm not holding my breath."

Momentary silence. Lisa starts to pour herself another glass of milk but instead opens the last bottle of beer. Éric raises an eyebrow.

"And the new apartment—how is it?"

"Poorly insulated."

"Electric baseboard heaters?"

"No. There's a kind of central furnace, in the basement, but I'm starting to think it doesn't work. Can you hold on a minute? I'm gonna put on a sweater."

She goes down the corridor, strides over the tools, bumps

her feet against the unscrewed heating grate (she makes a mental note to screw it down, but first she has to find a screwdriver), pulls on a sweater and comes back.

"The landlord is a numbered company. My neighbour tells me they haven't done any repairs in ten years. They buy dilapidated buildings and wait until they collapse to collect the insurance money and build condos."

"Speculating on catastrophe."

"Hm."

"I don't understand why you moved."

"The tools, my dear. The tools."

"You could have rented a storage space and stayed in your old apartment. Even if you factor in the fees for the storage, it would have cost you less."

Lisa doesn't know what to say. Her life is not an Excel spreadsheet; the numbers don't necessarily have to balance. Maybe she just wanted to finally have her own space. The tools provided a convenient pretext; the cost was a secondary consideration. What's more, she's declined Éric's many offers of financial aid. Her apartment may be broken-down, but her ego is made of reinforced concrete.

Éric also moved, two weeks ago. Despite Lisa's repeated requests, he still refuses to show her around the property. However, she did notice several monitors and enormous bay windows. The beast has taken up residence in a control tower.

"You know, I don't understand, either, why you moved. Your room in the attic was pretty nice. I liked the rafters. Were you and your mother not getting along anymore?"

"We got along just fine, she and I. I moved for tax reasons. If you want all the details, I can put you in touch with my accounting department."

Éric announces he's going to make himself a third cup of coffee. He disappears for a minute, and she can hear cups clinking, steam hissing. A budgie flits across her field of vision. He comes back with a steaming macchiato that Lisa greets with an admiring whistle.

"The good life! It hardly looks as if you're the head of an empire."

"I delegate."

"Isn't that a cliché?"

"I swear, both of my companies get by quite well without me. I'm still amazed. I do three or four video conferences a week, I'm couriered papers that need signing and that's about it. Everything runs on automatic pilot."

"Retirement sounds pretty sweet."

The question of retirement is a running joke between them, even though, in reality, there's nothing to laugh about. Éric is bored stiff. He lacks stimulation. For the past few months, his free time has been devoted to creating a new company, a curiosity called eQ, but for the time being it's just an empty shell. Éric has hired just one assistant and a programmer, both part-time. The new company serves mainly as an excuse to doodle on a whiteboard with a blank look on his face.

Lisa wonders how you can run three companies, be a

multi-millionaire and still be bored. This must be one of the downsides of achieving success at the age of eighteen.

Monday, 8:30 a.m. Lisa wakes with a start. There's no time for breakfast, no time to take the bus. She jumps into a pair of jeans, strides over a box of shaper cutters, grabs her backpack, her computer and her course notes.

Outside, the temperature has dropped another few degrees. It feels like snow. On the way, Lisa buys a coffee and a muffin at the Colmado Real, and then climbs into her car, whose starter has been groaning more and more insistently. Chronicle of a breakdown foretold.

When she steps into the hardware store five minutes late, brown paper bag in hand, she gets the distinct impression that, as the saying goes, "nobody gives a shit." She could be ten, twenty or forty minutes late—at her discretion. Business has been slow of late, the phrase *of late* referring to the last ten years.

"Morning, Ed!"

"'ning."

For nine months now, Lisa has been working at the HardKo hardware, and she still doesn't understand why she was hired. Edwin Schwartz belongs to that breed of shop owner who doesn't need employees or customers. He has the personality of a prophet and the looks of Isaac Asimov, and he spends his days in a tiny office on the mezzanine overlooking the sales area. He arrives early in the morning, goes home late at night and never leaves his office unless it's absolutely necessary.

The hardware store has been at the same address since 1954. Although the fixtures and fittings have never been modernized, the shop has the reputation of carrying extremely rare securing systems and is thus assured of the fanatical patronage of aircraft and sewing machine technicians. Behind the cash register, in a tarnished frame, hangs a photo of the Pioneer 12 space probe. Legend has it that in the spring of 1976 Schwartz senior provided NASA with three tungsten-cobalt alloy screws, which are presently in orbit around Venus.

There is nothing terribly exotic to be found on the ground floor shelves; all the specialized material occupies an occult section situated below ground level, where Lisa herself is not authorized to enter. When a customer asks for ten 17-millimetre, number six, niobium Torx screws, it's Edwin who, holding his set of keys, leaves the mezzanine muttering Biblical imprecations, unlocks the door and goes down to the cellar.

Lisa would willingly venture down there from time to time. It would make for a welcome change of place.

She hangs up her coat with a sigh. This day is going to be like all the days before, she can feel it. Work eight hours at the hardware store. Place screws on the shelves. Study for a math exam. Do the laundry. Go to Huntingdon. Help her father. Fill up the tank. Drive back from Huntingdon. Chat with Éric. Jog five kilometres. Talk to her mother. Promise to see her soon. Eight hours at the hardware store. Tell white lies. Eat ramen, drink coffee. Go to Huntingdon and back. Discuss dirty laundry with the CLSC nurse. Wash the dishes. Let the week roll by. The weeks. The months. Wonder about the meaning of life. Brood.

Lisa lives her life in the imperative.

She takes up her position at the cash register. Generations of forearms and packets of screws have polished the venerable wooden counter; you take your seat behind this piece of furniture as you would at the helm of History itself. She looks at the menu of the day: sort out the merchandise delivered yesterday afternoon. Nothing important, otherwise Ed would already have taken care of it. So it can wait another ten minutes.

She unrolls the paper bag and takes out the muffin. No sooner has she lifted the lid of the coffee cup than her mobile phone rings. Private number. At the other end, a husky female voice asks for Élisabeth Routier-Savoie.

"Yes, speaking," Lisa answers as she bites into the rim of her muffin.

"Sergeant Perrault of the Sûreté du Québec. Are you the daughter of Robert Routier?"

— 26 —

ON THE XENAKISES' FLOOR, the squabbles have grown more frequent and more intense. Coincidentally, it's been several days since a buyer came by to visit the apartment. There's a downward price adjustment in the air.

Jay is oblivious—too preoccupied with the Éric Le Blanc case. It turns out the young man is a celebrity of sorts, not just in Denmark but in the global subculture of intermodal transportation as well. Jay has just spent two days digging up dozens of articles on gossip and business sites; articles in English, Portuguese, German, Dutch, and a large number of articles in Danish, all translated using translation engines. Jay now knows that the Danish word for *container* is *skibscontainer*, that *portalkran* is a gantry crane, and that *bølgede galvaniseret stål* means galvanized corrugated steel.

Éric Le Blanc, with or without the accent, sometimes spelled Erik as per the journalist's whims, and occasionally converted to Erik Weiss for local colour, attracted public attention early on as a programming prodigy. He arrived in Copenhagen at age fifteen and, despite having almost no grasp of the local language, quickly secured a number of contracts. Years later, some of his clients admitted they had never met their mysterious partner in person and knew practically nothing about him, especially not his age.

Éric works and has fun, hardly distinguishing between

the two. Thanks to one of his early contracts, he discovered a passion for the shipping industry. In his spare time, he developed a management tool midway between reality and fiction. His work has been compared to an intermodal SimCity, where containers, terminals and ships are like the neighbourhoods of a vast moving metropolis.

After two years, he gave up freelancing and founded his first company. XYNuum offered a software suite enabling "the vertical and horizontal integration of the different spatiotemporal dimensions of the intermodal continuum." Still SimCity but translated into business jargon. Not only did the financial crisis not hurt him, it actually helped him to expand his share of the market. All across the globe, hundreds of thousands of empty containers lay stacked in terminals, hibernating. The industry needed to optimize every detail of its operations, and young Éric's customers soon included a few behemoths like Maersk and CMA CGM.

A year later, the kid celebrated his eighteenth birthday and sold XYNuum for 190 million euros. He could have retired, but he didn't.

In the ensuing years, he founded a number of companies, among them Weiss PSL (container terminal management), T2T (refrigerated container tracking) and eQ, a micro-company whose function remains unclear. Despite searching high and low on the Web, Jay has found no information on this company; there is no way to find out what goes on there or even where its offices are. No website, no postal address, no telephone. Oh well.

Aside from his professional activities, Éric Le Blanc has made generous donations to a host of Danish organizations helping homeless youth, drug addicts and people with mental health issues, and has established various scholarships and funds to encourage emerging talent in the fields of science and technology.

In spite of his philanthropy, Éric appears to keep his distance from society. Many articles underscore that he has no known political affiliations and has never made any statements about the country's public or economic affairs. He turns down most requests for interviews, never speaks in public and does not belong to any club or chamber of commerce.

In short, he would seem like a somewhat bland young man were it not for the scores of rumours and urban legends circulating about him.

The only one that has been confirmed is that for years his agoraphobia has kept him from leaving his house. He conducts absolutely all his operations from inside the private sphere, and, what's more, because very few photos of him have come to light, his situation is paradoxical: he was ranked eighth in the annual list of the most famous Danes under thirty, but he could go out in the street without running the risk of being recognized.

The more articles Jay reads, the more dissatisfied she grows. This Éric Le Blanc would be the ideal suspect if only he could leave his house. The question remains, why would a young software genius residing in Copenhagen come spend his vacation in an old garage in the Saint-Laurent industrial park?

Reviewing the press eventually becomes repetitive; Jay drags the bottom of the Web and discovers a variety of tidbits concerning Éric Le Blanc. An abandoned blog in which he published a manual on the art of launching a balloon into the stratosphere. An abandoned Flickr account filled with shots of budgies taken with an infrared camera. An abandoned GitHub account containing a plan for a drone piloting application. An abandoned Twitter account with three insipid tweets. This avenue looks more and more like a series of dead ends.

Jay falls back on the young prodigy's 103 Facebook friends, an altogether modest number, given his celebrity. Yet these 103 represent a substantial number of trails to be combed, probed and classified, and while Jay still does not feel a great affinity for manual labour, no part of this chore can be automated. She is reduced to slogging through the Scandinavian names while questioning everything, including things that should be obvious, such as this Asløg, whose profile picture is a sequoia—is (s)he a man or a woman?

Besides, how did a notorious agoraphobe manage to surround himself with such a bevy of jet-setters? A selfie taken at the international airport in Hong Kong, a large latte ordered at the Starbucks in Dubai, someone baring their soul at the Marriott Rio de Janeiro. Increasingly, Jay has the feeling she is going around in circles in different languages.

Hvad har du på hjerte? No que você está pensando? Again and again, back to square one: all people are alike even in their differences. It took twenty years of GeoCities, Tumblr and Facebook to arrive at this collective conclusion.

Among Éric Le Blanc's 103 modern and globalized friends, only one account refers to that backwater of Western civilization's hinterland called Montreal: the one belonging to a young woman named Lisa Baskine.

On her spartan home page, the young Baskine states that she was born in Huntingdon, a geographic detail that in itself should be enough to convince Jay this is the Individual with a capital *i*, but she mistrusts geography and capital *i*'s, and anything stemming from the Web in general. In fact, she wonders if Lisa Baskine is really a young woman and not some paunchy philosophy prof with a satyr's goatee. Whom can you trust? It's getting close to midnight, and after forty-eight hours of intensive searching and four potfuls of Earl Grey tea, Jay is starting to experience severe paranoia coupled with colour separation on the periphery of her field of vision. Everywhere in the room, objects are fringed with the double pink-blue halo of old 3D films. Jay is burned out.

How to find this flesh-and-bones Lisa? According to 411, the closest Baskines live in Washington, D.C., and Miami. Jay could hack into Lisa's Facebook account, but there is no guarantee of finding the slightest bit of useful information. The only definite links with the real world are the IP addresses from which the account was accessed, and to obtain them one would have to consult the Facebook and ISP registries, which would require several warrants to be issued as part of an official investigation.

Up to now, Jay has found nothing concrete, aside from a cracked camera and numerous bits of evidence. She is resourceful, of course, but her personal resources are laughable compared with those of the RCMP machine, and she is beginning to feel a little worn out.

Lying on the floor, she gazes upside down at the Canon on the living room table. The camera's blank eye holds her gaze impassively.

— 27 —

IT'S SEVEN IN THE MORNING when Robert Routier is intercepted at the Covey Hill customs office sitting behind the wheel of his old black Dodge Ram in his pyjamas. Mr. Miron had hidden the keys, but there must have been a spare set somewhere in a loose change bowl or at the bottom of a drawer.

When the customs officer steps up to the window, Robert is unable to show any kind of ID. The fact is, he never owned a passport. The officer would later describe him as "confused but courteous." When asked about his destination, Robert declares he would like "to go to 1978," which arouses a certain degree of bewilderment.

"I'm sorry, sir. You'll have to park your vehicle over there and come inside with me."

What happens next is marked by calmness and docility. The customs officers install Robert in a waiting room with some coffee and an old issue of *Fly Rod & Reel* and call the Sûreté du Québec to report that an incoherent Canadian national came knocking at the gates of the Great Empire and it would be very nice of them to come fetch him. The upshot is that Robert now finds himself at the hospital in Valleyfield.

Having come as fast as her Honda could bring her, Lisa listens to the policewoman's account of the exchange between Robert and the customs officers.

"He said *what*?"

"That he wanted to go to 1978."

Lisa is perplexed, not only because the incident reveals the extent of her father's illness, but also because 1978 means nothing to her. What in the world took place that year that would make her father want to return there? He had just turned thirty-seven. What did he do, where did he go? Whom did he meet?

Evidently, Robert Routier also had secret passages hidden in his walls.

An hour later, Lisa thinks back to her father's words as she rummages through his drawers. She pitches his clothes into either an old sports bag or the laundry hamper, according to the smell. Clearly, Robert was finding it increasingly difficult to draw the line between dirty clothes and clean clothes. She adds his toothbrush, a few magazines and—after hesitating momentarily—a framed photo of father and daughter, proudly posing on the staircase of some sad bungalow.

Lisa doesn't even know how long her father will be away from his house or, for that matter, if he will ever come back to it. She found their conversation at the hospital disturbing. At first he seemed to recognize her, but the more they talked, the more Lisa got the impression her father was actually speaking to a hybrid person who was part Lisa, part Josée Savoie.

She looks up, and what she discovers in the mirror is an exhausted young woman with a lined forehead, who appears to have aged ten years that day. True, she has her mother's eyes, but who does she take after? It's not easy to rise above yourself, to gain altitude so as to see yourself objectively, as others see you. She searches for her parents' features in her own, as if this could attest to the emergence of a personality. Will she be bipolar like Josée or get Alzheimer's like Robert?

Once she has collected the essentials, she checks her watch and sets about cleaning the house. She can't believe the place could have deteriorated this much in a few days. She does three loads of laundry, mops the floors, scrubs the counter. The situation in the fridge is toxicological. She jettisons whatever has passed—or is about to pass—a best-before date, leaving only a bottle of plum sauce and a tube of Krazy Glue.

Cleaning up in the bedroom, she discovers a few hundred little white pills dumped in the nightstand drawer.

Lisa estimates that this amounts to a dozen bottles of Ebixa. An entire year's worth of prescriptions that her father refused to take. So that explains it.

While the third load of laundry is tumbling in the dryer, Lisa tackles the spare change box, where Mrs. Miron deposits the mail she retrieves from the mailbox each morning, and which Robert has neglected to open. It's a mishmash: flyers, pizzeria ads, two Christmas cards, New Year's wishes from the New Democratic Member of Parliament, a few unpaid bills (Lisa is surprised the telephone and electricity haven't been cut off), papers from the CLSC, random newspaper clippings. There's even some mail for her: an offer for a platinum credit card (low fees, competitive rates) and a delivery notice from Canada Post.

Lisa considers the notice, at once intrigued and annoyed. She will have to make a detour to the Huntingdon post office, and this doesn't suit her. The day is slipping away and she would like to spend another hour with her father before heading back to Montreal. She still has to review her notes on advanced circuitry for the exam tomorrow evening, and she can't see where she will find the necessary time and energy.

Outside the window, a light snow has begun to fall.

When the time comes to leave, the Honda reaches its expiry date. It looks serious this time. One could scarcely imagine a worse moment for this to happen, and Lisa is too exasperated to think straight. She mistreats the starter for a few minutes, until a dark silhouette appears beside the car. Lisa lets out a sigh and rolls down the window. Mr. Miron leans toward her. His moustache is speckled with snowflakes, which soon transform into tiny water drops.

"How's your father?"

Lisa gestures. All right. It'll be okay.

Mr. Miron extends his forefinger with a set of keys swinging on it. "Take the Dodge. I'll take care of your car."

Lisa feels she's about to double up. She presses her temple against the rough back of Mr. Miron's hand. She could go to sleep right there, with the snow softly gathering on her head.

When she finally arrives at the Huntingdon post office, there are big dry snowflakes dashing against the Dodge's windshield like airplane debris. It's about ten minutes before closing time. The place is dead, the atmosphere muffled by the snow and the Christmas music. An old woman is having fifty or so greeting cards postmarked. In a corner, an employee is assembling a pink artificial Christmas tree one branch at a time, verrry slowly. The scene is all Lisa needed—now she is completely depressed, and suddenly her only wish is to be shut inside her apartment with a beer and her laptop, watching a kung fu movie. She turns toward the window and wonders if going out on the highway is a good idea. The outline of the Presbyterian church across the street can barely be made out.

If her mother still lived nearby, Lisa would gladly invite herself over for the night, but Josée has moved to the South Shore with a new boyfriend who does not like IKEA.

"Next!"

Lisa hands the delivery notice to the clerk; he straightens his glasses.

"This is dated September."

"I know. My father forgot to give it to me."

"Normally, we hold on to packages for three weeks."

"Oh, okay. No problem."

"I can still go take a look."

Pinching the notice between his index finger and thumb like a used tissue, he disappears into the back, where Lisa can hear him shuffling boxes. He comes back with a look of surprise and a large bubble wrap envelope, which he turns this way and that.

"No sender's address."

Lisa looks at the Parkinsonian letters written on the yellow paper:

Madame Routier
46 rue de l'Allégresse, RR 5
Huntingdon, Québec

There is nothing recognizable about the handwriting. She tucks the envelope under her arm and goes out to face what looks more and more like a storm. Five minutes in the post office was enough to bury the van. Lisa gets in behind the wheel without clearing the snow off the windows, starts the engine and turns the defroster on full blast. Then, in the half-light of this cocoon, she tears open the envelope, rips out some bubble wrap and tugs at what clearly appears to be packaging material.

Her fingers react at the first touch. The tactile sensation is at once so familiar and so strange that Lisa perceives it as an electric tingle. Her left hand grips the wheel, as though seeking to ground her. She pulls out the packaging, which in reality is the greyish silk of several shirts that once belonged to an opera singer. The parachute slides slowly out of the envelope, and suddenly everything spills onto Lisa's lap: Mrs. Le Blanc's PowerShot, the GPS beacon and the piece of cardboard on which Lisa wrote her address. Scribbled on the reverse side, in the same seismic calligraphy, are the words *found at Thetford Mines, September 9.*

In disbelief, she turns the camera around in her hands. Acting on an irrational reflex, she squeezes the shutter release button. No response. Corrosion has welded the batteries together in their compartment. Lisa ejects the memory card and examines the connectors. Good as new.

She opens her bag, grabs her laptop and inserts the card in the SD slot. The spring makes the satisfying click of parts falling into place. The computer hesitates but eventually displays the card's contents: a number of folders nested one inside the other, and containing the 253 photos—253!—taken by the camera.

Lisa keys in ⌘-*A* and launches the slideshow.

She and Éric appear in the cornfield at dawn. The pictures are slightly underexposed, but it's still possible to make out the heads of the two stratonauts: young, dishevelled and hard at work. Next are several shots of corn, a sea of egrets and leaves. Then the field shrinks. The balloon rotates and the camera, borne along by the wind, immortalizes at random. The Ouimet hog farm. The Domaine Bordeur. Route 209. She spots their respective houses, and a microscopic orange dot that must be Gus Miron's Datsun.

Now Lisa scrolls through the pictures at high speed. The balloon gains altitude. Whole swaths of the region appear. Huntingdon surrounded by a grey and yellow mosaic, Cleyn & Tinker's Mill No. 2, Vermont. Vast tongues of forest slashed by the line of the river. The mosaic grows blurry. Boundaries and details fade. Roads and buildings can no longer be distinguished. The wind tosses the camera about in every direction. The horizon takes on an increasingly curved shape. From time to time, the sun explodes in the lens.

In the very last photo, the balloon floats at such a great height that the true nature of the Earth is clearly visible: a large, bluish bowling ball, streaked with cirrus clouds. Near the top of the picture, the sky turns dark blue. This is where space begins.

— 28 —

JAY MOUNTS THE STAIRS AND exits from the Lionel-Groulx metro station. Above ground, it looks like Monday morning. It snowed the entire weekend and now it's raining, and pedestrians are scurrying on all sides like climate refugees.

She walks alongside the line of buses thrumming at the stops and begins her daily ascent to Westmount. Every morning she contends with gravity to get to her workplace, and every evening gravity pulls her down toward the metro. She tries not to read any hidden meaning into this.

She climbs Greene Avenue and its houses with their sedimentary facades, walks under the Ville-Marie expressway with her nose turned up. If she's going to be struck by a piece of a span or a dead pigeon, better to see it coming. True to her morning routine, she notes the damaged underbelly of the expressway, the missing slabs of concrete. The rush hour vibrations spread through the piers and down beneath her feet. Overhead, the southern roadway slowly crosses her field of vision, followed by a narrow strip of grey sky, followed by the northern roadway, followed by the wooded belt of the escarpment and then the CPR viaduct. Each morning, she walks through the same sequence, strip after strip—concrete, sky, concrete, wood, railroad—like a bar code that holds the secrets of the city.

When she arrives at the corner of Dorchester, the traffic light is red. She looks up toward the headquarters of C Division. A pure expression of 1970s brutalism, the vindication of natural concrete and the line of the formwork. Welcome to your workplace.

The floor of the vestibule is covered with brownish water, which the janitor is mopping unhurriedly. It's past the rush hour, and Jay is alone in the elevator. She waves her access pass, goes up to the seventh floor, waves her pass again to go through the glass doors. Officially, she has two (2) years, two (2) months and twenty-eight (28) days left to serve.

She heads for the coffee machine, absent-mindedly greets a colleague from Fraud, grabs a coffee along the way, turns the corner, crosses the microclimate of the photocopiers and takes the home stretch toward the Enclave.

At a distance of twenty metres, she knows everyone is there: Sergeant Gamache, Laura and Mahesh, all stationed in front of the latter's computer. Sergeant Gamache is on the telephone. The closer Jay gets, the easier it is for her to see what's happening on the computer screen. She could recognize a Google page from a hundred metres away: the logo, the list of search results, the royal blue of the hyperlinks, the apple green of the URLs. Mahesh has just brought up the grey and yellow mosaic of a map. A few more clicks and there he is on Google Street View.

Jay stands motionless on the threshold of the Enclave, but even at this distance she recognizes the photo of Autocars Mondiaux, located at 230 Gibson Street.

TWO

— 29 —

AT THE END OF FORTY-EIGHT hours in the purgatory of the hospital, and after a series of blood tests, X-rays and MRIs, urine and mucus samples, examinations and consultations and forms, it is obvious that Robert Routier will not be going anywhere. The subject under investigation does not understand why he's being prevented from going home or, even better, back to 1978. (When questioned in this regard, his answers remain evasive.)

The doctors are unable to ascertain the exact name of Robert's illness. They talk about *invasive near-borderline sclerosis* and *degeneration of the temporal walls*, but, clearly, all this mumbo-jumbo comes down to pure speculation.

Be that as it may, the next step is a long-term care facility. Lisa finds the expression *long-term* quite inadequate for a man who has already forgotten what he ate for breakfast. A perpetual-now care facility—that's what her father needs. Whatever. While waiting for a place to become available, they catapult him to the Westmacott Building in Saint-Anicet, twenty-five kilometres west of Valleyfield.

Her father's new room is dingy and cramped. Left behind by the previous patient, who either died or was transferred, are a miniature Christmas tree on the windowsill and an imitation potpourri air freshener plugged into a socket. "Greensleeves" plays in a loop in the corridor. Lisa feels as though she is living in a slow-motion horror film, but she puts her head down, clenches her teeth and does what needs to be done. She makes sure her father has enough socks, underwear, T-shirts. She encourages him to eat. She brings in a spider plant, knowing it doesn't have a chance. When it dies, she'll get another.

December sweeps down, grey and ugly, over the St. Lawrence Lowlands. Lisa ponders the meaning of life and declines her mother's repeated invitations for an IKEA outing. She resists the intruder. Éric has been incommunicado for three days, no doubt busy with holiday preparations. Lisa was quick to show him the 253 photos taken by the probe as it rose above the cornfield toward the stratosphere. She can't help feeling a kind of cognitive dissonance whenever she looks at the spectacular images—as though, all at once, their dreary adolescence at the Domaine Boredom had been transmuted into a *National Geographic* article. Éric, for his part, had a strange reaction when he saw them.

Edwin Schwartz decided to close the hardware store for two weeks without giving notice or an explanation. Lisa finds herself temporarily with neither income nor employment. She eats plain macaroni and draws up long, more or less methodical to-do lists: buy her father slippers (point number three), write to the Attorney General of Quebec (point number eleven), study for the final exam that she had deferred until late December "due to a family emergency" (point number twenty-three), start to empty out her father's house (point number eight), terminate the telephone service and pay the electricity bill (points fifteen and sixteen). The list grows longer and more complex from day to day, from hour to hour. Everything is complicated and overwhelming.

On December 24, shortly before midnight, Lisa finds herself alone in her one-bedroom apartment. She turned down her mother's invitation on the pretext of celebrating Christmas Eve at the Domaine Bordeur. The big lie went unnoticed; Josée Savoie is unaware that her ex-spouse is in the hospital, and Lisa has no intention of setting her straight. She prefers to keep the different zones of her life walled off. Each person in their own compartment.

The people upstairs can be heard shouting as they tear into the presents. Sitting on her bed under several layers of quilts and blankets, Lisa checks the airfares to Copenhagen (point number seventy-four) for the twentieth time. They shot up for the holiday season and won't drop again before late January. Her findings show that reasonably priced tickets are available if she agrees to lay over in Toronto, New York, Paris and Brussels, a total of forty-seven hours in airports and fifteen hours of chartered flights with four different airlines. But even under such insane conditions, she can't afford to take off for Denmark. She converts the fares into euros, US dollars and yen in search of a currency that would make the amount seem smaller. Oh, for those bygone days when you could cross the Atlantic by toiling away in the galley of a liner.

Anyway, there's no point in dreaming about hasty departures. Lisa doesn't even have a passport, and after thoroughly studying the steps involved in getting one (point number seventy-three), she has come to the conclusion that Passport Canada's mandate is to prevent people from leaving the country.

Lisa closes all the tabs and then the browser, and takes a peek at Skype, just in case. Éric is still perennially offline. He must be stuffing himself with *æbleskiver*, stirring a pot of *gløgg* or introducing Lærke to German board games, lying flat on his stomach in front of a cluster of wooden meeples.

She folds down the screen of the laptop. It will soon be midnight, and the tribe upstairs can again be heard making a racket. Someone has just received an iPad or mitten warmers or a programmable slow cooker. Lisa is starting to wonder if it was a mistake to turn her nose up at her mother's invitation.

Through the window, where she has yet to hang curtains (point number thirty-one), Lisa can make out the pinkish light of the neighbours' Christmas decorations across the street. She gets up from under the quilts and, shivering, goes to press her forehead against the frozen pane. A mist of delicate snowflakes is falling over the neighbourhood, turning the massive silhouette of Notre-Dame-de-la-Défense white.

Down below, in front of the church, the old Dodge Ram is gradually disappearing under the snow.

— 30 —

"IT'S A DODGE RAM," Sergeant Gamache repeats. "My brother had the same model."

Mahesh has his doubts. According to Wikipedia, it could be a Plymouth Voyager or a G-Series Chevrolet. Laura reserves judgment. Jay shrinks into the background.

For the last three days, the Enclave has been buzzing with excitement. Having traced Rokov Export through an (unpaid) electricity bill, and after placing the former premises of Autocars Mondiaux, located at 230 Gibson Street, under intensive surveillance for forty-eight hours, the RCMP launched operation Spur, which involved emptying out the garage with brushes and tweezers and packing everything into thousands of little zip-lock bags. The photographs are piling up on the RCMP server, and Laura observes the process with an air of disapproval. The operation was put under the command of a colleague she does not overly appreciate. She shakes her head as she scans the index of evidence.

"They need to be more discriminating. It's like they're emptying out the Collyer brothers' house."

Up to this point, the most interesting find has been the hard disk of the surveillance camera of the warehouse next door, from which 3,700 hours of nothing-very-much has been retrieved. Using an epic manoeuvre to which he alone is privy, Mahesh managed to assemble all of it in one interminable feature-length film that plays continuously on one of the screens, like an experimental film shot in black-and-white with a webcam and a cheap wide-angle lens. The infinitely slow scenes show the same four loading docks, where the occasional tractor-trailer arrives and leaves. In the upper left corner of the frame, almost outside the field of vision, a corner of the Autocars Mondiaux garage is visible, and parked in front is a black—black or very dark-coloured—van, whose licence plate, at this distance and resolution, is distinctly illegible.

A Dodge Ram, according to Sergeant Gamache, but Mahesh is not prepared to concede the point so easily. His screen is covered with pictures of vans that he is comparing to the security camera film.

"It could also be a GMC Savana, or a Vandura. Or even a Beauville Sportvan."

Sergeant Gamache slaps his thigh. "A Beauville Sportvan! Why not a Westfalia, while you're at it?"

Laura stares at the van, squinting. "And it spent the whole summer there?"

"Yup. It shows up every morning around 7 a.m. Disappears late at night."

With his finger on the mouse, Mahesh speeds up the film. The days and nights alternate in quick succession, along with the comings and goings of the trucks and tractor-trailers; meanwhile, the van appears and disappears from the parking lot at 230 Gibson, always driven by the same individual (five feet eight inches, Caucasian, short hair, indeterminate gender) lugging boxes, bags, two-by-fours, instruments and tools.

This business continues until October 9, the date the van disappears for good. On the morning of October 11, a tractor-trailer arrives and backs into the garage. Ten minutes later, it re-emerges pulling a trailer loaded with a perfectly white refrigerated container, on whose side one can make out the code PZIU 127 002 7.

"Do we know how long the container was inside the garage?"

"The videos start in July, but we know Rokov Export rented the garage as of June. A six-month lease, paid in advance. Transferred in cash. Oh, hi, Micheline!"

"Hello, port people!"

Micheline Saint-Laurent enters the Enclave, distorting the magnetic field around her. This diminutive, grey-haired woman is the founder, the soul and the brain of the Mechanical Forensics Unit. She has the reputation of being a human computer, capable of analyzing, with no apparent effort, tire tracks, a shard from a tail light or a flake of paint from a vehicle.

Her arrival lays bare the subtle hierarchies of the Enclave. She starts by greeting everyone with a single neutral nod, after which she directs a little wink at Laura and exchanges a robust handshake with Sergeant Gamache. Mahesh gives her a respectful two-finger salute, while Jay plays the invisible woman. Finally, Laura greets her with a vaguely Japanese bow. Micheline is her sensei, her mentor, her model. When Laura entered the RCMP as a naive intern, she started out in Mechanical Forensics. In her eyes, Micheline Saint-Laurent is the supreme über-librarian.

Once the ritual salutations are over (duration: five highly concentrated seconds), Micheline's steel-grey eyes scan the troops, while a teasing smile plays at the corners of her mouth.

"I get the feeling there's been some betting."

"Let's say a slight disagreement between Maurice and Mahesh."

"Well?"

"Dodge Ram."

"Are you sure?"

"A hundred percent. The shape of the grille. The diagonal between the headlights and the bumper, the angle of the windshield. I factored in ten parameters, the margin of error is nil. Dodge Ram B Series, 1981 or 1982. As for the colour, the choices are black, burgundy or blue. Personally, I lean ten-to-one toward black."

Sergeant Gamache is jubilant. Mahesh immediately looks up an image on Google and compares it to the video. He has to admit it: he was wrong and will be buying the beer. Laura does a mental calculation.

"A Dodge Ram '81 or '82—that narrows it down, doesn't it?"

"Sort of. I put in a query before coming up here. There

are two hundred and twenty-three of them still on the road in Quebec. If you include all those registered east of Manitoba, the number is upwards of four hundred. They were indestructible machines."

"My brother-in-law still had his last year."

"Okay, Maurice. We got it."

"As for the second van, it's a Ford Econoline 2007."

Everyone turns toward Micheline in unison.

"What other van?"

"Could you go to November 25, Mahesh?"

Mahesh moves the scroll bar to November. The dates flash by then slow down. Eventually, an ashen sun rises on Sunday the twenty-fifth. There is so little action on the screen that the image seems frozen. At 7:17, a white Econoline stops in front of Autocars Mondiaux and backs up in front of the garage.

Standing behind Mahesh, Jay feels as if she is in free fall.

No one says a word. Three minutes forty seconds elapse without the slightest movement. Then, at 7:20, someone wearing overalls gets out of the van, their face hidden under the visor of their cap, and disappears behind the corner of the garage. The image becomes perfectly static again; Mahesh fast-forwards it. The person comes back out of the garage at 7:39, dragging a garbage bag, and loads it into the Econoline. Sixty seconds later, the van moves off and vanishes from the screen.

Mahesh rewinds and stops at the exact moment the driver is shown dragging the garbage bag. "Weird, isn't it?"

"Weird."

"A black truck, then a white truck. It's like a game of chess. Black always plays first."

"White always plays first in chess."

"You sure?"

"Maybe it's the same person in a different van."

Mahesh is puzzled and replays the sequence in slow motion. "What could he be hauling in the bag?"

"No idea. Maybe he was cleaning up."

"Cleaning up? Did you see the state the garage is in?"

"He stayed for twenty minutes."

"It looks heavy, anyway."

They watch the person heaving the bag into the van as slowly as a tectonic plate. The scene goes on forever and is on the verge of becoming farcical. Mahesh freezes the frame, and Micheline shrugs.

"Ford Econoline 2007. Possibly 2008—it doesn't really matter. Hardly any white ones like that belong to private owners; there's an 85 percent chance it's a rental."

She adds nothing more and, after the customary goodbyes, slips out.

Mahesh replays the film backwards in slow motion and watches the suspect very slowly getting out of the van, followed by the enormous garbage bag. Knitting his brow, he leans his whole body toward the screen and analyzes the sequence frame by frame, as though trying to recognize someone. Jay feels an urgent need to find a diversion.

"And, uh . . . any progress with the search at the garage?"

Laura brings up a photo gallery on the screen. The crime scene has been recorded from every angle: workshop, washroom, reception, roof, and the surrounding lot within a radius of twenty metres. All that's missing are satellite pictures. There's even a panoramic shot of the workshop, which appears oddly familiar to Jay, even though she spent no more than twenty minutes there. Some minutes are more intense than others.

"Have they found anything so far?"

"Trash. Scraps of wood and steel, paint-stained tarps. And some empty Empire apple crates. Footprints. Lots of fingerprints, none of which match anything in the databases. They also sent some biological material to the lab."

Jay stiffens. "Biological material?"

"Hair and some blood, I think. We should have the lab report by this weekend."

Jay takes a few steps back in the direction of the corridor. "I'm going down to the cafeteria. Anybody want anything?"

"Negative."

"A sticky bun, if there are any left."

Jay's legs are shaking as she backs out of the Enclave. Above all, don't succumb to panic. She'll go down to the cafeteria and bring back a large coffee and two buns and act perfectly normal. She automatically checks if her pass is hanging from her belt and heads toward the elevators. Down to the cafeteria is where she's going. A coffee and two buns.

Though, on second thought, maybe she'll go down to the main floor and very calmly walk out the front door, whistling, hail a taxi, and ask the cabbie to drive to Vancouver.

— 31 —

LISA AND ROBERT WALK THE length of the only corridor in the Westmacott Building and back, three slow kilometres on beige carpet punctuated by sporadic dialogues. They exhausted all the conversation topics some time ago. Robert lives in a closed circuit; he can no longer ask questions about current events, his daughter's daily life or even the weather. Occasionally, bits of conversation surface from the past, anachronistic and intact, like a core of prehistoric ice.

When Lisa goes back out into the open air in the late afternoon, she's in pretty bad shape. The sun has just set on the St. Lawrence Seaway. The parking lot is empty. She sits down behind the wheel of the Dodge, breathes deeply for a long while, eyes closed, and gradually regains her composure. Then she starts off toward Huntingdon.

The landscape is ink black under a new moon, but Lisa knows the slightest curve of this road by heart. She passes Hinchinbrooke, crosses the little steel bridge, drives past the yellow light blinking at a deserted intersection. She can just make out the alternating fields and thickets, discerns the distant light of a farm, its silos standing like rockets ready for takeoff. She slows down imperceptibly in front of the dark and boarded-up Baskine house, where, if it were light, a RE/MAX sign that has been yellowing for months could be seen nailed to the door. Lisa gives the big barn of a place a discreet nod.

It's Friday, and the residents of the Domaine Bordeur have already shut themselves indoors for the evening. As she parks the Dodge, Lisa notices a peculiar Christmas decoration in front of the Mirons': the Datsun has been adorned with strings of lights, and Santa Claus is sitting behind the steering wheel wearing imitation Ray-Bans. Lisa bursts out laughing; the Datsun is ready for Burning Man.

Inside the house, it smells of death and stale air. There's the sound of water dripping in the kitchen sink. Any property left on its own naturally tends to fall into ruin. Lisa has to sell this place fast. As soon as she receives the certificate attesting to her father's incapacity. As soon as she can find the time. As soon as.

She shuts off the valves under the kitchen sink and turns up the thermostat a few degrees. While the place warms up, she sets up some boxes. On the first, she writes, *For Papa*. On the second, *For the Mirons*. On the third, *Salvation Army*. Placing the felt marker on the fourth box, she hesitates. From this point on, it's the trash can.

She switches on the radio and scans the dial from end to end. All the receiver can pick up is a folk music station. Well, at least it's better than silence.

As she makes her way to the bedroom with the *For Papa* box, Lisa stops in front of a framed picture. Under the glass stand daughter and father, aged eight and fifty-eight, wielding handsaw and drill, looking like a pair of outlaws. The photo was taken in Huntingdon at Robert's first building site. Who was holding the camera? Josée perhaps. The frame drops into the box. Maybe the photo will jog his memory, wring a smile from him. Lisa no longer knows how to clear a passage in her father's brain.

The evening goes by in this way, interspersed with insignificant discoveries. While emptying out the bathroom, between two bottles of shampoo, she stumbles on a pair of dice. What are they doing there? Lisa pictures her father rolling dice while sitting on the toilet. Maybe he used them to make difficult decisions during his moments of relaxation.

When the boxes are full, the time showing on the kitchen clock is 10 p.m. It's already Saturday in Denmark. The sun will be rising, and Éric too. Lisa loads the boxes into the Dodge. She turns down the heating in the house, shuts off the lights and locks the door without looking back.

Once she's home, Lisa jumps into her pyjamas and, taking her computer, slips under the mountain of blankets. Éric is online for the first time in a week. Without even thinking about it, she clicks on his picture. The connection is successful and the young man appears on the screen, sitting at his desk in a room flooded with morning light. Lisa points an accusatory finger at the camera.

"Where were you, sir, for the past week?"

"I haven't left my house for three years."

"You were doing the incommunicado thing."

"We had family visiting with us. I did some reading. Everyone needs to unplug from time to time. You wanted to talk?"

"Yes. No. Nothing special."

"You're up late."

"I just came back from Saint-Anicet, with a stopover at the Domaine Bordeur."

"How's your father doing?"

Lisa's gesture says, "topic off limits." And anyway, what could she say? The room is small. The staff seem competent. Her father's brain is atrophying. It's been weeks since he uttered Lisa's name, and she now suspects he has forgotten her.

"Am I disturbing you?"

"No. Quiet Saturday morning. Lærke is spending the day here."

The little girl's head, with ruffled hair and a freckled nose, pops into a corner of the screen. She scrutinizes Lisa closely and, having satisfied her curiosity, goes back to her occupations.

"What are those drawings behind you?"

Éric swings halfway around toward a big whiteboard covered with sketches and a tangle of sentences.

"Nothing. Just some work-related notes."

"I thought your companies operate all on their own."

"Um, yeah, but this is something else. Research and development."

Lærke moves through the background waving a Lego vehicle that's halfway between a flying cigar and a Soviet shoebox.

"Research and development for your new company? What's it called again? Iq?"

"eQ. With a lower-case *e* and a capital *Q*."

"What does it mean?"

"It's the abbreviation of *Encefaliseringskoefficient*."

"*Encefal* . . . excuse me?"

"I'm kidding. It doesn't mean anything. I asked the marketing team to come up with something for me."

"What's it going to do, your new company?"

"You've heard about drones?"

Lisa settles into her pillows; with an introduction like that, the story promises to be complicated.

"There's an outfit in New Mexico that builds solar-powered drones capable of flying at an altitude of thirty thousand metres for years without any kind of refuelling."

"A perpetual drone."

"Better than that: a self-guided drone. It's linked to an operational centre via microwaves. You just need to upload the raw data—weather forecasts, pressure systems, winds—and the drone makes its own decisions. You feed it a destination and some data, and the optimization algorithms do the dirty work."

"Wow!"

"Exactly. Soon this thing will be seriously competing with low-orbit satellites. I've heard that a major Mountain View company is set to invest in it big time."

"Okay. And the connection with eQ?"

Éric takes a sip of coffee. "I read an article on the subject last year, while I was working on T2T . . ."

"You like short names."

". . . and it gave me an idea."

Another sip of coffee. He needs to gather momentum.

"Refrigerated containers currently occupy the top rung of the evolutionary ladder. A conventional container is essentially just a big corrugated steel box. Reefers are somewhat more advanced: they're equipped with GPS beacons, webcams, motion detectors. The atmosphere and temperature are determined according to the environment, and the data is sent to the exporter in real time. If a customs officer in Hamburg opens the door of a reefer, an alert sounds in a Hong Kong office. The exporter can see if the door stays open too long, if the interior temperature drops . . ."

"A smart container."

"The marketing department would probably use that sort of term, but basically it's still just a big stupid box with a wi-fi connection."

Lærke suddenly appears over Éric's shoulder with a warlike expression.

"*Jeg er suuulten!*"

"*Cheerios er på bordet.*"

"Can I have some apricots? *Vær venliiig?*"

"They're on the cabinet. Help yourself. Hey, you can't imagine how much a four-year-old can eat. It just doesn't stop. A genuine industrial shredder. She asks me for something every ten minutes. Fruit, cereal, milk. Sausage, ham, pickles. And bananas! A dozen bananas a day! Okay, so where was I?"

"Big stupid box, wi-fi connection."

"Ah, right. Most reefers sail on weekly lines, with hyper-regular schedules. No changes, ever. Industrial and agricultural zones have stable production cycles. Climatologists can predict the dates of grapefruit harvests ten years in advance. *But.*"

"But?"

"But *even so*, there are unforeseen events. A late ship. A typhoon. A longshoremen's strike. An outbreak of the H5N1 virus is all it takes for Taiwan to tighten its import laws, and your exporter is stuck with fifty containers of frozen Brazilian chickens quarantined in power stations at a hundred dollars a day per box."

"So the schedules are theoretically fixed, but there are always adjustments to be made."

"Exactly. For a company that moves sixty thousand containers every day, it's a real problem. Ideally, the container would make the adjustments on its own."

"A container with a sense of initiative."

"A semi-self-guided drone."

"Can it be done?"

"Almost everything is already automated. Robots have

been moving containers for years. The industry operates like a three-dimensional database. The only thing that isn't automated yet is the consumer."

"My mother is working on that part."

"So to answer your question, yes, it can be done. Theoretically. The container could hook itself up to the terminal's network and manage its schedules by integrating the environmental parameters: weather, traffic jams, shipwrecks, delays, strikes, quarantines. A swine flu epidemic? The container could calculate the costs, assess the risks and automatically direct itself to another market or a less costly transition port. Even the paperwork would be done and sent by the container—bill of lading, customs forms . . . Shit. Hold on a second!"

Éric disappears. The sound of crockery and a French-Danish dialogue on the law of gravity can be heard in the background. The only thing showing on the screen is the whiteboard covered with notes, and Lisa uses the opportunity to try to decipher the jumble of phrases and equations, but the image resolution is too low, unless it's Éric's handwriting that is deteriorating. She takes a screenshot so she can study it at her leisure.

Éric comes back and sits down in front of the camera with a new cup of coffee filled to the brim. He takes a sip and gives Lisa a worried look.

"Are you okay?"

"I'm cold."

"You seem depressed."

"I'm cold and I'm depressed."

"Why?"

She draws the sheets up to her chin. It's the only warm spot in this damned apartment. If not for her being in the middle of a video call, she would pull the pile of blankets right over her head, the way she used to long ago when she played submarine under the sheets, armed with a flashlight.

On the screen, Éric is still waiting for an answer. Lisa lets out another sigh.

"Every time you talk to me about containers, I get the feeling you're describing a major achievement of human-kind. Like the roads of the Roman Empire, but better. It's almost as though our civilization had created an artificial continent, but an invisible one, hidden in the walls."

"That's a good image."

"Your semi-self-guided container—that's a tour de force. It involves optimization algorithms, risk management systems. It reminds me of the Voyager probe. Do you see what I mean?"

"I see what you mean."

"Except that instead of visiting Saturn, your drone-containers will ship Bic pens and toilet brushes. The smartest guy I know is racking his brains so that Mrs. Ouimet can buy flowery cushions and bananas . . ."

"You underestimate the importance of bananas for our society."

"I'm serious. We're living in fucked-up times, where every fabulous invention ends up becoming insignificant.

Technology ought to, I don't know, push against the limits of the human experience, right?"

Long pause. Éric makes an ambiguous gesture with his head, as though pondering the question.

"Fine. Okay. Forget about the banana and cushion industry. Suppose the semi-self-guided container were a Leonardo da Vinci kind of idea, though I should point out that Leonardo da Vinci also had his bananas and cushions moments. Suppose eQ were to be used to push back the limits of human experience. How would we go about it, in your view?"

Lisa takes a deep breath and looks at the ceiling. You would first have to determine exactly what human experience is. She thinks about her mother, standing at the centre of a vast IKEA, and her father napping in his long-term cubicle; she thinks about the Domaine Bordeur and Mr. Miron trying to start his Datsun, and even about Edwin Schwartz in his mezzanine, and thinks about herself, gloomily seated in a windowless classroom, assimilating equations and constants. Then, suddenly, *it* strikes her, every inch of her, from the top of her skull down into her spinal cord, travels through her vertebrae like a string of pearls, descends into her right leg and exits through her big toe, leaving behind a sensation of numbness and the smell of charred leather.

Lisa is struck dumb, mouth agape, eyes wide open, transfixed. Her lips articulate empty words, while she visibly attempts to take the measurements of the new space that has just opened up in a remote area of her brain.

Éric, leaning toward the screen, one eyebrow raised, waits for her to recover her ability to speak. Lærke shows up stage right, with a mulish expression, and mutters, "I'm still hungry." She turns toward the screen and sees Lisa, paralyzed.

"What's the matter with her?"

Éric rubs his chin in bemusement. "An idea, I think."

— 32 —

JAY CAN CLEARLY RECALL THE day she was processed. She had hardly stepped into the airport when her mug shot and fingerprints were taken. The policía nacional already had everything, of course, but the basic deportation package deal did not include the transfer of legal data, and the RCMP had to do the work all over again from scratch. After-sales service was on the decline in every sector, Jay thought as she contemplated the blue ink on her fingertips.

And there was more: they still had to take DNA samples. Jay shrugged. She was back in Canada; they could take whatever samples they wanted. The procedure lasted no more than a minute. A technician wearing nitrile gloves unwrapped a cotton bud on a long stick. She asked Jay to open her mouth and rubbed it against the inside of her cheek. Jay hated the texture of the cotton wad.

Jay mentioned the episode when she met her new lawyer that same afternoon. The small, feisty woman immediately flared up and declared she would have the "abusive, invasive and illegal" procedure nullified. Jay was not sure of what it all signified. She was already in prison, wasn't she? What difference could it possibly make?

Her lawyer made further inquiries and learned that the judge had authorized the procedure on the pretext that the offender had been found guilty of *piratería* and *subversión*, and that Canadian law allowed DNA samples to be collected for this type of crime. Case law, however, was imprecise on the subject of sentences handed down outside Canada, and the lawyer planned to exploit this lack of precision to have the ruling annulled. The case would no doubt be heard on appeal, but it was a bit late; Jay's saliva cells had already been collected and the sample processed. Though she failed in her efforts to have the data destroyed, the lawyer had succeeded at least in having their entry into the National DNA Data Bank suspended.

Consequently, Jay's DNA hibernated on a hard disk pending the outcome of a trial that most probably would never take place. Seven years on, Jay does not know where exactly the data is located, and, given this uncertainty, it makes sense to assume the RCMP entered it into the system nevertheless, which means that the traces of blood found at Autocars Mondiaux are liable to trigger a long series of causes and effects, like a steel ball dropped into a vast Rube Goldberg machine, which would make its way from the judicial laboratory to the database and from the database to Jay.

It's only a matter of hours before they question her and, worse, search her apartment. The detectives will quickly find the big cardboard box chock full of pieces of evidence classified with the loving attention of a museologist: bundles of invoices pressed flat and arranged in chronological order, lists scribbled by an unknown hand and, especially, the old, battered, inoperative Canon. They will triangulate, they will deduce.

It will be the end of an era—and maybe that would be a good thing, Jay muses as she climbs the stairs to her apartment. Her life will return to where it stopped seven years ago, with her imprisonment, the investigation, the legal procedures and the criminal charges. And she will finally recover her old name, her true identity. She is almost eager to see the news reports about her arrest. A former hacker employed by the RCMP, suspected of complicity in a terrorism case. This time, she won't be upstaged in the media by a hockey story.

When she reaches the top of the stairs, she flips the light switch. Nothing. The Malayan light fixture has already died. Through the floor comes the sound of a long monologue in Greek and the noise of broken dishes.

For an instant, Jay has the urge to let go, to let events take their course. Then she pulls herself together. She takes the box of evidence out of the closet and carries it to the trash can in the kitchen.

Inside the box is a stack of about twenty envelopes, organized with dividers. Jay pulls out the envelopes one at a time and unceremoniously throws them into the trash can, like pieces of a puzzle that will no longer be of use. Farewell, mysterious sketches and diagrams. Farewell, invoices and illegible lists. Farewell, precious Canon PowerShot. Garbage you were, and to the garbage you shall return.

Soon the trash can is overflowing. Tonight Jay will go toss the bag into a neighbourhood Dumpster, as long as she can find one that's not locked.

The only thing left at the bottom of the box is the *Miscellaneous* envelope, where Jay recalls having classified whatever defied classification, the crumbs, the shreds. She is about to chuck it when she suddenly stops short. She opens the envelope, pokes around amid the scraps of paper, and harpoons a Park'N Fly receipt for three months of parking, long-term rate, dated October 11.

Jay leaps to her feet, trembling. She checks her watch. She still has half an hour to run out and buy a suitcase.

— 33 —

ÉRIC SAID HE WOULD THINK about it, and he is probably thinking about it, the bum, thinking very hard about it, since his answer is as slow in coming as the fulfillment of an election promise.

It will be ten days tomorrow since Lisa was electrocuted by the idea of the century, ten days during which the two protagonists have ruminated on either side of the Atlantic, which proves that the two kids have become (at least theoretically) adults; six years earlier, the decision would have been made on the spot, live. Now everything is complicated, every question turns into a maze. They're not fifteen anymore.

Left to her own devices, Lisa draws up plans and diagrams in her head. The idea gnaws at her twenty-four hours a day, in the shower, at work, on the road to Saint-Anicet-de-Kostka, and even in the string of jumbled dreams in which she gets entangled at dawn.

As for Éric, there is no way to imagine what is brewing in his brain.

Yet the situation is not all that complicated. Lisa's idea was either excellent or mediocre, and, all things considered, Éric's hesitation provides a crucial hint. Why would he hesitate if the idea is an excellent one? No, this endless waiting points to only one possible conclusion: it's not going to happen. His company will perform its initial function: inject smart containers into the global economy. The limits of human experience will not be pushed back. Lisa curses bananas and flowery cushions.

In any case, she has no time to lose over this. She has to keep an eye on her father's sock reserves, memorize the history of Babylonian electronics, greet the hordes of customers at HardKo and refill the bottomless tank of the Dodge Ramosaurus; the fact is, she made a rough calculation of how much it would cost to realize her idea, how many hundreds of Leica IIIs in excellent condition would need to be sold on eBay to finance the project. Bottom line: forget it.

Éric does not like her idea, time and money are lacking—okay, message received: everything militates against the project, and Lisa immediately stops waiting for the answer. In her mind, the plans and diagrams fade like old sales receipts left lying in the sun. Tonight she will make a Montreal–Copenhagen video call to officially put an end to her blues.

But why the hell does she have the blues?

The question floats in the background of her mind while she stands in the doorway of the room and looks at her father looking out the window. On the other side of the glass, there is Route 132, powdery snow and the dark line of the river. No ship in sight, the St. Lawrence Seaway is frozen solid, closed until March. Lisa wonders where her shipbuilding forebears ended their days. She sweeps her eyes around the room with a twinge in her heart. This clearly is not the lap of luxury. Each time she visits, she discovers a new problem: a peeling piece of wall, a loose tile, a warp in the baseboard, a dripping faucet in the bathroom. Everything is falling apart, and Robert, the shadow of the man who was Robert, couldn't care less.

Look, the radiator cover is half unscrewed. A little tug is all it would take to open it partway. With some help from Murphy's Law, Robert will surely end up stuffing his dirty socks in it and setting the building ablaze. The problem should be brought to the superintendent's attention; on the other hand, it may be three weeks before he gets around to this small repair. Better handle it herself.

In the lobby, the receptionist is focused on a sudoku. Lisa steps up to the counter.

"Could I borrow a screwdriver from you?"

The woman jumps, as if she's been asked for a plasma welder or an industrial riveter. She opens a drawer that for years has served to keep sundries and in which Lisa glimpses bits of string, watches, pencils, dentures and greeting cards. The woman triumphantly waves a tiny screwdriver. Without touching it, Lisa looks it over.

"Is that all you have?"

"You don't like it?"

"It's a Robertson. I need a Phillips."

"A Phillips?"

"A star-shaped screwdriver."

"There are different kinds of screwdrivers?"

Lisa sighs and gestures "never mind." She'll take care of the matter some other day. So long as, in the meantime, her father doesn't burn the place down.

The sun sets and Lisa drives back to Montreal at proletarian speed; the price of gas has risen again. She feels as if she has run an ultra-marathon. She must be coming down with a cold. It's too warm for January, there's a miasma in the air, the streets are dirty, and brown snow clings to the cars.

Stepping into the vestibule of the building, Lisa collides

head-on with a UPS driver, who looks her up and down.

"What's your apartment number?"

"Six."

"Lisa Routier?"

"That's me."

He hands her a large brown cardboard envelope. The phrase *Ultra Express Parcel* in red Helvetica takes up the lower third of the envelope, and in the Sender section there is Éric Le Blanc's name above an address full of ø's. The customs invoice is marked "gift—value $20."

A gift? That would be a first. Christmas has come and gone, and her birthday is still six months away.

She signs absent-mindedly on the device held out by the driver and shakes the envelope, which feels empty. Climbing the stairs, Lisa struggles with the supposedly easy-open strip, conceived by some malevolent designer to poison the lives of his contemporaries. She gets nowhere with her fingers and resorts to her teeth.

Grunting like a Neanderthal, she finally manages to open the envelope and halts on the second floor landing, under the blinking fluorescent light. The damned envelope really *is* empty. What is this joke supposed to mean? Standing directly below the light fixture, Lisa pulls the envelope apart to give it a closer look. There may be something at the bottom after all.

Lisa turns the envelope upside down, and what flutters out and scatters on the landing is, without the shadow of a doubt, the much-awaited answer.

— 34 —

IT IS 6 A.M. WHEN the woman parks her rental car at Trudeau airport. She wears a grey pantsuit and Ray-Ban sunglasses and pulls a trolley suitcase still bearing the price tag from the Royaume de la Valise ($24.99 plus tax).

She enters the terminal and proceeds downstairs to the arrivals area. The first international flights have started to come in, and the passengers trooping past run the gamut of fatigue and jet lag. Some flight attendants are having coffee. A man goes by holding an enormous bunch of roses.

The woman moves past the arrivals area, exits the terminal through the revolving doors and follows the Park'N Fly signs. The shuttle is parked at the far end of the walkway. The driver is puffing on a cigarette. He greets the traveller with a nod.

"Which lot?"

"Express A."

He does not ask to see a ticket, and the woman climbs into the bus. The radio is playing softly. Three passengers already ensconced in their seats are immersed in their telephones. One of them resembles Gandhi. He is discussing the price of Kevlar per linear metre and supply time frames.

On the sidewalk, the driver consults his watch. He flicks away his cigarette butt, which ricochets off a post and explodes into sparks. He sits down behind the wheel and moves off. In a single manoeuvre, he cuts off a taxi, drives onto the ramp and turns up the radio. It's the news bulletin, and amid the grind of the gearshift come fragments of a report on drones in Pakistan.

The first stop is Express B, a small parking lot alongside the Côte-de-Liesse highway. Gandhi gets off and climbs into a Jaguar XK. The Kevlar trade is thriving.

The bus continues on its way, and a few minutes later they arrive at Express A, which covers a far larger area. The shuttle drives around the entire lot. Sitting next to the window, her sunglasses lowered slightly, the woman keeps an eye out for surveillance cameras. Best to assume that every inch of the parking lot is monitored.

Suddenly, the woman grabs her suitcase with one hand and pulls the stop request cord.

"I get off here!"

Muttering, the driver applies the brakes. The woman gets off the bus, nearly loses her footing—stupid high heels—and the doors close behind her. The next instant she is alone in the parking lot, face to face with the old black Dodge Ram. With its two very round headlights and the smirking shape of the grille, you would swear it was expecting this traveller.

She steps closer and, using her hand as a visor, looks through the windows. Imitation wood, dials, vinyl seats patched with electrical tape, eight-track tape player. A paper coffee cup forgotten in the cupholder. The back seats have been removed to free up more room, and the floor has disappeared under the tool boxes. A handyman's van.

The woman tries the door handle. Locked, of course. On the passenger side too, the lock button has been pushed down. She opens her suitcase and takes out a piece of wire hanger carefully cut and bent. It's been years since she opened a car door this way. Luckily, there's YouTube.

She adjusts her gloves, wiggles her fingers and, her expression tight with concentration, inserts the wire between the rubber seal and the window and pushes it inside the door. The mechanism resists, but the woman has lost little of her touch and, on the second try, with a small additional twist, the button pops up.

Not wasting a second, the woman tosses her suitcase onto the passenger seat, climbs in behind the steering wheel and shuts the door.

The van has been sleeping in this parking lot for almost two months, but it still smells of coffee, wood, oil and old carpeting, and another distant scent, rounder, indefinable, a human scent. The olfactory signature of the owner.

The woman opens the glove compartment and picks through its contents: a flashlight, a toothbrush, a road map of Montreal and a grimy car registration. The vehicle is registered in the name of Élisabeth Routier-Savoie.

The woman delicately grasps the certificate. Smiling a little, she raises it to her lips and gives it a kiss.

ROBERT ROUTIER'S EYES, IN THE past, when he was hunting wild bungalows . . .

His manic spells invariably started with the careful perusal of the newspapers and real estate catalogues, with black coffee and red pencil close at hand. Yet Robert never found what he wanted on paper and always ended up combing the region in the Dodge, looking like a highway robber, stopping for a long time in front of properties for sale, jumping fences, poking his nose between the pales. This time, he would ferret out the deal of the century, *el fabuloso bungalow*, which would replenish his bank account and allow him to move up to the next level: the luxury home market.

His eyes would glint back then with a worrisome craving, like those of a compulsive gambler sitting at a blackjack table. He hovered, cut off from the world. He would lose sleep over it, and his appetite.

These episodes persisted for as long as Robert did not buy a house and begin working on it. In the meantime, he soared in the upper atmosphere on automatic pilot. Physically present, certainly—able to cook spaghetti, wash the dishes, do the laundry, pay the damned bills and answer the phone—but somehow not there.

This morning, Lisa dropped her Applied Mathematics 2 course. She left a message on the hardware store's answering machine saying she would not be coming to work today or in the future. She will not return her mother's calls anymore, especially if they involve IKEA.

She feels light. She walks on the walls and ceiling, and flits about in the living room.

She has transformed her kitchen (the only place in her apartment not cluttered with tools) into an operations centre. She folded the chairs, pushed the table into a corner, pinned up cryptic sketches and lists, pages torn out of her notebook, a whole galaxy of little papers that she will have to convert into vectors, points, plans. For ten hours a day, Lisa bombards the computer with queries in a sibylline dialect. She talks in volts, calories, CFM and lumens, and when she happens to catch her own gaze in the chrome of the toaster, what she sees are her father's eyes, fevered and serious and focused.

Her eyes consumed by that same worrisome craving.

— 36 —

JAY HAS NOT SET FOOT in this neighbourhood for twelve years.

It is 7:15 a.m. when she parks in the shadow of Notre-Dame-de-la-Défense, still attired in her camouflage-grey pantsuit, with the Ray-Bans perched on her nose.

She shuts off the engine, and in the ensuing silence her stomach emits a long rumble. She's just officially digested the last molecule of the grapefruit devoured at five o'clock this morning. She should have had a bite to eat at the airport. She sees a *dépanneur* on the corner of the street. *Colmado Real, bière, vin et livraison.* It will do.

The cashier is drowsily listening to an Italian radio show. Jay catches the gist: low-pressure system moving up from Ontario, gradually clouding over, twenty centimetres of snow in the Greater Montreal area. She walks all around the store but without any real appetite. She counts ten varieties of panettone, lingers in front of the salami, examines a bag of ruffled vinegar-flavoured chips. In the end, she opts for a coffee loaded with *molto* cream and, after first checking the best-before date, a box of Whippets.

When she arrives at the counter, she realizes she has no cash.

"Do you take plastic?"

"Yeah. Give me your card. The chip reader is broken."

The cashier completes the transaction behind the counter and hands Jay the receipt, which she signs absent-mindedly.

Back in the truck, she rips open the box and bites into the cookie. Over-sweet chocolate, gooey marshmallow and red-flavoured jam. It tastes of 1983: soft and melancholy. She eats a Whippet, slurps a mouthful of coffee. Wonders if this sort of breakfast is still reasonable at thirty-nine-going-on-forty. Then she puts on her gloves and gets out of the truck.

The neighbourhood is still quiet. Jay scans the addresses, swings around toward the north and spots a small apartment building on the verge of collapse. Lisa lives in number 6.

The scene in the lobby is straight out of Beirut. It smells of wet plaster and cigarettes. The mail for apartment 6 has not been picked up for a while. Jay presses the buzzer. No answer. The door leading to the stairs is not locked, and Jay decides to go up and have a look around. There isn't a sound in the entire building except for the click of her high heels on the cracked terrazzo.

The apartment number has been torn off the door, leaving just a screw hole and the silhouette of the number 6. Jay examines the peephole and the deadbolt lock. An old four-pin tumbler, easy to pick. She tries the handle and knocks. The echo resonates through the stairwell.

Back on the sidewalk, Jay has no intention of going away empty-handed. She walks to the entrance of the back lane, which has not been cleared of snow. She advances despite her high heels.

The apartment building has no backyard but, instead, an asphalt strip bounded by a Frost fence—occupied by a barbecue and bicycle locked together—and a battered trash can. There is a wrought iron fire escape leading up to the balconies. The place is visible from all sides.

Jay pushes the gate open and sizes up the fire escape. The steps are covered with snow; climbing them in high heels would be suicidal. She should have changed clothes at the airport, but it's pointless to beat herself up. She grips the guardrail, hesitates, is about to turn back. Even at thirty-nine, she is too young to die.

Then she notices some tracks. A cat went up the steps before her, imprinting its delicate pads on the snow. Jay decides this is a good idea. She removes her shoes and starts up the fire escape in her stocking feet. A thin crust of ice covers the snow, producing the sensation of stepping on crushed glass.

Jay climbs the steps four at a time up to the third floor, leaving the very clear impression of her toes on the snow. The back door of apartment 6 has not been opened since the beginning of winter. Shading her eyes with her hands, Jay looks inside. No one in sight. The kitchen is tidy. No dishes on the counter, no corpse on the tiled floor.

On the balcony by the door are a garbage can (empty) and a recycling bin (full). Jay sweeps away the crust of snow, pushes aside the cookie wrappers and yogurt containers, and finds a layer of papers at the bottom of the bin. Her eyes fall on a UPS envelope sent by Éric Le Blanc, København Ø, Danmark, and addressed to Élisabeth Routier-Savoie.

The envelope is empty, but the customs invoice is marked "gift—value $20."

Jay feels a surge of enthusiasm that almost makes her forget her predicament. To the west, the charcoal-grey band of the storm front is approaching, laden with several million tons of snow. On the opposite side of the lane, people are eating breakfast. At any moment, someone will look up from their bowl of porridge and notice the madwoman in a light grey pantsuit rummaging through the trash on the balcony across the way.

She takes hold of the bin and goes back down the steps looking nonchalant, as though she were leaving for work (which is not entirely off the mark). The nylon of her left stocking has a hole in it, affording a glimpse of a big toe gradually turning blue. Once she has safely arrived at the bottom of the fire escape, she puts her shoes back on, limps her way out of the lane and deposits the bin in the trunk of the car.

Then she starts the engine, turns up the heat full blast, and, after making sure no one is around, removes her pantsuit and slips into her street clothes. With her feet resting against the heating vent, she munches on Whippets and sips her lukewarm coffee. Her morale is like a roaring furnace, in spite of the troubling lack of sensation in her toes. No, things are going not so badly, after all.

She is slightly late getting to work, not even enough to be noticed, and walks into the Enclave whistling, with the box of Whippets under her arm. She comes face to face with Laura, dishevelled, overexcited, ready to break out the champagne.

"Shenzhen has released the data!"

— 37 —

FEBRUARY DESCENDS ON MONTREAL. The winter rages on and the building's central heating is a triumph of inefficiency.

Wearing several layers of wool, Lisa sips chicken broth. She goes out now only when absolutely necessary: to get provisions, jettison recyclables and trash, de-ice the Dodge.

She travels to Saint-Anicet-de-Kostka only on Saturdays. Robert apparently hasn't noticed. Nor has she returned to the Domaine Bordeur. Over the telephone, Gus Miron assured her that he would shovel the staircase and the doorstep. Good old Uncle Gus. In the background, Sheila asked if the little one needed something. No, the little one has everything she needs.

Lisa toils away for fifteen hours a day and does the job of a small commando. The sketches grow rare on the kitchen wall, pushed out by electrical diagrams and blueprints drawn by computer. The atmosphere increasingly resembles that of an engineering firm, with dirty dishes.

The situation on the Scandinavian front is just as hectic. Éric has assembled a team of programmers who churn out code day and night to rough out the various modules of the piloting software. He reassured Lisa, who was surprised to see him subcontract such incriminating work: in addition to signing non-disclosure agreements as long as the Old Testament, the programmers don't know each other—at least, they don't work in the same place—and each of them has been tasked with a different module. Only Éric enjoys a comprehensive view of the project, and he will personally code the most critical segments, assemble the modules and debug the finished software.

In any event, there was no other choice: the only way to have a functional system by the f all was to delegate. Preliminary estimates put the total number of lines of code for the software, tens of thousands of which would be customized, at fifteen million, and this huge mass of text was not going to write itself. The latest reports indicate that automation has not yet been automated. Éric would have been informed.

Meanwhile, the UPS envelopes keep arriving from Copenhagen with clockwork regularity, twice a month. The content never varies: twenty lovely banknotes issued by the Federal Reserve of the United States, each of them bearing the head of Benjamin Franklin, that great electrocutor of kites. Phrases float around his head like the balloons in a graphic novel. "One hundred dollars!" Franklin seems to be exclaiming. And also, in a tone of insinuation: "This note is legal tender for all debts, public and private!"

"Private debt"—the expression always brings a smile to Lisa's face.

Every second Tuesday, she converts the loot, each time at a different foreign exchange office, and then stacks the bills at the bottom of a Cheerios box, under the bag of cereal, in a corner of her pantry. A bank transfer would simplify the procedure, but every envelope from Éric contains a subtext not lost on Lisa: it's not so much a matter of laundering money as dirtying it. The two confederates use sums acquired legally to finance illegal (or, at the very least, questionable) activities, while trying not to soil their hands in the process. It follows, therefore, that all project-related expenses must be paid with old, crumpled banknotes. Above all, no plastic—what is a credit card these days other than a sophisticated geo-localization device?

When Lisa was seven years old, her father made all his purchases in cash. Even back then, Robert Routier's money clip was an anachronism, an accessory from another generation, handed down perhaps by his own father, which he persisted in using for obscure reasons: for the sake of elegance, out of nostalgia or an absolute distrust of banks, or quite simply because the object exasperated Josée. In any case, he had given in to plastic, like everyone else, and the money clip ended up at the bottom of a drawer, along with a handful of Mexican pesos and some unused cufflinks, before eventually vanishing from the face of the earth.

Lisa hasn't seen her father's money clip in years and has resigned herself to using a large pretzel-shaped paper clip. She loves to feel the slight bulge on her left buttock made by a dozen bills folded in half. Whenever she pulls out her paper clip, she feels all-powerful and invisible, by virtue of an otherwise archaic technology. "An elegant weapon for a more civilized age," Ben Kenobi would say.

But more important, for the first time in her life, Lisa does not have to worry about money. Everything seems possible, as if the laws of physics were suspended. Beyond a certain critical mass, money creates its own reality, like a locomotive able to lay down its own tracks, and the tracks appearing before Lisa are strange indeed. A few hours earlier, she would not have had any idea where a bold consumer might acquire a forty-foot refrigerated container, yet here she is, easily navigating through the industrial want ads, as one might have run one's finger over a globe long ago.

Blurry pictures taken all over the world with cheap telephones stream past on her screen. Walls of containers rusting in the rain in Newark. With peeling paint in the port of São Paulo. Anonymous white containers in Chongqing, Abu Dhabi and Tunis. Reefers in Qingdao, Shenzhen, Tianjin and Rotterdam. Oversized containers in Hamburg, Pakistan, Kuwait. Dented boxes fit for the junkyard, and others transformed into luxury condos, canteens, offices, clinics. Available in different sizes, multiple attractive colours, for sale or long- or short-term lease, single or multiple units, legal documents on demand, some conditions apply, safe and confidential transactions, easy payment via bank transfer, credit card, PayPal. Eighteen months interest-free, satisfaction guaranteed. Collect the whole set.

On the video chat, Éric simply shrugs his shoulders. "A side effect of the financial crisis, comrade. There are still half a million containers sleeping in terminals in Western Europe. Hong Kong gets thousands of empty boxes every day. Shipping companies have a whole fleet anchored off the coast of Malaysia. Hundreds of container ships, bulk carriers, tankers. No one on board for months. The industry has stalled."

"I feel an urgent need to shop for a refrigerated container."

"Don't succumb to impulse buying."

— 38 —

THE NEWS WENT OUT AT NOON, Beijing time, when everyone in Montreal was asleep: the Shenzhen port authority had agreed to divulge some strategic information.

When Laura came in to work at around 8 a.m., she found a summary of the situation among her messages: Papa Zulu had indeed arrived in Shenzhen on November 24 with a transshipping code. According to official records, it supposedly was loaded three hours later onto the *Sea Master Evergreen*, but the captain claimed he had never taken this box on board (a claim yet to be verified). The Shenzhen port authority having "physically ascertained" that PZIU 127 002 7 was no longer to be found in its terminal, the bothersome container had necessarily departed again aboard one of the seven ships docked during those few hours.

Jay is almost disappointed. "Is that it?"

"Well, it's not bad. It narrows the search. The port of Shenzhen processes about fifteen container ships a day. With every passing twenty-four-hour period, the search area grows by 40 percent, with about a 5 percent overlap." She opens an Excel file filled with names and calculations. "I tracked each of the seven ships. In total, they stopped in nineteen ports of call since November 24. The CIA should be able to obtain data on each of those ports, though that may not even be necessary. If we can determine the specific ship the container was on, that would be enough to limit the search to three or four ports."

"So the investigation is progressing."

"That's quite a radical verb. Let's just say it's not regressing."

On the opposite side of the Enclave, Mahesh is quietly busy on Google Earth, where he has traced Papa Zulu's course over the past fifty-eight days, from Montreal to Caucedo and from there on to Panama, then across the Western Hemisphere to the waters off the Aleutians and Japan. From Shenzhen, the line splits into a multitude of possible paths, which, without too much of a stretch of the imagination, looks like a bouquet of tentacles moving among the region's ports, stretching toward Manila, Singapore and Jakarta.

Mahesh, with an air of exasperation, twists the planet in every direction. "It doesn't work!"

"What doesn't work?"

He swivels 180 degrees and briefly loses his composure. "Are those Whippets?"

Jay holds out the box to him. Never stand between a programmer and his prey. She points at the screen with her chin. "What doesn't work?"

Mahesh chomps on a Whippet, obviously wondering where to begin. "We've been following Papa Zulu for three weeks?"

"Twenty-two days."

"Twenty-two days . . ."

Another Whippet disappears.

"At first it was a piddling little Montreal investigation. Not even Maurice took it seriously. Twenty-two days on, and Homeland Security and the CIA are on the case. Why do you think that is?"

"A lot of people think the next 9/11 will be industrial."

"The dirty bomb scenario."

"A classic."

Mahesh spears another Whippet and dreamily inspects it from every angle.

"Homeland Security would love to vet all the containers entering US territory, but that's impossible. Laura, how many container movements are there each day in NAFTA territory?"

"About a hundred and fifty thousand."

"A hundred and fifty thousand. And that's just ordinary business. The normal flow of trade, with the occasional load of cocaine or Cubans. Homeland is quite simply swamped. They can't keep up. So just imagine what they might think of a mutant box capable of erasing itself from the databases . . . The Americans don't want to find Papa Zulu; they want to catch the bearded guys holding the joystick. They see Rokov Export as the Canadian al Qaeda."

"They don't know Canada very well."

"If that were true, wouldn't Papa Zulu have entered the United States at Newark–Elizabeth?" Knitting his eyebrows, Mahesh gingerly removes the top of the Whippet's skull.

"Not necessarily. Papa Zulu goes unnoticed because security for transshipping is not very tight. It's not worth vetting a container that will be gone again in forty-eight hours. But moving a container into the hinterland—that is a different kettle of fish."

"Maybe the United States doesn't really interest them."

"So what does interest them?"

"Very good question!"

Mahesh swings around toward the screen and points his semi-trepanned Whippet at Google Earth. "Papa Zulu went through Panama."

"So?"

"It would have been quicker to go through Suez and Malacca. I just did the math: the route via Panama is four thousand kilometres longer."

Laura shakes her head. "The shortest route isn't always optimal in shipping. You have to consider schedules, fees and . . ."

"For a container travelling under normal conditions, that's true. But Rokov Export does not have to concern itself with schedules and fees. Anyway, even with some leeway, going through Panama is a valid option provided the final destination is in Southeast Asia . . . say, in China, or Indonesia . . ."

He bites into a shard of chocolate.

"But if the CIA finds that Papa Zulu continued on to Singapore . . . what would that tell us?"

"That it's going around the world."

"A sort of test flight."

Laura, decidedly skeptical, raises her hand. "Maybe they had their reasons for avoiding Suez. Regional issues, for instance."

"You're thinking Yemen?"

"Or possibly Sudan. That could explain the CIA's persistence. I'll see what I can find out about that."

So Laura goes back to her keyboard to compose elegant inquiries. Silence falls over the Enclave once again. With an earnest expression, Mahesh sucks out the Whippet's brain.

Jay spends a seemingly endless morning mining credit cards and chomping at the bit. In her mind, she tries to organize the events of the past twenty-four hours, to no avail; the clues have been piling up so quickly that she finds it hard to draw any conclusions, and she is afraid she won't succeed before being run down by the lab results.

Standing by the windows, a handful of managers drink coffee and watch the cold front slowly bear down on Montreal.

At lunchtime, while everyone else is momentarily distracted, Jay slips on her coat and steals outside. She parked the car at a safe distance from the office. A providential layer of snow has already covered the windows. Jay takes the recycling bin out of the trunk and installs herself in the back. It's cold and dark, but private.

What is immediately obvious is that the recycling bin paints a more intimate portrait than the trash from 230

Gibson. Élisabeth Routier-Savoie eats margarine, bagels and blueberry jam. She cancelled her Internet package during the month of July. She ignores the Publisacs, full of flyers and circulars. She has recently suffered from migraines or menstrual cramps. She has dry skin.

As she rummages, Jay wonders what people might think of her own garbage. Trash has always been a significant marker of social class. In bygone days, piles of manure attested to a farm's prosperity. Today, everybody is secretly afraid of producing boring garbage, which would be evidence of a dull life. The trash can is the height of personal expression, and Mark Zuckerberg should take note: say goodbye to statuses of food and music; the posts of tomorrow will show the contents of our trash cans.

Jay makes a mental note of the idea. She should get it patented. It will give her something to keep herself busy, after they lock her away.

Right now, she still has to sort out Élisabeth Routier-Savoie's recycling bin. Some finds are disconcerting, such as the receipt for a pair of imitation sheepskin slippers, three pairs of men's XL underwear and twelve toothbrushes. And what about the dozen or so UPS envelopes, all sent by Éric Le Blanc and bearing a customs invoice marked "gift—value $20"?

But strangest of all are, without a doubt, the innumerable medication packages. It's as if the young woman had robbed a drugstore: analgesics, antihistamines, antibiotic and anti-hemorrhoid ointments, multivitamins, vitamin

D, omega-3, eye drops, proton pump inhibitors, antifungal creams. Jay is starting to suspect she is dealing with a hypochondriac. No one buys this much medication all at the same time. There are even some obscure products that Jay has never heard of, like this collyrium wash, or these scopolamine patches.

Holding the scopolamine package, Jay suddenly goes rigid. A hair's breadth from going into shock, she reads and rereads the words printed in red on the box: *ScopoMax— fast and efficient treatment for seasickness.*

— 39 —

LISA EMERGES FROM HER RETREAT in late May, pallid and shaky, but with that unmistakable gleam in her eye. Here she is, pacing back and forth in front of Autocars Mondiaux, beneath a broken sign representing a Greyhound Scenicruiser circling the globe. She parked the Dodge by the side of the cracked asphalt road, and from time to time she looks down the street and at her watch. She is waiting for something to happen or for someone to arrive, or both. She once again steps up to the garage and peeks through the windows, grimy almost to the point of opacity. Some abstract shapes can barely be made out in the half-light. And that's good.

Renting this place turned out to be amazingly simple, although she did have to track it down first. Garages large enough to accommodate a forty-foot container are not all that common on the Montreal rental market. As soon as she saw the pictures of the garage on the MVGR Global Rental website, she rented it without even paying a visit. The pictures were flattering. The lease was signed via fax, and Lisa paid six months in advance.

There is just one detail left to take care of . . . and there it is just now appearing on the horizon, racing down Gibson Street and screeching into the Autocars Mondiaux parking lot. The tiny car makes an elegant turn and comes to a halt near Lisa. The courier rolls down the window, smiling, Rastafarian-ish.

"Isabelle Boucher-Boivin?"

"Present."

The girl reaches toward the back seat and lifts out an envelope that she hands to Lisa. "Your signature. Right here."

She holds out the terminal and a plastic stylus. Lisa puts a random mark on the screen, and the squiggle is instantly propelled to a server in Bangkok or Tucson.

"I need to see some ID."

Lisa feels a stab of anxiety; she of course does not have any ID in the name of Isabelle Boucher-Boivin. It's something she came up with on the spur of the moment, for the sake of the lease. And to think she laughed at Éric and his Rokov Global Import Export. Isabelle Boucher-Boivin. Pathetic. She taps her pockets with a grin, but the courier gestures for her to stop. No problem, comrade, forget it. Lisa draws the money clip out of her hip pocket and pulls out a tired twenty-dollar bill. The girl pockets the tip, gives Lisa a vaguely lascivious wink and immediately speeds off toward new adventures.

As she watches the car drive away, Lisa wonders what exactly that wink meant. She unseals the envelope, lets a set of keys drop into the palm of her hand and opens the glass door of what was once the reception area of the glorious Autocars Mondiaux. The lock could use some oil.

It's like walking into an archaeological museum. *Come see the wonders of the twentieth century, with its peanut vending machines, its waiting rooms, its management culture! Admire the gloss of linoleum and vinyl!*

Lisa tries the light switch. No electricity.

She crosses the workshop, preceded by the echo of her steps. The place is empty. A vehicle lift once occupied the centre of the workshop, right where eight large rusted screws jut out now, and a hoist, whose track is all that remains, ran along the ceiling. All the implements of the mechanic's profession were sold off, but there is still some robust steel shelving left, as well as a huge garbage drum, a steel workbench sturdy enough to support a tank turret, and a big sink with a petrified cake of soap resting on the rim. Lisa opens the tap, which sputters and spits brownish water. She lets it run.

The ring-shaped stains on the floor suggest leakage during heavy storms, and the cracks between the cinder blocks point to structural problems, probably irreparable. In a word, the building is just about ripe for demolition. It's perfect.

Lisa presses the button that controls the garage door. Nothing happens. That's right: no electricity. She'll definitely have to take care of that. She opens the door manually, using the chains, and then she backs the Dodge up to the threshold to unload her equipment. She has brought only the bare essentials. Five tool boxes, extension cords, a drill, a mitre saw, several kilos of various screws, a portable light, her computer, clamps. She makes a tentative list of what's missing. Work lamps. Radio. Trestles. Anvil. Vise. Coffee maker.

She takes a cardboard tube out of the van and pulls out ten large-format blueprints, which she proceeds to tack up on one of the walls. She arranges them in chronological order, like the storyboard of a film, to properly represent the project timeline.

Plans A, B and C are the most technical; they show the modification of the refrigeration unit to provide electricity, and the installation of the central electrical panel, the wiring, the breakers and power outlets, the lighting.

Plan D tackles the problem specific to the Faraday cage: how to communicate with the outside world from inside a corrugated steel box. The solution is a complicated diagram of unobtrusive antennas installed on the six sides of the container, so that every need as to wi-fi, radio and GPS is fulfilled.

Plan E deals with flow-through ventilation: carbon filters at both ends of the system, air cooling and heating, dehumidification.

Plans F and G delineate the main living areas: living room, kitchenette, storage room, drinking water and waste water tanks, trash and toilet space, and a wall of phony Empire apple crates to serve as a screen. The design also involves building an emergency hatch through the refrigeration unit.

Plans H and I represent the fine details of the design. Lisa drew her inspiration from the cabins of sailing yachts; everything is compact and convertible. The bunk transforms into a bench. The chart table is tiny but functional. In the kitchenette, each cubic centimetre was calculated and then recalculated. The extremity of the container, near the doors and just before the wall of apple crates, will be taken up by the dry toilet (concealed in an elegant wooden closet) and a trash compactor that can crush garbage into nice high-density cubes.

Finally, Plan J is more in the way of a perspective drawing. It represents what the finished container would look like if its sides were removed. There is a computer on the chart table, a VHF radio, an abundance of full-spectrum lighting, the library, the unfolded bunk, a trunk for clothes. Some peanut sauce is simmering on the electric stove. The bread maker and rice cooker are discreetly doing their jobs, and the germination machines are luxuriant under the ultraviolet lamps. The plan does not show everything; it leaves much to the imagination, with which Lisa gladly conjures up mellow, baroque details, cushions edged with pompoms, a samovar, a polar bear skin, even one of those padded armchairs in which the great explorers of the

Victorian age, bushy-bearded and sharp-eyed, struck a pose before sailing away to perish Britannically in the heart of the Arctic icefields.

Once Plan J has been tacked to the wall, Lisa takes a few steps back and, hands on hips, contemplates the general effect. These plans represent seven months of intensive work: the past three months and the four months to come.

Speaking of the future, she looks at her watch. No time to daydream—she has an appointment with Piotr.

— 40 —

DESPITE HER NORDIQUES TOQUE, THREE layers of sweaters and rubber boots, Jay is shaking. It's 1 a.m., and there's a bitter wind sweeping over the Canadian Shield.

The little girl has just turned ten and still lives a thousand kilometres downstream from Montreal in the village where she was born. It's mid-October and, as is true every mid-October, she accompanies her father to watch the last sailing of the *Nordik Express*. The ship won't be back before March, when the river thaws. Until then, there's always the Ski-Doo.

Jay has never set foot on board the *Nordik Express*, and she looks enviously at the crew, the captain and even the three or four late-season tourists half asleep in their fuchsia windbreakers, who clutch the guardrail to keep from being carried off by a gust of wind.

The gangway is still resting on the wharf, and Jay

wonders if it would be hard to steal aboard. Stowaway—
now there's an interesting idea.

She follows the operations, shivering. The dockers are
loading an old container.

All of a sudden, Jay feels sad. She goes back to sit in the
pickup, out of the wind. Long before the *Nordik Express*
leaves port, she is already asleep.

— 41 —

LISA IS IN THE MIDDLE of the Jacques Cartier Bridge
when her phone rings on the passenger seat. Her hands
grip the wheel a little more tightly. She has learned to
dread this sound. Since December, the only incoming calls
have been to inform her that her father:

1) has tried to cross the US border;
2) cannot return home;
3) will be transferred to a faraway transitional facility;
4) has lost his partial dentures and damaged his TV.
It won't be long before he:
5) runs away;
6) has a stroke;
7) breaks his hip.

Lisa darts a sideways glance at the phone and sees the
name Josée Savoie. With her finger on the button, she briefly
considers not answering.

"Mom?"

"Glad to see you still remember me."

There's a hint of reproach in her voice. How many weeks has it been since Lisa last called her mother? She's lost count.

"You're busy?"

"I'm driving."

"Busy in general?"

"Oh, yes. Yes. Pretty much, yeah."

Lisa takes a passing look at the odometer: ninety-five kilometres an hour. Her mind struggles passively to wriggle out of this conversation.

"I was in Montreal yesterday afternoon. I went by HardKo. Your boss said you quit your job during the winter."

"New job."

"Oh? Where are you working now?"

"I'm *going* to get a new job. Soon. I want to finish my term first."

A studied micro-silence—Josée takes a sip of something. She decides to get to the point of the call.

"Are you coming to IKEA with me this Sunday?"

Lisa suppresses a sigh. Her mother is afflicted with an ironclad karma: her new boyfriend isn't fond of IKEA, like the previous boyfriend, and the one before that, and Robert back in the day. At this rate, no matter how many partners she has, Josée Savoie is likely to solicit Lisa for Sunday visits to IKEA for the rest of her life.

Incidentally, which piece of furniture does she want to replace this time?

"My coffee table."

"Your coffee table."

"The top is all scratched."

"We bought it together, when was it . . . two years ago?"

"I know."

"I'm driving right now. Is there anything else you wanted to tell me?"

"I'll come pick you up Sunday morning."

"I have to go."

"Okay. See you Sunday. You'll have supper with us after?"

"I didn't say yes."

"Nine thirty."

"I didn't say yes!"

Surplus Industrials Peter is exactly how Lisa pictured it: a vast empty lot in the sub-suburbs of Montreal, strewn with obsolete farm machinery, M35 Canadian army trucks and reinforced concrete pipes. Nothing is new. Everything containing ferrous metal is slowly taking on an orangeish hue, and the company's office is housed in a trailer in the same tones.

Piotr speaks English with an accent only a Slavophile linguist would be able to pinpoint on a map of Europe. He leads Lisa to the far end of the yard, where the obscure object of desire lies between an old snow blower from the Saint-Lambert municipality and a batch of PVC cisterns. It's a large white container bearing the seven-pointed star of Maersk and speckled with rust. Lisa inspects the refrigeration unit with excessive care. Piotr bangs the steel with his fist.

"Mint condition!"

He opens the doors as if this were a precious coach. Lisa turns on her flashlight and climbs inside.

"Mint condition! Only one former owner. Need CSC certification? I can arrange."

Lisa listens with half an ear. Under her feet, the plastic embossing is as abraded as a dance floor. Lisa pictures millions of pallets of grapefruit and bok choy waltzing back and forth on this floor. She sniffs the air and thinks she detects a faint scent of strawberries. The walls are clean, no trace of mould. A few minor dents. She trains her flashlight on the ventilation grilles. No rust.

Outside, Piotr stands around, takes a phone call, converses in Croatian or Bulgarian, lights a cigarette, interrupts his conversation to mention something to Lisa about the paint, the hinges, the rivets. She nods.

It starts to rain. Piotr flicks away his still-smoking cigarette and takes shelter inside the container. The smell of wet tobacco overlays that of the strawberries.

The negotiations are fierce and trilingual. The phone rings, Piotr ignores it. Lisa offers twenty-five hundred. Piotr pretends to rip his heart out and throw it on the floor—the refrigeration unit alone is worth thirty-five hundred! Give me a break, Lisa's smile replies, this wreck is almost as old as I am . . . The phone rings again. Slavic swear words. Different amounts are uttered. Pouts and grimaces. They agree on thirty-one hundred, to be paid on the spot.

Outside, the cigarette butt persists in smoking despite the rain.

They shut the container and dash toward the trailer to finalize the payment and sign the documents. Even here, in the small intestine of the industrialized world, there are forms to fill out, stamp and initial. Paperwork rules the world. Lisa shivers in the rain. Fucking paperwork.

The rain gives way to aggressive sunshine, and the interior of Autocars Mondiaux is stifling in spite of the wide-open door. Time for a drink. A FedEx truck drove by ten minutes ago; since then, nothing.

Lisa downs her second litre of mineral water sitting cross-legged on the doorstep of the garage. She looks at the containers parked across the street. A guy perched on the edge of a loading dock is having a cigarette. Lisa wonders what exactly goes on in that anonymous beige warehouse. The containers are nameless. They could hold electronics, winter boots, hashish or Romanian nationals. There's no way of knowing. Opacity is the cornerstone of modern capitalism.

The sun is relentless, and Lisa feels she is about to fall asleep when, suddenly, the starred white container—*her* starred white container—comes into view down the street. It looks enormous, twice as long as it did at Surplus Peter, and tall beyond reason. The big rig nearly drives right by, slows down all the same and parks in the street. The truck driver looks like an appliance repairman: blue uniform and matching cap, ballpoint pen in his shirt pocket, magnificent moustache. He looks at the document on his clipboard.

"Rokov Export?"

"That's me."

Lisa feels herself blushing slightly. She can't bring herself to take the name seriously. Éric was the one who suggested using Rokov & Co. Global Import Export Inc. For some mysterious reason, he found it amusing. Corporate humour, no doubt; she didn't make an issue of it. Since then, whenever she has used the name—to rent the garage, open an account with Hydro-Québec or have the container delivered—she felt as if she were asking for a bank loan wearing a clown costume and holding a bunch of balloons.

The driver points to the Autocars Mondiaux sign with his clipboard. "That's misleading."

"We're going to change it soon."

They shake hands. Then the driver pushes up the visor of his cap and eyes the garage door. "Do I back it inside?"

"Will it fit?"

Without saying a word, he climbs back behind the wheel and starts the manoeuvre. The trailer describes a flawless curve and rolls through the doorway on the first try, while Lisa looks on in amazement. The driver brings the trailer to a stop in the exact centre of the garage. A perfect fit, with just enough room left to open the container doors and work unimpeded. Lisa suppresses a surge of claustrophobia.

The driver cranks away at the handle and lowers the trailer's landing gear, disconnects the compressed air tube and electrical cable connector, and releases the fifth wheel. No wasted moves, no hint of effort or hesitation. The demeanour of someone who has done this millions of times. Just before leaving, he holds out the clipboard with the inevitable forms to sign.

"Here and here, and your initials here."

He leaves Lisa the yellow copy and wishes her good day.

The tractor disappears at the corner of the street and the garage is again plunged into silence. Lisa contemplates the container, doing her best to realize it is really and truly there in front of her. Just as she closes the garage door, Lisa remembers Éric's special request: a picture of the whole beast, "not a close-up."

Right from their initial discussions in February, Éric made known his intention to document every single stage of the project. He wanted it all: CAD files and sketches on napkins, every version of the plans, the technical remarks, the inventory of parts and tools used. When Lisa announced the work was officially getting under way, he made her swear she would photograph everything. Lisa takes a few steps back, points her telephone at the garage and captures the big box for posterity in both portrait and landscape formats. She looks at the results and frowns. This old Nokia never did take terrific pictures.

She sprints over to the Dodge, opens the glove compartment and grabs Mrs. Le Blanc's camera. She hasn't checked to see if it still works, but if it does, Éric will appreciate the nod. Walking back to the garage, she inserts two AA batteries taken from a flashlight. The suspense is short-lived. The PowerShot does not respond. As dead as a brick.

Lisa removes the memory card and slips it into her pocket. Then she lobs the camera into the garbage drum, which resonates for a long time, like a gong in a Buddhist monastery.

She rubs her hands together: there's work to be done. She punches the huge red button, and the garage door comes down over the scene amid the jangle of pulleys and poorly oiled steel.

— 42 —

JAY GOES BACK UP TO the seventh floor, still half dazed. She waves her access card and walks through the glass doors. She has the feeling everyone can readily decode the thoughts imprinted on her face. She cuts across to the washroom and examines herself in the mirror. She splashes some water on her face, rubs her eyes. Good enough.

It's dead calm in the Enclave. Mahesh is finishing off the box of Whippets with the glassy gaze of a heroin addict. Laura is sipping some herbal tea. Sergeant Gamache's office lacks Sergeant Gamache. Jay stumbles on the short pile carpet, recovers with a little pas de deux that takes her to the coffee machine and, while she's there, pours herself a cup. Then, cup in hand, she sidles up to Laura, trying to act as casual as possible.

"So tell me, you wouldn't, by any chance, have a dossier on stowaways?"

Laura shoots her a peeved look over the top of her glasses. "No, I don't, *by any chance*, have a dossier on stowaways."

Still sitting in her office chair, she propels herself with a skilful kick over to the grey filing cabinet, of which she is wholly and exclusively in charge. She takes the key hanging from her neck and unlocks a drawer, which opens with a panzer-like rumble. Squeezed neatly inside are some thirty bulky files.

"What is it you want exactly?"

"I don't know. How are things classified?"

"Location, vehicle and year."

"Vehicle?"

"Ship, truck, wagon, landing gear . . ."

"Container?"

"I have that."

She extracts a thick binder and hands it to Jay. It contains hundreds, possibly thousands, of articles, mostly in English, arranged in chronological order. The oldest ones were taken from microfilms dating back to the sixties; the resolution is muddy, there are words and lines missing. The quality gradually improves, with the most recent articles printed directly from the databases. Laura gestures somewhat apologetically.

"The last five years are missing. It's not worth printing them, since I'm going to digitize everything when I find the time. And then"—she gives the file cabinet a little kick—"I'm getting rid of this fossil."

Jay hefts the binder. "There are only articles here?"

"I appended some photos, and some documents that are more technical. Reports from the government, the RCMP, FBI, Homeland Security."

"Can I borrow it?"

"For as long as you want. It makes pretty interesting bedtime reading. Ever hear of Amir Farid Rizk?"

"No."

"October 2001. It's worth a peek."

— 43 —

A WEEK HAS ELAPSED SINCE Lisa closed the garage door, and she won't be opening it again.

The young woman is suffering from structural paranoia. After the cash, the fake IDs and bogus company names, after the intricate logistical schemes and the VPN encrypted messages, she has now deliberately shut herself in. Éric insisted on compartmentalizing? Well, Lisa is compartmentalizing. It's out of the question to open the garage door again. She hasn't even washed the windowpanes. Security through grime.

She keeps at it fifteen hours a day in what feels like a poorly ventilated sauna—a most peculiar sauna, actually, where the radio plays very softly and the smell is a blend of coffee and tin solder. She has just spent a week modifying the container's refrigeration unit.

As soon as she unscrewed the panels, she could see the

machine hadn't been cleaned in years. The circuits were plastered with tropical grunge—bits of leaves, dust, flies and even a huge yellow and black spider, shrivelled up in a corner. The creature ended up in an old pill bottle; Lisa couldn't bring herself to throw it in the trash. It was a stowaway, a colleague, really, and therefore deserved a minimum of deference.

When he saw the picture of the creature, Éric's jaw dropped. He wasn't likely to stumble on anything like that sitting at his keyboard. He had never seen this sort of spider—by the way, what sort of spider was it? He would do some research, if he found the time.

Having cleaned everything out using compressed air and then a vacuum cleaner, Lisa got down to the real work. First, she had to make sense of the jumble of coils, accumulators, ventilators and bundles of wires. The wiring diagram glued to the inside of the panel was oily and partly illegible. Lisa had to make do with a user's manual found on the Web; it was pixelated and fuzzy, but better than nothing.

In any case, her aim was to dismantle as few parts as possible—a short-circuit or a Freon leak can happen in the blink of an eye. Theoretically, just one or two wires needed to be disconnected for the machine to stop producing cold and confine itself to providing electricity and ventilation. A hatch also had to be fashioned behind one of the control panels so she could enter the container after locking the doors.

Ten litres of strong coffee and two sleepless nights later, Lisa can see the light at the end of the tunnel. She's completed the modifications, and the time has come to plug in the golem.

She unseals a package that arrived from Hong Kong two days ago, containing a fantastically specialized electrical cord designed to connect a nautical refrigeration unit to a 220-volt outlet. Lisa wonders how many people in the world would need a cord like this. At the bottom of the box, she discovers a legal notice in English and Chinese, which she skims over distractedly. *Responsibility limited to manufacturing defects bla-bla-bla manufacturer cannot be held liable for bla-bla-bla in the event of electrocution, explosion, fire or any other material damage or physical injury due to incorrect use.*

Lisa crumples the paper and tosses it over her shoulder.

Holding the adapter cord, she steps up to the refrigeration unit. A few centimetres from the outlet, Lisa hesitates. She recalls the Sunday morning her father got a 220-volt shock: the odour of burnt hair, his arm numb for ten minutes. Many years on, he still has a pinkish scar running across his hand. "Always respect electricity, Lisa," he would often repeat, and as Lisa plugs in the container, she tells herself that right now a chemical extinguisher would be an excellent sign of respect. She'll try to keep that in mind next time. If there is a next time.

She turns on the switch and the ventilator starts up, generating as much noise as a Cessna. Lisa looks at the control panel. The thermometer will have to be tampered with to permanently display three degrees Celsius.

She straps on her headlamp and climbs into the container. A light puff of air brushes across her forearms. The beam from her lamp shines on the newly installed electrical distribution panel, bristling with wires neatly coiled and tied, like a spiderweb waiting to unfurl.

Lisa opens the panel door and, clenching her teeth, throws the main switch. No sparks or crackling sound. She flips the breaker switch of circuit number three, and a light bulb at the end of one of the electrical wires comes on at her feet.

The beast is alive.

— 44 —

HAVING DITCHED THE RECYCLING BIN in an alley, driven the car back to the rental agency and gone crosstown by bus, Jay comes home to a real-estate marathon in full swing. Alex Onassis has decided he is going to sell the damned duplex tonight or never. Jay doesn't care—she's hungry.

Owing to the events of the past few weeks, domestic affairs have been somewhat neglected; there's nothing left but five and a half partly sprouted potatoes, two cans of beer, a bottle of habanero sauce and some cat kibble.

Speaking of which, how long has it been since she last saw Erwin?

She scans through the menus on the fridge. Everything looks repulsive. She sets about cooking the potatoes in the last clean pot. Alex Onassis comes and goes, reciting his sales pitch: great exposure, five-minute walk to the metro, elementary school. Roofing redone ten years ago. Electric heating on every floor, two balconies, new asking price. Any questions?

Jay conspicuously ignores this farcical parade. Seated on the sofa like a queen with her potful of mashed potatoes and a cold beer, she turns her attention to the binder on stowaways. The dossier is both exhaustive and stripped-down: no table of contents, no index, no page numbering. Zero ornamentation. Just raw information, recto and verso. Laura Wissenberg, through and through.

The oldest articles date back to the late fifties—the dawn of containerization—and the rate of publication steadily increases over the subsequent decades. Jay assumes at first that this curve follows the rising number of stowaway cases, but she soon notices that the articles grow more and more detailed over the years. The specialized vocabulary becomes commonplace, various concepts become implicit. Containers become grist for the media from the moment they crystallize in the collective imagination.

After all, how can a story be narrated when it unfolds in a place no one can conceptualize?

Jay knits her brow. Is a container a place? No, not really. But neither is it an ordinary box, or a vehicle, or the trans-continental equivalent of an elevator. It functions at once as object and infrastructure, corrugated steel and database; it falls within culture and the law. For centuries, human beings have been familiar with geography, with concepts such as road, territory, border; but the container eludes geography. It operates on the periphery of the collective consciousness. Thousands of Romanians and Cubans and Chinese enter, or try to enter, North America and Western Europe crammed inside boxes, and no encyclopedia mentions this historic migration.

"Excuse me . . ."

Jay looks up from her reading and finds an exhausted Alex Onassis. To all appearances, the poor man is having more and more trouble conceptualizing the duplex.

"The visits are over for tonight."

Without waiting for an answer, he gives a little wave and, as he goes out, walks under the intermittently blinking light fixture. Dramatic music, roll credits.

Jay stretches and thinks she ought to tackle the mountain of filthy dishes. There's no reason to nurture disorder now that the visits are over. But then she thinks better of it. There may be more visitors tomorrow and, if so, she won't have time to dirty enough plates to make a bad impression.

What's more, she has something more pressing to do. She has just recalled Laura's recommendation to read the articles about a certain Amir so-and-so, from October 2001.

First surprise: the file on this guy—Amir Farid Rizk is his name—is a good centimetre thick, some fifty documents in all. The beginning of the story is unremarkable: a man gets caught at the Gioia Tauro terminal in Italy aboard a container newly arrived from Cairo. A longshoreman heard someone yelling and banging against the sides. Not the first time a stowaway lacked air. Some had suffocated.

The security people were called and immediately came to cut the seals and open the doors. The poor wretch staggered into the open air blinking his eyes, a little dazed but in good health. A quick look was enough to conclude this was not a typical stowaway; he was fitted out like a secret agent. The police dispatched to the scene discovered a satellite telephone, fake credit cards, access cards for Canadian, Egyptian and Thai airports, and a Rome–Montreal plane ticket.

The individual's name was Amir Farid Rizk—with a *z*, he insisted—and he was a Canadian-Egyptian national. Yes, fine, okay, but what was he doing in the container? That part was not so clear. Grilled about this, Rizk launched into a sketchy account. He asserted he was the victim of religious persecution, claimed that his powerful brother-in-law had made threats against his life. He was looking for an unobtrusive way to return to Canada.

The attacks against the World Trade Center were still front-page news, and Rizk became an overnight microphenomenon in the media. Airport surveillance had been boosted threefold, but what about seaport facilities? In the United States, some observers predicted terrorist attacks involving ships, speculated about the existence of a clandestine intermodal network for the conveyance of Taliban kamikazes and bacteriological bombs. Amir Farid Rizk, they said, was quite simply a sign of things to come.

Except that, having completed their investigation, the authorities acknowledged that Rizk did not belong to any terrorist cell and was not preparing any attacks. He was, in short, and despite appearances, a harmless stowaway. Immediately on being released, the fellow vanished from Italy, from the media and from the face of the planet.

Jay skims through the articles. This character was a unique case. As a rule, stowaways move in more or less disorganized groups. Rizk travelled alone and was well equipped: in addition to a satellite phone and an assortment of tickets and passes, he had brought provisions and drinking water, a bed, a bucket that served as a toilet, a laptop computer, clothes and a dishwasher.

Rizk was so well prepared, in fact, that he easily might have reached Canada without a hitch had he not run out of air. Even the most organized travellers can neglect a detail such as breathing.

Jay wonders if Élisabeth thought of it.

— 45 —

SEVEN WEEKS HAVE ELAPSED AND, apart from the weekly runs to Saint-Anicet-de-Kostka, Lisa devotes herself body and soul to fitting out the container. The passenger compartment is taking shape, and the workshop of Autocars Mondiaux is full of studs. The floor is strewn with blond shavings, and the atmosphere is saturated with a fine mist of sawdust streaked with the sunrays passing through the skylights.

Lisa is touching up a plank. She measures the depth of the tenons for the third time and climbs into the container. A hook scale and the computer, showing an Excel spreadsheet, have been placed inside the doorway. Having weighed her plank, Lisa keys in the result. Everything that enters the container must be weighed, from the wood and hardware to the electrical appliances, the mattress, the food and drinking water, the teapot and teabags, right down to the slightest pompommed cushion, not to mention Lisa herself. The net weight must not exceed twenty-five tons, otherwise the container will start to groan and bend. According to Lisa's calculations, the final structure (including the drinking water) should amount to about ten thousand kilos, but everything has to be weighed all the same because the merchandise weight must be specified on the forms.

Inside, there are three white-hot floods casting a harsh light, but the ventilation makes the atmosphere bearable. Lisa catches herself appreciating the narrowness of the box. The great discovery of the summer: you can't suffer from claustrophobia in a cell you build yourself. The partitions are already up, and Lisa has moved on to assembling the cabinets. Furnishing the container is probably overdoing it, but Robert Routier's daughter won't settle for plastic crates stacked on shelves made of two-by-fours.

The project is a little behind schedule, but this is not entirely due to familial tendencies. The fact is, Lisa had to revise her plans to take into account certain unforeseen properties of containers.

It all started when Lisa noticed that some studs were slightly twisted. The wood warped in the damp heat of the workshop. In itself, this was in no way surprising. Everything in the universe warps and changes: wood bends and twists, concrete buckles, plastic cracks and sags, bones grow porous and muscles stiffen, polymers decompose, steel rusts—come to think of it, Lisa wondered, wasn't the container itself apt to crumple? The heat and cold aren't likely to cause significant fluctuations, but what about the handling?

Two minutes on Google was all it took for her to learn about the mysterious and terrifying deflection factor.

The attachment points of intermodal containers are located at the corners, and when the cranes take hold of the big boxes—the forty-footers in particular—they sag in the middle somewhat and undergo all kinds of torsion of varying degrees of severity. Lisa hadn't considered this. She had designed the passenger compartment as one long unit, like a tree house. If the container twisted even a little, the whole thing could collapse.

Lisa saw herself again at the age of eight, perched on a trestle, watching her father assemble a kitchen cabinet with dowels and a wooden mallet.

"Why don't you use glue? Wouldn't it be faster?"

"To allow the cabinet to breathe."

"Cabinets breathe?"

"Cabinets breathe, the walls breathe . . . the whole house breathes. When you put a piece of wood under the microscope, it looks like a sponge. It's full of air cells."

Dowel. Three strokes of the mallet.

"When the wood absorbs humidity, it changes shape, and size. In summer, when the air is warm and damp, houses expand. In winter, they shrink. Like a lung. It breathes in then breathes out."

Lisa was a big girl now; she was the one wielding the tools and drawing the plans, and she had to ensure that her container could breathe.

She immediately sat down at her computer and modified plans D, E and F; the different sections of the passenger compartment would be independent, separated by expansion joints, and all the parts would be assembled à la Robert Routier: no screws or glue, but wooden dowels, which would allow the parts to give. (The new plans were immediately sent to Éric, for the archives.)

Lisa positions the plank. The tenons are a little wide and she has to work them into place. Once the piece is properly fitted together, she tests the four corners of the cabinet with a square. She drills the holes and inserts the dowels. Each dowel gets five strokes of the mallet. It's solid.

Just as she drives home the last dowel, Lisa realizes she is using the very mallet her father used twelve years earlier when he explained to her that houses breathe. She wipes her eyes with the back of her sleeve. Damned sawdust.

At midnight, her computer bleeps. Video call from Copenhagen. Éric obviously still has some time to spare between programming blitzes, as he has solved the enigma of the spider found in the refrigeration unit: it's a *Nephila clavipes*.

"Poisonous?"

"It would seem so."

"And what if it laid eggs somewhere before dying?"

"Vacuum extra carefully."

"Already have."

"Then there's nothing to worry about. But wait, it gets better. Do you know where *Nephila clavipes* is found? In banana shipments. I was intrigued, so I did some research on the container. Interested?"

"I'm listening."

He flips through a bunch of papers, off-camera. "Let's see, now. It was assembled in mainland China by the AC Teng company and registered with the International Container Bureau on March 19, 1997 by A.P. Møller—Maersk Gruppen. It travelled between Central America and the east coast of the US, Honduras, Venezuela, Guatemala . . ."

Micro-pause while he sips his coffee.

"It sat idle for about ten months at the Newark terminal during the financial crisis. After that, it shuttled between Guayaquil and St. Petersburg, with a dozen ports of call throughout the Caribbean and Western Europe."

"Guayaquil?"

"Ecuador."

"There's a shipping service between Ecuador and Russia?"

"Ecubex. Seven Class N container ships that do the round trip in forty-nine days. Weekly sailings. Total capacity, ten thousand containers like yours."

Lisa tries to imagine the volume represented by ten thousand containers stacked one atop the other, linked end to end, piled sky-high. You could fit St. Peter's Basilica in there and still have some room left over for a few hands of bananas. A knock-down St. Peter's, with the parts spread out between Guayaquil and Russia.

Éric continues to rummage through his papers. "It stayed with Ecubex for five or six months before being decommissioned last January, when Maersk modernized its stock. The old boxes were replaced by controlled-atmosphere StarCare models. Yours was part of a batch put up for sale by a Russian wholesaler and bought by a Ukrainian Canadian who went bankrupt. The containers were resold all over the map."

"Where did you get this information?"

"I have my sources."

Lisa yawns. She's had a long day and it's time for bed.

"Already?"

"It's midnight here. Was there something else you wanted to tell me?"

"Yes, actually. I have a confession to make."

"A confession?"

"I've been trying to figure out how to say it for weeks."

Lisa wavers between curiosity and apprehension. She sits back to get comfortable. "I'm listening."

"It's about the balloon."

"Which balloon?"

"The balloon we launched into the stratosphere."

"Oh, yeah, I remember you had a funny expression when I sent you the pictures."

"I had a funny expression?"

"The same one you have now."

Éric pauses as if to think about the expression he's wearing. He takes a long sip of coffee. "Right. Do you remember when we waited for the GPS to send us its coordinates?"

"Yeah. The three longest weeks of my adolescence. We wondered if the GPS was to blame or the batteries."

"It was neither."

"Oh?"

"The GPS beacon was working fine. I was the one who changed the phone number at the last moment."

Silence.

"Which number did you enter?"

"No idea. I punched in a random number. It didn't matter."

More silence, but longer, interspersed with distortions from the software, crunching and encoding tiny background noises. Lisa finally waves it off; she understands. There's nothing more to say.

After they sign off, Lisa gets up and, among the boxes of screws and rivets, fishes out the pill bottle with the dead spider. She takes a marker and writes *Nephila clavipes* on the cap in neat cursive script.

MORNING RUSH HOUR ON THE Orange Line, and the density level is nearing five humans per square metre.

Compressed into a corner of the metro car, Jay focuses on her reading. She spent the night reading about stowaways and was unable to sleep, one thing having no doubt led to the other.

Her first intuition was borne out: media coverage over the years doesn't rise just because of the growing number of stowaways but also because of the cultural ubiquity of containers. Containers gradually become more commonplace, and this acts as a filter; with the passage of time, the media increasingly regard only the most spectacular cases as newsworthy: Chinese dead of hypothermia, asphyxiated Moroccans, dehydrated Filipinos, Guineans thrown overboard by the crew, catatonic Guatemalans crammed pellmell amid clothes, dead bodies and garbage. And the Ivorians poisoned by the rodent control products sprayed between the containers. The Colombians whose flashlights went out one after the other and who had to live for ten days in absolute darkness. The Dominicans who, having bored a tiny hole in the side of the container, literally killed each other for a breath of air. The young Americans roasted alive in an overheated container. Jay tried to take a peek at the appended photos, but she quickly gave up. She doesn't have the stomach for it.

The train stops at Bonaventure station. Three people get out, five get in. The car smells of bacon and deodorant.

Jay realizes there is one question to which Laura's press clippings binder has no answer: how many stowaways make it to their destination alive and undetected?

Which gets her thinking again about the young Élisabeth Routier-Savoie.

Everyone is trying to locate Papa Zulu—the RCMP, the CIA, Homeland Security, CISC, not to mention the database administrators of all the ports of Southeast Asia—but no one actually knows what the object of this vast hunt really is. Only Éric Le Blanc, in his Copenhagen bunker, and Jay, in a metro car beneath downtown Montreal, know the truth: a young woman is hiding aboard Papa Zulu.

Lucien-L'Allier station. A man is determined to get on with a double baby stroller. The interior pressure climbs to nearly 30 psi. Jay feels her eardrums are about to burst. There are sure to be some strokes when the doors open. She resigns herself to closing her notebook—anyway, it's just two more stations. She twists her body and dips her hand into her coat pocket in the hope of discovering a scrap of paper that might serve as a bookmark. She fishes out the receipt from the Colmado Real *dépanneur*: a medium coffee and a box of Whippets for the modest sum of $42.12.

Jay would jump if she had enough room. Whippets at $39.90?! Colmado Real has blown a fuse. Forty dollars a box works out to $1.25 a bite. At that price, they should have been hand-painted by Jackson Pollock.

She shakes her head in disbelief. Not even a scammer would dare to jack prices up that much. It must have been a mistake. She tries to reconstruct the chain of events. The box was supposed to cost $3.99, but someone must have entered the wrong price in the inventory. Zero is next to 9. The person had large fingers. The mistake went unnoticed and the item ended up with two prices: $3.99 on the shelf and $39.90 in the database. The cashier was half asleep and swiped the bar code without even glancing at the screen; come to think of it, she didn't say the total amount out loud. To top off this long series of blunders, Jay signed the credit card receipt without paying much attention. A typical blend of inattentiveness, human error and faith in the system.

Horacio always liked to say that love and faith are blind, but at least love serves a purpose.

Absorbed by this problem, Jay almost misses her stop. She alights from the car at the very last moment, the note-book pressed against her chest, and drops the receipt in the rush. ¡Adiós! Real. She mutters as she ascends the hill to C Division. After all those rented cars, Jay is starting to go soft. The process of aging happens one capitulation at a time.

The only one at his station is Mahesh, who leans toward his screen, engrossed in a manual for an intermodal man-agement system. The cross-section of a container ship shows the various boxes nested in their cells like Lego blocks. He turns toward Jay.

"Ah, finally!"

"You wanted to see me?"

"I'd like your opinion."

Caught off guard, Jay freezes. In the seven years they have shared this space, she does not recall a single instance of Mahesh asking for her opinion, except perhaps on the freshness of the buns in the cafeteria.

"My opinion?"

"I think I've discovered the secret of Papa Zulu."

— 47—

THE SUN IS SETTING OVER Montreal, and in three hours summer will be officially over.

Lisa has started the camouflage operation: having covered the tools and the floor with plastic tarps, she sealed the openings of the container, slipped into a coverall, duct-taped her wrists and ankles, pulled on a pair of rubber gloves, put on goggles and a dust mask, and set to work on the container with a belt sander. The old paint is tenacious, and the belt needs to be changed every five minutes, but that's not a problem—Lisa allotted a specific budget item to sandpaper, and as she grinds away, the white gradually disintegrates, the alphanumerical codes disappear, the big seven-pointed star fades. An immaculate dust rises into the air, like the pulverized memory of the container. The industrial brown of anonymous containers peeps out here and there on the steel.

Then, after washing the sides and letting the dust settle, Lisa sprays on two coats of paint.

As she sweeps a fine mist of titanium white over the steel, she wonders if it might be appropriate to name this, um . . . vehicle? After all, sailors give names to their boats. And truckers, their trucks. Lindbergh, his *Spirit of St. Louis*. The aerospace industry christens its orbiters, probes and satellites. So why not this container? She toys with various names— Stratos, Houdini, Seventh Continent, Lego—but none of them really fit. Containers aren't given names, but numbers.

When she finishes the second coat, around one in the morning, the container is absolutely anonymous, a perfectly smooth white. All that's needed now is to stick on the new codes; the pile of self-adhesive vinyl numbers and letters lie in a jumble on the workbench.

She and Éric chose the code following a long and lively discussion. They agreed on at least one thing: the numbers and letters couldn't simply be picked at random. For one thing, the code must conform to the ISO 6346 standard. For another, they had to make sure the code was not already used by a company or, at the very least, was not registered with the International Container Bureau. Lisa insisted all the same that the code have a certain aesthetic, whereas Éric was mainly concerned with its "forgettability."

"Imagine if we chose the code LULU 2323237—I'm over-simplifying, but you get my point. One glance and it's etched into your memory. We want a code that your eyes will just slide over."

Still, camouflage is not an exact science, and their deliberations went on for some time before they could agree on PZIU 127 002 7, which was both "reasonably forgettable" and "fairly aesthetic." The new code would serve every purpose: entry into the databases, visual tracking, company identification. It would be used by customs, shippers and exporters, dockers and port administrators. It would be entered on forms, bills of lading, receipts and invoices. The code would identify the container and make it invisible, at once unique and like the others, lost in a sea of numbers and letters. Security through mimicry.

But before Lisa can stick on the codes, the paint must dry. This gives her forty-eight hours to deal with a headache that won't go away. The accumulated smell of everything that was splashed, sprayed, rolled, spread, injected, cut and daubed in this garage since June is enough to kill an ox.

Lisa scans the workbench. She runs her hand over a row of jars containing nails, screws, rivets, a poisonous tropical spider, and stops on a bottle of ibuprofen. She pops it open, drops three capsules into her palm, lifts the top of a cooler full of cans and ice cubes, and grabs an iced tea.

Then she does what she has not dared to do since the month of June: she punches the big red button, and the garage door opens amid a clang of metal.

Lisa steps away from the door and removes her mask. Even at a distance of ten metres, she can smell the toxic vapours flowing out of the building—worlds apart from the fragrance of mahogany and beeswax. Lisa massages her temples. This place is going to make her sick. She looks at the door; there are whorls of fine particles floating against the light of the floods, and she suddenly doubts she'll be able to go back inside.

It's a busy night across the street: some fifteen containers are parked at the loading docks. A few tractors wait with their trailers attached and their engines purring. The foam block seals around the docks keep any light or sound from filtering out. There's no way of knowing what is going on inside that warehouse.

Sitting in front of the main door, Lisa opens her iced tea with the hollow sound of aluminum being stove in. She swallows her ibuprofens and takes a sip of tea. Every two minutes, a plane roars off runway 24B, its huge shape looming against the bluish glow of the airport. The voyage beckons you, one way or another.

Twenty hours elapse: twelve hours of fume-coloured sleep and eight hours of chores. Lisa grimaces as she pushes a cart brimming with sacks of rice and flour, dried fruits, sugar, oil. She is the last customer in the supermarket. The ambient music playing on the loudspeakers is interrupted:

"Dear shoppers, the store is about to close. Please proceed to the checkout counters."

Lisa consults her notebook, where pages and pages of shopping lists have been progressively crossed out. Okay, this should do it. Counting the frozen and freeze-dried foodstuffs she bought earlier today, nothing seems to have been missed.

She briskly pushes the cart along, negotiates a tight turn and heads straight for the express checkout, where she recognizes the passive-aggressive cashier and the narcoleptic bag boy. This is the seventh such cart that Lisa has filled this evening, and she is getting to know the staff. She didn't take paranoia to the point of shopping in different stores. After all, what's so suspicious about buying three thousand dollars' worth of non-perishable foodstuffs and paying in cash?

The cashier scans the bar codes and sighs, and her helper stuffs the items haphazardly into the bags. On the cash register screen, the total keeps climbing until it finally stands still at $555.99. Taking the money with the utmost indifference, the cashier counts the bills twice and hands the change to Lisa, who then propels the cart toward the exit while the bagger looks on blankly.

There are just three or four cars left in the vast parking lot. Lisa empties the contents of the cart into the Dodge already crammed to the roof with foodstuffs, which have spilled over onto the passenger seat. She has to use her shoulder to get the door to close. Better drive cautiously: if she should brake suddenly, Lisa is in danger of being flattened under a half ton of provisions. She drives away leaving the cart abandoned in the middle of the parking lot.

It's late at night when she finally loads the last bin of food aboard PZIU 127 002 7. She hangs it on the scales and enters the weight in her computer, something she has done ten million times since June.

The opening of the container is almost completely filled up with the wall of apple crates intended to dupe a possible inspector, but Lisa isn't fooling herself: these people won't necessarily be put off by appearances; they're perfectly capable of emptying an entire container on the slightest suspicion.

She slips along the narrow passageway left open between the dry toilet and the trash compactor, steps through a sliding door and ends up in the pantry. She strides over the hose snaking across the floor to convey drinking water to the port-side tank. She glances at the level as she goes by. It's rising one millimetre at a time. In about ten minutes, it will be full.

Around her, the deep shelves are laden with sacks of flour, dried fruits and nuts, dried sausages, pasta, yeast for use in the bread machine, packets of spices, jars of honey, and freeze-dried meals. There are even some treats: a bottle of Haitian rum, some Swiss chocolate bars. The freezer is chockablock with frozen strawberries and mangos, orange juice, ravioli, cheese and tofu. The ample medicine cabinet is replete with ointments and drugs for a host of ailments and illnesses, even those she has never experienced, as well as a dozen tubes of toothpaste and several kilometres of toilet paper. In a large chest, there are tools for sewing, others for soldering, gluing, sawing, screwing, spools of thread and string, twelve kinds of adhesive tape, a voltmeter, three flashlights and many packages of batteries.

Lisa slides the last bin into place and leans back against the water tank to contemplate her work. Everything is carefully stowed away; not one centimetre has been wasted. Nothing could have escaped her attention, and yet she's afraid she has overlooked some silly thing, an obvious or obscure item—a corkscrew, pipe cleaners, Hungarian paprika—that will turn out to be essential in the middle of the Indian Ocean.

She exits the pantry through the other door, crosses the kitchen and continues on to the wardroom. The room is compact but comfortable. The bed has been converted into a sofa, and the place looks like any other living room. The arrises are rounded and edged with wooden moulding, and the room is bathed in a cozy light. A bookshelf running the length of the partition is stocked with books and periodicals, in particular a set of *Life* magazines from the sixties purchased on eBay. On one wall Lisa has hung a photo of the stratosphere taken by Mrs. Le Blanc's PowerShot and a shadow box containing the *Nephila clavipes* pinned to a block of cork.

A circle of light encompasses the chart table, illuminating the VHF radio, the GPS and two small dials indicating the time on board and the time in Copenhagen. The computer is in the middle of a download, and the progress bar, now showing 57 percent, advances a fraction of a pixel at a time.

After six months of intensive development, Éric finally announced that version 1.0 of the piloting software was operational. Improvable, of course, but operational. Lisa received a download URL in the late afternoon. Installation instructions would follow. "There's going to be a learning curve," Éric warned.

The monster's name is He_2, which Éric described as more than just software, comparing it to a Swiss Army knife with hundreds of tools. The computer has been struggling for two hours to download the files. Lisa feels as though she is torrenting an entire floor of the Alexandria library. At this rate, the sun will be up by the time she's received the whole software package, but no matter: time zones will soon be irrelevant.

She makes a mental list of what still needs to be done. Not much, actually. Collect the tools. Make sure no evidence is left behind in the garage. Install He_2 and learn how it works. Routine stuff.

She stretches out on the sofa, adjusts a cushion behind her back. Comfortable. She's done good work. She shuts her eyes and breathes in the fragrance of wood. For a girl supposedly afflicted with inborn claustrophobia, she has a strange sense of freedom. Now, how about a shot of that Barbancourt?

All at once, she opens her eyes and sits up. There's one more crucial thing she needs to do.

— 48 —

JAY ISN'T THE ONLY ONE to benefit from Laura's good turns—nor is she the only one to go without sleep because of them. Apparently, Miss Wissenberg passed along to Mahesh documents obtained by the CIA, which, despite being redacted with a shotgun, proved to be a mine of revelations. The poor computer analyst left the office late last evening and, after a brief and troubled night, showed up at the RCMP building at dawn. If the empty sugar packets littering his desk are any indication, he has just downed his fourth coffee, and he has clearly not yet recovered from yesterday's overdose of Whippets. (*A dollar twenty-five a bite!*)

Jay stays calm. She unhurriedly deposits the press clipping binder on her desk, slings her bag over the back of her chair, hangs up her coat and turns on her computer. Then she gets to unlacing her boots, while Mahesh fidgets, waiting for her to finish these exasperating preliminaries. Jay finally wiggles her toes.

"Okay, so, about this secret?"

He rubs his hands. "How does Rokov manage to move Papa Zulu around?"

"By modifying the databases, right?"

"They use a blend of exploits and social engineering. First, they send real fake forms—or fake real forms, depending on your point of view—and then they directly manipulate the databases. This combines the best of two worlds: it allows the container to disappear and reappear, to erase its tracks, and at the same time to look perfectly straightforward on the administrative level."

"Bonus points: social engineering makes it possible to skip some steps. It's quicker than brute force."

"Exactly."

Mahesh grabs his Pyrex mug and visually assesses the toxicity of the centimetre of coffee sloshing around at the bottom. He decides to risk it.

"What interests me is the alteration of the databases. There's nothing in the CIA documents about that, but you don't have to be Gary Raskapov to draw a few conclusions."

"Kasparov."

Ignoring the remark, he tears open three sugar packets, which he taps against the side of the cup to eject every last crystal.

"The main conclusion is that there was no infiltration. At this point, it would have taken dozens of infiltrators in four or five countries. Actually, I saw the list of procedures. Injection, sniffing, brute-force attack. The databases are altered sometimes through direct queries, sometimes with the same software as the port administration—which in itself is surprising, since the ports all use different software."

He tastes the coffee. It's the Attila the Hun of morning beverages. He decides to add a fourth sugar.

"Still, what's happening is no surprise. I've said it before, but it's been known for a long time that the industry is poorly prepared. Everyone assumes compartmentalization makes the systems secure, so we inevitably end up with every mistake in the book: weak passwords, three-year delays in updates, suboptimal configurations, badly filtered queries. But even given all that, Papa Zulu moves fast. Rokov needed eighteen hours to get into the system in Montreal. Twelve hours in Caucedo. Fifteen hours in Panama. Three hours—*three hours!*—in Shenzhen."

Sip of coffee. The hairs on the back of his neck stand on end.

"This can't be the doing of just one person working manually. It's too fast and too diversified."

"So you think there's a team working on this?"

"Precisely. Possibly a dozen hackers. Each specialized in a different area. They don't even need to know each other. They could be subcontractors, with a coordinator."

"Distributed hacking."

"You can farm this out to people in Belarus for a song."

Jay is about to add something when she catches sight of Maurice F. Gamache and Laura Wissenberg marching up the corridor. Even at this distance, she can tell they are deep in conversation, and when she notices the sergeant is not carrying his usual bag of bagels, Jay realizes it's serious. Mahesh has followed her gaze and instinctively stands up.

Without slowing down, the two colleagues enter the Enclave all smiles. Maurice F. points a triumphant finger skyward and lets out what could pass for an altogether acceptable battle cry.

"Singapore!"

— 49 —

ALL'S QUIET AT THE WESTMACOTT Building. Apart from the staff's cars, there's only a black Dodge Ram in the parking lot. A nurse greets Lisa with an intrigued smile.

"You're early today!"

In response, Lisa nods ambiguously. The nurse watches her as she walks off down the corridor. She finds there is something oddly solemn about Lisa, and it takes her a few seconds to understand why: for months now, Lisa has shown up at the residence in dirty overalls and steel-toe boots, with blackened hands and sawdust in her hair. This morning, she's wearing a clean pair of jeans, a spotless pullover, and sandals. Her sunglasses are perched atop a freshly washed head of hair.

Lisa saunters up the corridor. It smells of coffee, toast and strawberry jam. The doors of the rooms are open; the residents are eating, watching TV, doing sudokus. A lady lying on her bed is having a discussion with the ceiling.

Lisa arrives at number 19. From the doorway, she watches her father rock in his chair, facing the window. He is dressed but wears his old bathrobe over his clothes all the same, and he has put on a John Deere cap that doesn't belong to him. Lisa feels a knot tightening in her stomach. She notices all at once how much thinner he is, how prominent his cheekbones have become. Against the morning backlight, he's like a skeleton.

Not only did her father not fully recover from his stroke in late July, but his condition has steadily declined. According to the doctor, he's constantly at risk of another episode, and the slightest cold could be fatal. His complexion is pale and he has the life expectancy of a beetle. He doesn't leave his room anymore, not even at mealtimes, and hardly touches the food they bring him. Lisa looks around the closet-sized room, where nothing is left of the few souvenirs she salvaged from the Domaine Bordeur. Trinkets, photos, knick-knacks—Robert chucked everything in trash cans all over the residence. The third spider plant has disappeared from its hook, probably dead from lack of water. Without these particular objects, there's something fragile about the atmosphere in the room. Yet Lisa realizes her father will never be transferred anywhere else. He won't last long enough for a spot to become available in a long-term care facility. This cramped room will be the last place he'll see.

"Hi, Dad."

He turns toward the door, sees his daughter. He gives her that hollow half-smile, his only smile now, and Lisa knows right away he doesn't recognize her. Still, he lets himself be kissed on the cheek. There's an abandoned breakfast tray in front of him. He's nibbled the corner of a slice of toast, hasn't touched either his tea or the piece of orange. Soon he'll have to be fed intravenously.

As is her habit, Lisa drives away the uneasiness by busying herself. She asks questions, talks about the weather or the state of the room. She inspects the drawers to make sure everything is all right, that there are no hamburger patties hidden among his T-shirts. She notes the inexorable disappearance of his underwear. Robert is oblivious, hasn't noticed a thing. He's no longer interested in the present; he lives in the past—or, rather, in several simultaneous pasts.

It's hard to tell if he is in 1978 or 1991 or 2007. His memory has different floors, and he circulates among them through secret stairways and invisible trap doors.

The drawers are in order, although Lisa detects a faint odour of urine emanating from a source she is unable to locate. She goes around the room sniffing the air and gives up. She finally sits down beside her father and plays nervously with her earlobe. She casts a glance at the door. Too late to duck out.

"Dad . . . Remember that big house we renovated, in Hinchinbrooke? The Baskine house?"

Lisa doesn't expect an answer. Her father nods purely as a reflex. He appears to have no memory of the Baskine house or Hinchinbrooke. Unfazed, Lisa continues regardless.

"You found a passageway inside the larder, behind the wallpaper. A passageway between the walls, with a ladder going up to the second floor."

Robert moves his chair, obviously incapable of grasping the subject of the conversation. Surrounded by people who carry on monologues, maybe he's forgotten the very nature of a dialogue. Lisa's insistence bothers him. He squirms a little, averting his gaze.

"I went into the passageway with a work light and climbed up the ladder, and when I came back, you asked me if I'd seen anything, and I told you no, that there was nothing to see."

Silence. A man in the next room can be heard singing "Love Me Tender" very loudly and slightly off-key.

"I lied. There was . . . a secret room. With an old flashlight, an ashtray, some magazines. A cushion. A bottle of rum. It had been deserted for years, but long ago, in the fifties, someone had hidden there. A woman, I think. A woman who spent hours hiding inside the walls."

Robert starts to search around, looking for something, to no avail. He grumbles. Lisa sees the remote control peeking out from under the rocker's seat cushion. She hands it to Robert, who presses down on the big red button, the only one whose purpose he can still remember. There's a morning show on the TV. Today, they're blind-tasting different balsamic vinegars.

Lisa kisses her father on the forehead, presses her head against his for a long time and goes out of the room.

SLOUCHED IN HER ERGONOMIC CHAIR, Jay remains aloof from the celebration. It seems as if the entire floor has agreed to meet up in the Enclave. There's Laura and Mahesh, of course, and Sergeant Gamache, who's on the phone, and three colleagues from Narcotics who came to see what was going on, and Micheline Saint-Laurent, and an officer from Commercial Crime. Even the person in charge of the recycling bins is loitering in a corner, casting an occasional glance back over his shoulder. People come and go and talk cheerfully.

Amid the hubbub, Jay catches the key bits of information: Papa Zulu was off-loaded in Singapore eight days ago with a transshipment code for Jakarta. Ever the instructor, Laura explains that Singapore is the world's biggest transshipment port, with 15 percent of all the containers on the globe transiting there—that is, twenty thousand containers a day filled with latex gloves and plastic beads, handbags, mica powder, canned beef, ink, USB connectors, wrapping paper, galvanized sheet metal, Christmas lights and potassium silicate. What's more, the port is equipped with seven thousand hookups for reefers, which makes sense considering there are three billion digestive systems within a radius of four thousand kilometres.

In a word, it's the ideal location for disappearing from view.

Right now, everyone is speculating about whether Papa Zulu was really sent to Jakarta (near-zero probability) or kept on standby in the port of Singapore (average probability), cleared through customs (negligible probability) or re-dispatched to an as-yet-unspecified destination (high probability).

Laura has already brought up on her screen the map of all the intermodal ports within a radius of 2,500 nautical miles. Standing at the whiteboard, Mahesh scribbles equations to compare the surface area (S) and the density (d) of Papa Zulu's potential dispersion (Pz) in relation to the number of ports of call (Np) through time (T). In sum: a large number of ports of call means slower forward progress but a more complicated investigation.

Jay, meanwhile, is thinking back to the little ten-year-old girl she once was, standing on a pier wearing a Nordiques hockey toque. Laura suddenly notices her.

"Are you okay? You're white."

"I'm white?"

"As a sheet. Did you have anything to eat this morning?"

"Um . . . yes."

"You need a vacation."

Jay nods, slowly at first, then more and more vigorously. A vacation? All things considered, that is an excellent idea.

— 51 —

LISA IS READING WHEN THE lights abruptly go out and the ventilation stops. Everything goes dark and silent, except for the battery-powered devices, whose indicator lights are visible here and there. Lisa can hear nothing now but the distant sound of machinery intermingled with that of her pulse throbbing in her eardrums.

A metallic jolt reverberates through the container, which rises and sways a little. The interior compartment creaks but does not crack; as planned, the various modules yield to each other. Another jolt, and then a vibration. The container is in motion. Lisa could turn on the GPS screen and track its path, but she does nothing of the sort. All is quiet in the darkness, and she doesn't feel like budging.

The container moves for a while, turns left, then left again, and comes to a stop. There's another metallic jolt: the gantry crane grasps the corners of the container and Lisa suddenly feels herself being lifted several storeys and set down on a ship. Banging and vibrations; the hooks are released and everything goes silent again.

After a minute or two, there are new noises: a container lands on the port side of PZIU 127 002 7, then another on top, and still another nearby, like so many pieces in the hands of a giant. Lisa hears the metallic banging of the securing operation, the lugs being locked, the hoist slings being attached to the corners of the box. Then more jolts, farther and farther away, not so much noise as waves. This container's soundproofing is surprisingly effective.

Then, all at once, the interior comes to life again. The lights come on, the ventilation starts up and the freezer in the pantry can be heard purring.

Lisa leaps to her feet and sits down at the chart table. She keeps calling it that even though it's not strictly speaking a chart table. Actually, there aren't any geographical maps on board; such maps are designed for navigating in a real territory, and Lisa is about to enter a whole other kind of space, at the intersection of management and economics.

She wakes the computer with the tip of her index finger. Eight windows appear on the screen and the action is as hectic as in a NASA command centre. In the foreground is the loading layout of the ship in real time, as seen by the port personnel. The containers are being stacked one on top of the other, little yellow tiles nicely assembled in rows, each in its own slot. The OOCL *Belgium* is a fairly average

Panamax, with a capacity of fourteen hundred containers. Lisa's was placed aft, with the other reefers.

Bay 26, Row 01, Tier 82: this will be her address for the next five days.

Lisa relaxes somewhat. Éric gave her a lengthy presentation on the dangers associated with being positioned in an outside cell. If the ship starts to list or is struck by giant waves, the lateral containers are the first to go overboard, something that occurs more often than one might think. Furthermore, all the dangerous or flammable products are positioned on the periphery. Better to be in the middle, with the teddy bears and the baking soda.

She pictures the high wall of containers rising toward the stern of the ship. If the partitions weren't so well sound-proofed, she would be able to hear dozens of air conditioners humming like a gigantic beehive. Lisa jumps onto the bunk and places her nose near the ventilation grille. The air carries a faint odour of grease. Of course ships smell of grease—what was Lisa expecting? From the bottom of the hold to the tops of the deck winches, this industry is steeped in grease, oil and bunker fuel. With a little luck, as soon as they reach the channel, the prevailing wind will hit the wall of containers and the smell of the river will take over.

She sits back down in front of the computer and reviews the list of things to do before they weigh anchor. She still has to remove the traces she left in the databases, access the ship's routers to be able to use the network once out to sea (He_2 is already on it) and listen to the VHF radio to find out when the loading will be completed. Then she can begin to tackle the medium-term tasks: plan the transfer at Caucedo, examine the departure schedule for Panama, fill out and send the paperwork to the port authorities, shipping companies and customs. Voyage to the Centre of the Bureaucracy.

Right now, everything is fine. She has power and passwords, and she'll soon be holding a beer in her hand. Tonight's menu: rice noodles with shrimp, mango salad and fresh vanilla tapioca pudding.

She really can't see what could go wrong.

— 52 —

"WHICH COMPANY?" THE CAB DRIVER ASKS.

Jay shrugs; she bought her ticket so quickly that she's forgotten which airline she'll be flying on. She points to the first sign that comes up. Lufthansa. That will do.

The car slips into a vacant spot. Jay holds out two twenty-dollar bills—keep the change—and springs into the open air. A snowflake splatters onto her nose. Towing her bag, she slaloms between the baggage carts, steps through the doors and finds herself back at square one: the concourse of Trudeau airport. Around her, people are moving in every direction, each of them following their own straight line.

Jay pokes around in her pocket, looking for her transaction statement, and steps up to a check-in kiosk. Adult passenger. Window seat. No checked baggage. No, she's not carrying any weapons, fireworks, solvents or compressed gas.

The machine spits out her boarding pass, and Jay heads toward pre-board screening. She overtakes a group of students on a language immersion trip, rushes into the screening area and instinctively looks around for the paranoid agent who inspects books by Jules Verne with a scalpel. Nowhere in sight.

Jay doesn't recognize anyone, no one recognizes her, and her passport doesn't set off any alarms. Even if an agent did decide to question her, he would find nothing suspicious about her taking an airplane. Unlike her previous flight, this time she is simply on vacation for health reasons. She claimed to be suffering from restless nights, poor appetite, and a variety of obsessions and compulsions—which, in a way, is the absolute truth. She ended up receiving a joint letter of authorization from the RCMP, the Parole Board and her immediate supervisor, who could easily get by without Jay while she took ten, twelve or even, if she liked, fifteen days off for some R and R in Spain—off you go.

But no one asks her for an explanation, and the letter stays tucked away in her pocket.

It does feel strange to be a normal person. This morning, standing in front of her closet with one hand on the shoulder of her pantsuit, she hesitated. Just as she was going to lift it out, she changed her mind. The pantsuit was not just a disguise; it was a suit of armour, and merely putting it on would amount to an admission of weakness. On second thought, a pair of jeans and an old T-shirt would do just fine. Jay would gladly have pulled on her old Nordiques toque if it hadn't got lost in the shuffle decades ago. Maybe it was still mouldering away at the bottom of a drawer in her father's house on the Lower North Shore.

Jay removes her shoes and belt, her jacket and watch, and empties her pockets. She places her Eee in a grey bin. Then she lines up in her stocking feet and watches the conveyor carry off her black suitcase, with the label of the Royaume de la Valise still attached. In front of her, an overweight businessman has to choose between an EHF scan and a frisk. He opts for the scan. You have to keep up with the times.

The agent finally turns toward Jay and motions for her to advance. She steps through the metal detector—no beeps—and shows her boarding pass. All clear, thank you, have a good day. Jay collects her belongings from the conveyor, puts her things back on and charges into the international zone. The worst is over. Directly ahead of her, the air is fragrant with fries and freedom.

There are still twenty minutes left before boarding, and Jay stops in a bookshop to buy a bottle of water. Standing in front of the science fiction section, she skims a few back covers. Everything looks insipid to her. She thinks about Élisabeth Routier-Savoie, who at this very moment is sailing in international waters on the far side of the planet, shut inside her container. Did she take along some reading material to while away the hours of rolling and pitching?

Jay leaves the bookshop with her bottle of water and a novel she won't read.

Gate 53. The travellers are crammed into every corner, in every possible position. Jay lays claim to part of a seat between a hockey equipment bag and an eighty-year-old Sikh man. In front of them, a built-in screen is showing offbeat news items. A rhinoceros adopts a brood of ducklings. A woman has let her toenails grow for fifteen years. An adventurer crosses the Americas all the way to Tierra del Fuego on a unicycle. Station identification, barrage of commercials, followed by an infotainment offering on the financial crisis in Abu Dhabi. Thousands of cars are gathering dust near the Dubai airport, left there by hordes of ruined Brits and Emiratis, who have fled to evade imprisonment for default. It appears that speculative culture and sharia law are hard to reconcile. The camera pans over Ferraris, Jaguars and Porsches abandoned on the side of the road or in underground parking lots, with the doors unlocked and the keys in the ignition. The hoods are covered with a yellowish powder, in which people have drawn phalluses and written insults in Arabic.

Jay feels a fierce need to be done with geography.

THREE

— 53 —

JAY AND HER COMPUTER ARE ASLEEP.

The night was spent hopping from one train to the next, first in Hamburg, then Lübeck—where there was a slight delay after the train had flattened a Fiat 500 at a level crossing—then Puttgarden, and finally in Rødbyhavn, where Jay ended up aboard the R4208, an exasperatingly slow Regionalzug. She would have saved precious hours by taking the plane from Brussels, but she chose to be discreet. She must follow the script.

After two hours of fighting off sleep, she finally succumbed with the Eee balanced on her lap and her hands on the keyboard. In front of her, the screen is a deep, deep black. She wakes up when the computer is about to slip off her lap, catching it just in time. To her right, the sun is exploding on the horizon, the light almost unbearable.

Squinting, Jay tries to understand the landscape streaming past the window. The train is apparently crossing a kind of sea arm on a threadlike bridge. The scene is straight out of an IKEA commercial.

It's been thirty hours now since she left Montreal, and if her calculations are correct, taking into account the time zone difference, in ten minutes she will officially turn forty.

She stretches her neck and sweeps her eyes around the train. Half the seats are unoccupied. Across the aisle, a couple is sleeping. The woman's head rests on the man's thigh; there's a telephone in his hand. Lying on the tray in front of them is a tourist brochure. A Coke can rolls from port to starboard in the curves. The air smells of vinegar and sweat. What a pathetic place to celebrate a new decade.

Forty. The last months have been so busy that Jay didn't even have time to go through the conventional moods: bitterness, anxiety, regrets. The fact is, she feels as though she's grown younger since November. Her senses are on the alert, and she has recovered her old skills.

Her Eee signals that a message has been received. Jay activates the screen with her forefinger. E-mail from Laura, who wishes her a happy birthday and a good time vacationing in Andalusia—population eight million, capital Seville, short-term weather forecast fabulous—and, while she's at it, brings Jay up to date on the latest news: a container called Papa Zulu is thought to have left the port of Singapore twelve days ago bound for Colombo. *Send us a postcard. Warmly, LW.*

Jay scratches the tip of her nose. Colombo? Called up to assist, Google presents a map of Sri Lanka. Utterly predictable. Élisabeth continued her voyage westward, crossed the Strait of Malacca and then the Gulf of Bengal. She has already covered three thousand kilometres since leaving

Singapore, and Lord knows how many since Colombo. She is speeding up—unlike this train, which seems about to slow down again.

The Coke can rolls to her feet. Jay slips the Eee into her bag and goes hunting for some strong coffee, assuming such a substance can be found aboard.

After forty-five minutes replete with fields and villages and cows, the train pulls into the little station in Roskilde. The environs have a suburban look about them. Around Jay, the passengers stir and stand up, collect their luggage. The train *slowly* pulls out. The tracks can be heard agonizing under the car's wheels; mobile phones ring here and there.

At last, they announce København H.

Standing near the door, Jay fidgets impatiently, as though wanting to alight while the train is still moving. As soon as it enters the station, she hops down onto the platform and merges with the throng. It's rush hour; tourists commingle with suburban workers. The ideal moment to go undetected. A clock shows 6:39 a.m., still too early to go knocking on people's doors, but first Jay needs to eat, to drink some coffee—the brew served on board the train was an affront to humanity—and get her bearings in the city.

She goes up the escalator and looks around. She notices the scent of coffee and pastries (to the right) and a sign with a suitcase (to the left). *Bagagebokse*, the sign says. Jay's vocabulary widens by the minute in this country.

At the entrance to the lockers hangs a notice with the rates and opening hours. The maximum storage time is seventy-two hours. Jay will need far less time than that. She shoves her suitcase to the back of the first available locker, keeping only her computer case, her passport and her wallet, which she now looks through. Tucked between two twenty-euro notes is a precious little scrap of a UPS envelope bearing the address of Éric Le Blanc, Stjernegade 3030.

She shuts the locker, pockets the key and goes off to track down that coffee.

— 54 —

ON THE LIVING ROOM WALL hangs a huge coloured map of the world, a hybrid Bonne/Lambert projection, where the continents fan out like banana leaves.

A line drawn with a red marker starts in Montreal, follows the St. Lawrence, exits the Gulf and descends to Caucedo, moves on to Panama, climbs up the West Coast toward Alaska and disappears at the upper left margin, among the dragons and sea spray, reappears at the other end of the map, brushes by the Japanese archipelago, lands in Shenzhen, cuts across toward Singapore, ricochets toward Sri Lanka, and ends in the Indian Ocean off the coast of India.

Standing in front of the map, Lærke Høj-Le Blanc lets her pinky slide along the line.

The little girl doesn't have school today, and since her mother had an important meeting scheduled, she has come to spend the day with Éric. Other options were available—day camp, music or drama school, private rock-climbing lessons, a chartered hot-air balloon ride—but Lærke would rather stay with her big brother, who doesn't object.

It should be noted that she is quite good at keeping herself busy. She draws sea serpents, builds Lego cities, turns the library upside down, empties the fridge, and, more often than not, plants herself in front of the enormous picture windows, armed with a giant pair of binoculars, to watch the comings and goings at the port. Nothing fascinates her more than the repetitive ballet of gantry cranes, trucks, ships and containers. There's definitely a virus going around in this family.

Despite her precocious fascination with containers, Lærke knows almost nothing about her brother's activities. It's grown-up business, so necessarily abstract, inaccessible and mysterious. The world map obsesses Lærke, and she constantly returns to it, perhaps simply because she wonders about the red line that each day grows longer. By way of explanation, Éric confines himself to telling her it's a board game, and no, she can't play, it's useless to insist, or, maybe, one day—he adds with a peculiar smile— when she's old enough.

Old enough—talk about an old guy's answer!

The map contrasts with the numerous screens and projectors in the loft. Like all primitive technology, it's safe from hacking, network malfunctions and power outages, but Éric uses a paper map for a somewhat less utilitarian reason: it's a way to remind himself that this whole undertaking is essentially poetic and outside his usual sphere of activity. Éric may have the technological expertise, but Lisa is the one who's calling the shots.

Lærke has grown tired of studying the red line, and she scampers to the kitchen to see if she can find something to snack on. Éric takes the opportunity to station himself in front of the map with a red marker. He locates latitude 15.205584 and longitude 71.036897—not an easy task with such an atypical map—and marks the point, which he connects to the red line. Just four hundred tiny kilometres left before Mumbai.

He caps the marker, takes a sip of coffee and sighs. The voyage is in its sixty-fifth day, and an unforeseen problem has come into view: time—more specifically, the length of time.

At first, the tasks involved in navigating kept Lisa very busy. She had to familiarize herself with the thousand and one functions of He_2, complete and send all sorts of forms, supervise the transfer of PZIU 127 002 7, doctor the databases. Lisa is a quick study, however, and all this work has become routine, especially since He_2 automates many of the steps in the process. With each passing day, she finds she has more free time on her hands. The on-board library contains twelve thousand digital books, six hundred feature films and thousands of hours of music, from Johann Christoph Bach to the Yeah Yeah Yeahs, but ultimately, Lisa has no great talent for idleness and meditation. Following an intensive Thai cooking phase, she tried yoga, scoured every surface and inventoried the supplies ten times. Last week, she granted herself a glass of rum—yo-ho-ho—which, turning half green, she immediately puked up in the dry toilet. She is so utterly bored that she is now considering taking apart the bread machine to see how it works—clearly a symptom that should be taken seriously.

The expression *to kill time*, Éric thinks, is taking on a whole new meaning: it now denotes a mortal combat.

As he ponders the problem next to the map, he hears the buzz of the intercom. He looks at the clock in surprise. Who could be coming by at eight in the morning? He steps toward the monitor, but Lærke dashes past, overtakes him on the left and plants herself in front of the intercom on her tiptoes with her nose pressed against the screen.

"Who is it?"

"Let me see."

Lærke steps aside. Éric doesn't recognize the woman standing at the building's front door—which in itself is unsurprising: the camera is fitted with a slightly spherical lens that makes people's faces bulge like a globe. He presses the button.

"*Ja?*"

"*Bonjour. Je peux parler à Éric Le Blanc?*"

Éric starts. A francophone? With a Montreal accent? This is something he was not expecting. He looks carefully at the image. No, he really doesn't recognize this woman. She looks around for the camera, obviously aware of being observed.

"Are you a journalist?"

"No."

"Because journalists have to go through my administrative assistant, at T2T. I . . . And besides, who gave you my address?"

"I fished it out of the trash."

"You're sure you're not a journalist?"

"I'm the exact opposite of a journalist."

The statement gives Éric pause. The opposite of a journalist? Sounds more like a riddle than an answer. He turns toward Lærke, but the little girl has already gone off to engage in more interesting pursuits. The situation is beginning to annoy Éric.

"What is it you want to talk to me about?"

The woman doesn't reply right away. She cocks her head to one side, as though looking for the right words.

"About Élisabeth."

Éric feels the goosebumps running up both his arms. Almost in spite of himself, he presses the button to open the front door.

— 55 —

THE ELEVATOR IS DISCREETLY LUXURIOUS: wood panelling, brushed steel, scientifically calculated lighting. The buttons are made of hand-carved black marble, and, starting on the eighth floor, each one is fitted with a lock. Éric Le Blanc occupies the last of these private floors.

While Jay is examining the tiny locks, the doors close and

the elevator starts to go up automatically. The takeoff is so abrupt that she feels her eardrums pop and her blood pressure fall. The doors open on the tenth floor—not at a landing, but directly onto the entrance hall of the apartment.

Standing in front of Jay, Éric looks calm and self-possessed.

Out of mutual curiosity, they study each other for an instant without saying a word. The most promising Danish businessman of his generation is barefoot and wears a plain T-shirt and karategi pants. He looks even younger than Jay had imagined him, and all at once she feels old. She was his age not too long ago, and here she is suddenly forty. What does she look like from Éric's point of view? An unknown, tired woman with messy hair, wearing a simple pair of jeans and a leather jacket. Hardly stunning.

"Coffee?"

Jay says yes, and the young man immediately goes off toward the kitchen. After a moment of hesitation, she decides to do in Rome as the Romans do, and removes her shoes. Holding her computer under her arm, she quietly steps into the enormous loft.

The place is surprisingly bright. Two whole walls consist of picture windows that create the impression of standing in a control tower. The bedroom is perched on a large mezzanine at the top of a glass staircase. The walls are bare and spotless except for a long, neatly arranged bookcase.

Jay hears a noise. She ducks her head just in time to dodge a budgie, then two more, which fly past in tight formation and land on the bookcase. A minuscule bluish feather spins in the air.

Somewhere to the left, there's the sound of the coffee machine's pump.

Jay continues to explore. She walks along an endless dark-coloured conference table fashioned out of a single slab of Douglas fir, which is encircled by ergonomic mesh-back chairs. A bowl of Cheerios and a comic book have been left in the middle of the table, confirming the ambiguous character of the place, midway between the professional and the domestic.

Right in the centre of the living room floor, hundreds of Lego pieces radiate out from a container ship under construction. Jay immediately recognizes the Maersk Triple E that made Mahesh drool last summer. The 1,500-piece set was not yet available in Canada, and her poor colleague contemplated buying it overseas for a small fortune. If only he could see this.

Stepping toward the picture windows, Jay comes upon a panoramic view of the port, three hundred metres away. What a surprise! On the ground floor, there was no way of knowing the waterfront was so close. As far as she can tell, it's a small terminal. She watches for a second as the gantry cranes off-load containers.

"*Hej!*"

Jay starts and swings around. A little girl (Lærke, she gathers) is scrutinizing her. In the background, a huge map of the world hangs on the wall. Jay's heart races as she immediately spots the line that starts in Montreal and ends in the Indian Ocean near Mumbai.

Lærke tilts her head to one side, unable to make up her mind about this woman who has come out of nowhere.

"*Hvad hedder du?*"

Jay tries to remember the only Danish phrase she learned, and especially its pronunciation.

"*Jeg taler . . . ikke dansk?*"

Lærke looks Jay up and down. A woman who pops up out of nowhere and doesn't speak Danish. The mystery deepens.

"You're a friend of my brother?"

Momentary silence. Jay mulls over the question.

"Yes, you might say that."

The reply seems to satisfy Lærke. She turns away without a word, takes hold of the huge binoculars and stations herself in front of the picture windows. Jay watches her confidently adjust the focusing wheels, not like a child at play but like a veteran lookout.

Éric comes back carrying a tray with two steaming macchiatos.

"Sorry about the mess. I'm usually told forty-eight hours in advance when guests are expected."

They sit down at the big conference table, on either side of the Douglas fir. Between them are centuries of growth rings, thousands of seasons compressed into a few centimetres, where an expert could pinpoint Columbus's arrival in America, the colonization of Africa and the Second World War. Éric pushes aside the cereal bowl and the comic book.

"Sugar?"

"Sugar."

Jay can't remember ever having had a better cup of coffee. The appliance that produced this beverage must be worth as much as her quarterly salary.

Éric drains his cup in three gulps. Despite appearances, he's nervous, and Jay decides to cut to the chase.

"I know everything."

There is a slight hint of doubt in Éric's gaze. "Everything?"

"*Nearly* everything. I know Élisabeth Routier-Savoie is travelling in a container bearing the number PZIU 127 002 7. I know she left Montreal on October 13 and crossed the Pacific on a ship bound for Singapore. When I arrived here this morning, I wasn't a hundred percent certain that you were somehow involved, but now that I've seen the map on the wall, you might say that, yes, I know *nearly* everything."

Éric's face betrays no emotion. The kid would do well at a poker table.

"Are you with the police?"

"Not really. I'm a civilian employee of the RCMP. I do data analysis. My area of expertise is credit card fraud."

Éric looks disconcerted. "I was expecting them to send an officer, actually."

"No one sent me."

"I don't understand."

"I carried out my own parallel investigation. In my spare time."

"Parallel?"

"I didn't follow the same trail as them. The RCMP and the CIA are also looking for the container, but they're not yet aware that Élisabeth is inside—that *anybody* is inside. They're expecting some explosive device remotely operated by a bunch of good old terrorists, bearded guys in tunics."

Éric rubs his temples while examining the milk rings on the sides of his cup. "I was sure the container would be invisible. What did I forget?"

"The accounts."

"The accounts?"

"There was an unpaid bill. Harbour dues or electricity, I think. Starting there, the investigators tracked down the delivery voucher, then they searched through the databases' backup copies—the servers record an image of the system every night. Using the successive copies, they were able to reconstruct the sequence."

Éric shakes his head in disbelief. "But . . . wait a minute. So you—how did you figure out there was someone on board?"

"Does it matter?"

"Humour me."

"The distributed trucking was what drew my attention. Using various companies to muddy the waters. That stuck out for me. The kind of idea a computer specialist would come up with."

"It was my idea."

"There are thirty-nine trucking companies in the Montreal area that handle containers. I visited all of them."

"Every one?"

"Let's say most of them. It led me to the garage where Élisabeth worked. That's where I collected some clues. The old Hansel and Gretel trick."

"I had no idea I'd left so many breadcrumbs."

"There are still a lot of grey areas left. For instance, no one understands exactly how you operate. You modify various database formats. You hack into wi-fi networks and extranets. You emulate all kinds of sorting software. You combine brute force and social engineering. A colleague of mine believes you farm the work out to Belarusian hackers . . ."

Éric bursts out laughing.

". . . but, personally, I think you just automated the process. With a program or a software suite. A sort of Swiss Army knife."

Éric nods. "It takes a big Swiss Army knife."

"How big?"

"Very big."

Silence. Jay pieces the puzzle together in her head.

"An operating system? Right?"

He nods, staring into space—but after a few seconds, Jay realizes he's watching Lærke. In a tiny voice, the little girl is singing "*simsaladim bamba saladu saladim*" under her breath—a strange contrast to Éric's industrial spying activities.

"There are already dozens of Linux distributions designed to perform specialized tasks. Controlling particle accelerators, piloting drones. Currently, home automation is the trend. Controlling fridges and coffee makers, lighting or heating systems." He turns toward Jay. "So designing a semi-automated navigation system was naturally the next step."

"It's even better than what I'd imagined. So there's power on board?"

"Lisa modified the refrigeration system."

"Of course!"

"She thought of everything. Kitchenette, freezer, ventilation, heating, air conditioning, trash compactor, dry toilet. She has enough drinking water and food to be self-sufficient for six months at sea."

"Fantastic . . . Fantastic . . ."

Jay is in a daze, as if she's forgotten her purpose in coming to this place. Éric clears his throat.

"So, you came here on your own?"

"Correct."

"The RCMP isn't aware that you're here?"

"Negative."

"The Danish police?"

"No."

"Then why exactly are you here?"

Jay toys with her cup, searching for the right words.

"*Så kom en hæslig jæger*," Lærke sings with her little voice, "*simsaladim bamba saladu.*"

"Because I've always had an issue with geography." She smiles. "I grew up in a tiny village on the Lower North Shore. Ever hear of Tête-à-la-Baleine?"

"Nope."

"I'm not surprised. Even Route 138 doesn't go that far. To leave the village, you have to take a boat or a plane, or a snowmobile in winter. The last I heard, the local population was in a nosedive."

Brief silence, sip of coffee.

"As a child, I suffered from claustrophobia. I was suffocating. When I went off to high school in Sept-Îles, things got a little better. But not much. I ended up running away to Montreal and . . . long story short, let's just say I led a double life. Ten years on, I had to leave the country in a hurry. Use a fake passport. That was still relatively easy at the time."

"Before September 2001."

"Precisely. But if I'd had this . . ." She punctuates her statements by rapping her knuckles on the table. ". . . a container that can go through walls . . . It's better than a road. Better than a passport. With this, geography no longer exists."

Long silence. *Simsaladim bamba saladu saladim.* Jay checks her watch, as if time has just resumed after a twenty-minute break. She finishes her coffee.

"But, to give you a more straightforward answer, I came to help Élisabeth. So here's the situation. The RCMP is running the investigation in Canada. They searched the garage on Gibson Street ten days ago. Lots of material, but no leads. No reason to lose any sleep. The CIA, on the other hand, is a whole other matter. They have access to the databases of every port in Asia, and pretty soon they'll get their hands on the container."

"Pretty soon?"

"When I left Montreal thirty-six hours ago, they were still analyzing the Singapore databases. This morning, on the train, I learned they had tracked the container as far as Sri Lanka. They're probably combing through the servers of the port of Colombo at this very moment."

Éric's fingers dance on the table as if it were a keyboard. "Which leaves us . . . three days."

"That's all? I'm really sorry. I wish I'd come sooner. Everything started to speed up."

Éric doesn't respond. He's here and elsewhere at the same time, staring blankly, already busy calculating parameters and working out a plan. He comes back down to earth momentarily, looking composed and focused, but distant. For the most part, his faculties are still tied up at altitude.

"Thanks for coming to warn me."

Jay gets the message. She stands up, and Éric mechanically shows her to the elevator. They shake hands without speaking. The young man appears unafraid.

As the elevator doors glide shut, Jay glimpses Lærke at the far end of the loft, backlit against the picture windows, still concentrating on her binoculars. *Simsaladim bamba saladu saladim.*

— 56 —

A TRAIN RUNS THROUGH THE night, bound for Spain with Jay on board. Weary of playing the spartan voyager, she booked a berth in a sleeping car at great expense: the perfect place for a bout of insomnia.

Stretched out on her back, she listens to the regular hiss of the rails. She tries to remember the last station they went through. A city with a name like a wine. Tourillon-sur-Rhône or something like that. They are approaching Valencia, and through the curtains she can make out the suburban houses piercing the semi-darkness.

Jay curls up in the fetal position. She can't stop thinking about her meeting with Éric Le Blanc, some fifteen hours earlier. She recalls every second spent in that huge loft, the slightest bits of conversation, and yet she's unable to dispel the disturbing sensation the episode never took place. The past forty-eight hours feel like a waking dream—an impression resulting no doubt from the pace of the trip in general and the lack of sleep in particular.

She constantly harks back to the large map of the world hanging on the wall and the red line running through it. The more she thinks about it, the more convinced she becomes of remembering exactly—fairly exactly, at any rate—where the line ended: on the west coast of India, not too far from Mumbai.

The train crosses a road, and the sound of the level-crossing bells brushes against the cars and then dies away in the lower frequencies. Everything in life ends up Doppler-ized. Even memories shift to red, if you wait long enough.

Jay pulls out her suitcase and gropes around for the comforting shape of her Eee. She leans her back against the pillow and logs on to the on-board router, whose Internet connection is the slowest in all of Western Europe. The smallest image takes forever to download, but Jay has all night.

She opens Google and searches for websites indicating the positions of ships in real time. There are dozens of them. ShipTrax will do the job. Jay clicks on India and zooms into the area where the red line ended. It's a busy corridor and the screen fills up with coloured vectors. Luckily, the map can be configured, and by checking a few boxes Jay eliminates all the cruise ships, fishing vessels, oil tankers, bulk carriers, naval ships and yachts. The map gradually grows more legible. Soon, there are only container ships left.

Jay clicks on each vector, looking for a ship that might have left the Colombo terminal December 8. There is just one: the *Guangdong Express*. The ship instantly appears in a thumbnail: a leviathan of the Malaccamax size, registered in Singapore, with a capacity approaching ten thousand containers. The picture makes her head spin. It brings to mind a floating city imagined by a mad Metabolist architect.

According to the data received eleven minutes ago, the *Guangdong Express* was entering the estuary of the Ulhas River, at the southern tip of Mumbai. Right now, the ship must be situated off the Nhava Sheva terminal. The helmsman has already taken up his position in the wheelhouse, and the tugboats are nudging against the sides of the ship.

Jay looks intently at the little red vector. Those few measly pixels represent a massive vessel located eight thousand kilometres away. This does nothing to ease her sense of unreality.

The train slows down. They are coming into Valencia station, and Jay finally feels sleep overtaking her.

She awakes at dawn, curled up around her Eee. She gingerly climbs down the berth's ladder and draws back the curtains. Outside, the world has been transformed. The thin patches of snow glimpsed the night before in the north of Germany have given way to the first tufts of parched vegetation of the south.

Jay slides her computer under the mattress and goes off in search of victuals.

It's still early and the passengers are sleeping in their seats in every conceivable position. The human species is highly adaptable. Jay makes her way to the dining car, where she buys a large coffee and a piece of apple strudel—though she doubts there are really any apples in the strudel or caffeine in the coffee.

Back in her compartment, she locks the door and sits down by the window with her breakfast and her computer.

The screen still displays the ShipTrax site, with the *Guangdong Express* in the mouth of the estuary. Jay hits Ctrl-R and the map refreshes very slowly, eventually showing the data from eight minutes ago. The *Guangdong Express* has already left the terminal and is bound for Abu Dhabi, but Jay knows very well that Papa Zulu is no longer aboard.

She bites off a corner of the strudel and loads the satellite photos of the Nhava Sheva yard: a vast ochre-and-rust-coloured world, composed of thousands of boxes, each one its own world or a fragment of another world, and in one of those boxes a young woman sits busily in front of her computer, maybe with a cup of coffee and some apple strudel.

Jay opens her e-mail to see if there's any news from the CIA. Nothing. Laura Wissenberg is asleep at this time, and Jay catches herself envying Laura. Despite her half night of sleep, she is still as tired as before. She thinks of the little hotel waiting for her in Barcelona, in the Barri Gòtic. Maybe there will be a bathrobe.

After one last glance at the warren of containers, Jay closes all the windows of her browser and erases the cache memory.

— 57 —

THE CONTAINER WAS OFF-LOADED around six in the morning. An absolutely nondescript white reefer without the slightest distinguishing feature. Even so, it has hardly been deposited in the yard when it draws V2's attention.

V2 is a basset hound specially trained to detect stowaways. Dogs have long been used to sniff out explosives and narcotics, but V2 is part of a pilot project. Accompanied by his handler, he trots up and down the entire terminal, including the areas reserved for reefers. More skittish dogs are averse to the din of compressors and fans, but V2 stays calm at all times. Besides, neglecting this area is out of the question: last month a dozen half-suffocated Romanians were discovered in a reefer. There are Romanians everywhere.

The container has just been hooked up to the power line when V2 passes in front of its doors and starts sniffing frantically. After the usual to and fro, the dog handler decides the box is suspect and makes a call to the supervisor.

As a precaution, before disturbing the border authorities, they put the container through the gamma ray scan. The image leaves no room for doubt: there is someone aboard. While the administration tries to contact the shipper, a company with a Russian name, the box is shunted to an isolated part of the terminal.

The absolutely nondescript white reefer without the slightest distinguishing feature suddenly becomes unique among the thousands of other containers, and the port security personnel eye it curiously while they have a smoke in the grey dawn light.

The Special Response Unit arrives an hour later in a black SUV. The officers talk in hushed voices while donning their bulletproof vests. A muted argument erupts concerning the security perimeter, which no one thought to set up.

A few calls are exchanged with the port administration office. No, they haven't been able to contact the shipper. Still, they're not going to wait around for his blessing.

A second sniffer dog is brought in, one specialized in firearms and explosives. The animal could not care less about the container. Well, at least that can be ruled out. A member of the Special Unit sounds the sides of the container with a stethoscope, but the insulation makes it impossible to hear anything at all. Pulling up the rear, two ambulance operators have parked their vehicle at a safe distance and are betting on whether they'll be dealing with carbon dioxide poisoning or bullet wounds.

Everyone finally gets into position: the ambulance operators on the sidelines, the police on either side of the doors, and three sharpshooters kneeling in the front row with their HK416s at the ready. At the signal, a police officer cuts the seal and they yank open the doors. Five flashlights and three assault rifles are trained on the opening of the container, inside which two young men, pale and red-eyed, are sitting in front of a laptop computer, fairly surprised by the turn of events.

"Policja! Nie przesuwa się o jedną!"

Minutes later, the two men are on their knees in front of the container with their wrists tie-wrapped. A light snow starts to fall, driven by the northeaster blowing from the Baltic.

The police inspect the crime scene. The container has been furnished with hammocks, lawn chairs and a coffee table. Screwed down in one corner is an old dry toilet, which, at first whiff, is leaking a little, and a heater is on full blast. The refrigeration unit has been rigged up to provide electricity, and an astounded officer examines the bundles of wires hastily assembled with plastic connectors and bulky adhesive tape. The fact that this setup hasn't already caught fire is a miracle. An ample supply of provisions was stacked in cardboard boxes, but even a cursory glance makes it clear that the pair of sailors have spent the past week subsisting on M&M's and Diet Coke.

The computer is still sitting on the coffee table, with many active windows open in plain sight. No one is able to figure out the purpose of all these applications. A police officer finally unplugs the laptop with due care, as if it were a bomb. Crucial evidence.

Sifting through the mess, the police discover a pair of Russian passports. In answer to a border official's questions, the two young men are co-operative and immediately admit that they embarked in St. Petersburg.

Q: *Do you have any weapons or drugs on board?*
A: *Um, no.*
Q: *Why have you come to Gdańsk?*
A: *We were just passing through.*
Q: *To go where?*

The question brings a giggle from the two men. They shrug.

A: *Brest, Liverpool, New York. Anywhere.*

The officer's eyes shift back and forth between the stow-aways and the container. *Anywhere.* What kind of answer is that? The Romanians at least knew where they were going.

— 58 —

WINTER GOES BY AND THE phenomenon continues to spread.

Everything started with the two Russians arrested in Poland aboard an old reefer. It was believed to be a one-off—two Muscovite jackasses hungry for a thrill—but the following week three Brazilians showed up in Miami the same way. A month later, two half-crazed Japanese were nabbed in Seattle, followed by an Australian in Singapore and a Lebanese in Anvers. Then the Chinese began to storm the West Coast, while the Romanians, with their customary sense of timing, took on the East Coast.

At present, that is, two days before the spring equinox, the tally is twenty-three such containers, not counting the cases that went unnoticed, and they all had one feature in common: a computer found on board, operating with Linux He$_2$.

The origin of the system was quickly tracked down; it had been uploaded to the Web by a certain Harry Houdini via an anonymous connection. One interesting coincidence was that the initial upload took place on October 13, the very day Papa Zulu left Montreal.

Harry Houdini was a person of few words. His description of He$_2$ amounted to two sentences: *A live USB Linux distro with tools and instructables to hack a shipping container, from the yard to the hold, and beyond. Use wisely.*

According to an old Persian proverb, you can't put the toothpaste back in the tube. The He$_2$ files were erased, and Harry Houdini's account was shut down, but new copies instantly reappeared on various mirror sites, GitHub and the Pirate Bay and obscure Russian FTP servers, whose links circulated in forums and on social media. Clearly, He$_2$ occupied a minor but vacant ecological niche, devoid of competitors or predators, a situation that fostered rapid proliferation. Harry Houdini, meanwhile, was conspicuously absent. With a name like that, he certainly was not about to let himself get caught.

The authorities couldn't even be bothered to hide what seemed to them a micro-phenomenon, one more incomprehensible fad that would soon peter out. In late February, a reporter from *Wired* launched He$_2$ on the extranets of a number of shipping terminals on the West Coast of the United States. The report struck a nerve: some ports were using laughable passwords, which He$_2$ succeeded in breaking in fifteen seconds.

By the time the story hit the mainstream media, derivative versions of He$_2$ were already in circulation—more powerful, faster, stealthier. Rumour had it some copies had been infiltrated by the NSA: the Trojan horse now contained another Trojan horse. No one knew if the rumour was true or just a conspiracy theory, or whether it had been started to undermine He_2's reputation. It all probably amounted to the same thing.

Early in March, Mahesh announced he would give a demonstration of the system in the conference room for the benefit of any interested geeks. The episode left a lasting impression on those in attendance.

Within seconds after it was launched, the system scanned the surroundings and identified not only the routers but also every software port, open or not, of the computers and peripherals connected to the network, the servers and telephones, and the lowliest smart gadgets. Only the coffee machine was left out. No need to touch anything; the whole process was automated—you just had to sit back and make yourself comfortable. He_2 triggered the interruption of the nearby connections one by one, like a mischievous child, and waited for the devices to reconnect so it could intercept the authentication messages, which it instantly set about decrypting. If left running for an hour or two, it would eventually obtain practically all the passwords in the vicinity.

The demonstration prompted a mild panic among the personnel on the seventh floor, who all of a sudden decided it was time to use more elaborate passwords.

Mahesh was in seventh heaven. He studied every nook and cranny of the system with teary eyes.

"They thought of everything!"

In addition to an astonishing arsenal of software, He$_2$ came with a vast reference library: hundreds of technical and theoretical texts, detailed maps of shipping terminals, user's guides, organization charts, immigration forms and bills of lading in a dozen languages, legal documents, and an address book with the contact information of lawyers and human rights groups in seventy-five countries.

But the crowning glory, naturally, was the *Claustronaut Cookbook*, a comprehensive handbook on the art of transforming a reefer into an intercontinental capsule, with plans covering the subject down to the last detail, from the power supply to the toilet. There were even a yoga manual, workout routines for tight spaces, cookbooks and a huge portion of the Gutenberg Project's catalogue.

He$_2$ was not a garden-variety dashboard: it was a manifesto, a challenge issued to humankind, an invitation to conquer a new continent. The message had been heard.

Within this sudden surfeit of clandestine containers, Papa Zulu remained in a class of its own, the stealthiest among the stealthy.

The CIA investigators were 100 percent certain of nabbing it at Nhava Sheva, but all they caught was a handful of wind. The databases in Colombo were categorical: PZIU 127 002 7 had been loaded aboard the *Guangdong Express* bound for Mumbai, but apparently the damned box was never off-loaded. Lost at sea, so to speak.

The analysts worked on the case for two weeks before hitting on an explanation: the container's identification number had been slightly modified. Starting in Mumbai, Papa Zulu began to travel under various codes: PZLU 127 200 7 or PZJU 217 020 7 or PZTU 127 002 7—making it difficult, even impossible, to search for it in the databases.

Laura was appalled. "They didn't even bother to repaint the codes showing on the container! No one noticed that the number on the container didn't coincide with the one in the databases?"

Mahesh didn't understand either, but Jay suggested an explanation.

"*Nobody* looks at the codes on the containers, Laura. Thousands of boxes are processed. They whizz by. Everyone trusts the system implicitly. And even if someone did decide to open their eyes, Papa Zulu's codes all look alike. It affects people like dazzle camouflage, you know, those old navy ships with zebra stripes? Same thing. It creates a moment of confusion, just long enough to steal away."

"The terminals don't use automatic code readers?"

"Not for transshipments."

"I think I already heard that somewhere."

"Human history is a long series of repetitions, Laura."

Having been apprised of this theory, Maurice Gamache grumbled that Jay ought to come work for the Port Enforcement Team rather than wasting her time on credit card numbers; without waiting to hear the concerned party's views on the subject, he got it into his head to follow this through. There's likely to be some gnashing of teeth, upstairs.

———

It's dead calm in the Enclave. Everyone has gone for lunch, except Jay, who, sitting on her desk, skims a report that Laura has passed on to her. She skips over several chapters and goes straight to the end—and to the peculiar epilogue to this investigation.

Three weeks ago, Papa Zulu was found, completely by chance, in an industrial zone of Athens. A scrap dealer had bought it on Alibaba for five hundred dollars, and the container sat in a forgotten corner of the yard waiting to be reduced to steel chips. The workers had quite a surprise when they opened the doors: the box was fitted out like a Westfalia! After posting their discovery on YouTube, they called the police. In less than twenty-four hours, the news had reached the CIA and, incidentally, the RCMP.

According to the report, Papa Zulu's occupants had carried off every last item that could have provided clues, and not a trace of He_2 was left aboard. The fingerprints and DNA were consistent with those found at Autocars Mondiaux but did not match any of the records at the National DNA Data Bank.

Jay flips through the report until she finally gets to what really interests her: pictures—ultra-confidential—of the container's interior. The truth was beyond anything Jay had expected. Unlike the makeshift constructions intercepted since January, Papa Zulu looked like the cabin of a luxury ketch, and Jay could easily picture Élisabeth sitting at her chart table, stretched out with a book, busily cooking a risotto.

She closes the report, lost in thought. She wishes she knew for sure that her young protege was all right. Two or three times, she has discreetly gone behind Élisabeth's apartment near Notre-Dame-de-la-Défense. Still no sign of life. For weeks, she has contemplated getting in touch with Éric Le Blanc—but she holds back. She must stick to the script and do what she has to do. She triangulates credit cards, she drinks coffee. She has started cooking ceviche and bacalao again.

And she has made a major decision: she'll give Alex Onassis a call and buy the old duplex that no one is interested in. She'll play hardball, bargain him down and boot out those loudmouths on the ground floor. No one is ever going to force her out of anywhere again.

She tosses the report onto Laura's desk, stretches and pulls on her jacket. She has one (1) year, eleven (11) months and seventeen (17) days left to serve—right now, though, it's time to eat.

— 59 —

IT'S MIDNIGHT, BUT ÉRIC ISN'T SLEEPY. Sitting in an armchair, his feet resting on the coffee table, he sips a glass of oolong. Around him, in the dim light, the floor is littered with Lego pieces.

Through the picture windows, Copenhagen seems to be deep in hibernation, but the port doesn't sleep, the port never sleeps, and gantry cranes are unloading an old Panamax flying the Lebanese flag.

Éric thinks back to that woman who came ringing his doorbell last December, the edgy woman with dishevelled hair, who lacked sleep and chafed at geography, and about whom he knew almost nothing, not even her first name. Now even her features are starting to fade from his memory. He could have traced her quite easily—it's not as if the RCMP in Montreal has thousands of people working on online fraud—but he thought better of it. He prefers to picture her wreathed in mystery, like a guardian angel paratrooper. A member of the elite commando of serendipity. A rescue worker of the improbable. Something like that.

He sets down his glass, rubs his face with his hands. The last months have weighed on his frail shoulders like so many decades. Tonight, sitting in the half-light with his weak tea, he might just as well be ninety years old.

He gets up and has a long stretch. And smiles, at last.

Side by side on the floor in front of the picture windows, Lærke and Lisa are asleep.

The traveller arrived in the late afternoon, tottering under her huge backpack, grungy and exhausted. Her trek across Eastern Europe had been an unexpectedly long and complicated expedition. She had declined Éric's help, obviously, and along the way had run into all kinds of problems in Greece, then Serbia, then the Czech Republic.

Her feet hurt, she hadn't really slept for three days, and the last thing she'd eaten was a doner kebab in Berlin, some ten hours ago. Sitting at the big conference table, as she wolfed down three platefuls of spaghetti with butter, she recounted her recent adventures, while Lærke devoured her with her eyes.

When she was about to collapse for the night, Lisa insisted on installing herself at the foot of the picture windows. She didn't care at all about the uncomfortable floor; she wanted to go to sleep with a view of the horizon. As for Lærke, she refused to leave her new idol. From that moment, they were friends for life.

The scene is perfect, like an Old Master, and when Éric finally turns off the light, the image lingers momentarily on his retina before it disappears.

ACKNOWLEDGEMENTS

I would like to express my gratitude to the following people:

Martin Beaulieu for his advance reads, his advice and his encouragement, and for steering me toward Émile Zola. Céline Bourdages and Raymond Dickner for their precious writing retreat in the 3rd Range. Luis Ferre for his expertise on Spanish grammar. Saleema Hutchinson for convincing me to buy Sekula's seminal book, back in Kassel. Martha Radice for her exotic documentary references. Antoine Tanguay for Alto. Hugo Tremblay for his advance reads and his technical recommendations. Marie Wright-Laflamme for her support, and for taking the risk of marrying a novelist.

Special thanks to my translator, Lazer Lederhendler, who gets even my most obscure allusions, and to Pamela Murray, my wonderful editor, for her confidence and support over ten years.

For those who wish to have a better understanding of the world of containers and modern maritime industries, I recommend the following:

Fish Story (1995), by Allan Sekula, sadly no longer with us; *The Box: How the Shipping Container Made the World Smaller and the World Economy Bigger* (2006, revised 2016), by Marc Levinson; *The Box* (2008), a special report by the BBC: bbc.co.uk/thebox;

Moby-Duck: The True Story of 28,800 Bath Toys Lost at Sea and of the Beachcombers, Oceanographers, Environmentalists, and Fools, Including the Author, Who Went in Search of Them (2011), by Donovan Hohn.

NICOLAS DICKNER is the author of multiple works. His first novel, *Nikolski*, was published in a dozen countries and was the winner of Canada Reads 2010. *Six Degrees of Freedom* won the French-language Governor General's Literary Award for Fiction in 2015.

LAZER LEDERHENDLER's work as a literary translator has earned him distinctions in Canada and abroad, including the Governor General's Literary Award in 2008 for *Nikolski* and in 2016 for *The Party Wall*, which was also shortlisted for the Scotiabank Giller Prize.

.